C. L. M.

Ebon and Gold

A Novel

C. L. M.

Ebon and Gold
A Novel

ISBN/EAN: 9783337001476

Printed in Europe, USA, Canada, Australia, Japan

Cover: Foto ©Andreas Hilbeck / pixelio.de

More available books at **www.hansebooks.com**

EBON AND GOLD.

A Novel.

BY

C. L. M.

"There are no shadows where there is no Sun;
There is no beauty where there is no Shade;
And all things in two lines of glory run,
Darkness and light, Ebon and Gold inlaid."

FABER.

NEW YORK:

G. W. Carleton & Co., Publishers.

LONDON: S. LOW, SON & CO.,

M.DCCC.LXXIV.

JOHN F. TROW & SON, PRINTERS,
205–213 EAST 12TH ST., NEW YORK.

Maclauchlan, Stereotyper,
145 & 147 Mulberry St., near Grand, N. Y.

To

𝕸𝖞 𝕯𝖊𝖆𝖗 𝕳𝖚𝖘𝖇𝖆𝖓𝖉,

WHOSE LOVING-KINDNESS HAS MADE ME FORGET

LIFE'S EBON IN ITS GOLD,

THIS BOOK IS DEDICATED

BY THE

AUTHOR.

CONTENTS.

CONTENTS.

EBON AND GOLD.

CHAPTER I.

MISS MARSHY! Miss Marshy! Miss Marshy (in a gradual crescendo)! "whar am dat chile hiding he'self, wi' ole miss a-waitin' for her dis bressed minit, and me a-callin' till dar ain't no call lef' in me!" and good-natured Aunt Phillis wiped her shining black face, shaking her head dolefully at the

1*

wilfulness of her troublesome charge. "Miss
Marshy!" she began again; but at the same
moment, she espied the object of her search,
and while she is making rapid strides towards
her, we too will take a glance at the truant.

Snugly ensconced in the forked limb of a magnificent shade-tree, she sat, so intent on the book
clasped in her hand, as to be utterly oblivious
of everything else. Her long black hair, floating
in a tangled mass about her shoulders, gave a
somewhat elfish look to a face which, while it
was certainly lacking in the rosy freshness and
rounded outline so essential to childish beauty,
could not be called plain, still less uninterest
ing. The features were regular enough and
finely chiselled, and there was a wondrous transi-
tion of light and shade as they caught the vary-
ing expression of the book before her. But the
charm of her countenance, was her glorious
eyes, a fact which we recognized at once, as, in
response to a vigorous punch from Aunt Phillis,
she started into consciousness, and turned them,
albeit somewhat unwrathfully, upon her.

"Come, Miss Marshy! git off dat roost!" exclaimed that much-abused individual; "I'se been
a'most screechin' my head off for ye, and dar ye

set, as innocent as if ye was as deaf as ole Uncle
Mose. I wonder if ye'll make out to hear when
de Lord Gabriel blows his horn!"

"I rather think the matter will not be left to
my choice," said the young girl, laughing, her
good-nature completely restored, while with a
bound she cleared her mossy seat and alighted
on terra firma. "But what's the occasion of all
this screeching, and why could you not leave me
to enjoy my dear, delightful 'Black Prince' in
peace?" and she glanced regretfully at the volume of Froissart still tightly grasped in her hand.

"Dear, delightful *Black* Prince!" sniffed Aunt
Phillis, holding up her hands in holy horror.
"Dat beats my time! To think o' a young miss
a-readin' and a-studyin' about *Black* Princes,
when dar's plenty o' white ones'll be glad enough
to run after her when she gits old enough to 'courage 'em."

"But I doubt if any of them are half as grand
as my Black Prince after all. But where is this
numerous train of admirers to come from? Not a
masculine ever enters our gates but the dear,
good old priest and ugly old Monsieur Moreau.
Surely, Aunt Phillis, he is not one of your white
princes?"

"Dat poor old critter! wi' one foot in the grave, and the odder jes' a *gwine!* No indeed! But bress your heart, honey, dars plenty o' time. You ain't but jes' fifteen, and the princes are sure to turn up right enough when you're ready for them!"

"Very well; I will hope so, at least, for I would like to take a peep outside these enchanted walls, and I believe princesses are generally supposed to do as they please. When I'm one, I'll have lots of books, and pictures, and statues, and a great organ such as they have in the grand old cathedrals we read about; and I'll go everywhere and see everything. And Aunt Phillis, you shall have the gayest of turbans, and gold ear-rings that will make your very mouth water, and nothing to do but to wait on me and lord it over the other servants."

"And won't I make that sassy Chloe stand around!" exclaimed Aunt Phillis, revelling in implicit faith in the coming Elysium. "Yes, Miss Marshy! you can 'fide in me to do the right thing. Old Phillis knows the grand ways dats fit for princesses!"

"And," continued the young girl, pursuing her day-dream, "good Father Baptiste shall have

a new suit of clothes every Christmas, and plenty
of money for his poor people, and a set of new
vestments for the church. As for grandma—"

" Lord ! honey, don't mention her," interrupted Aunt Phillis in breathless consternation.
" How she's a-tearing and a-pitching dis berry
minit. She sent me to fetch you right off, and I'se
done been a-talking about princes and princesses,
and sich, till I clean forgot all about it ! "

" My grandma sent you for me ! " exclaimed
her young mistress in a tone of genuine surprise,
before which all the airy castles crumbled at once
into dust. " What can it mean ? " she added bitterly, " for she is more apt to shun than to desire
my presence."

And Marcia Lyle was right. Little indeed was
the love and few the caresses lavished on her by
her stern old grandmother. Relentless in her
pride, she had never forgiven Marcia's mother for
marrying the handsome and talented but penni-
less Robert Lyle ; and even when a young heart-
broken widow she came home to die, leaving the
little orphaned Marcia to her care, she showed no
sign of softening or remorse, and took no pains to
conceal that she looked upon her helpless charge
rather as a burden than a sacred trust. Indeed,

the poor child would have fared badly, had it
not been that the servants, who still cherished
the memory of their lovely young mistress and
delighted to recall the days of her splendor,
were more than ready to transfer their allegiance
to her little one. Foremost among them was
Aunt Phillis, who, having been the nurse of the
ill-fated young lady, at once took the little
Marcia under her especial protection and upheld
her in everything she did, good or bad, even in
opposition to her stern old mistress herself. Not
that the old lady was capable of positively ill-
treating her unwelcome grandchild. She simply
ignored as far as possible her very existence;
and having provided amply for her physical
wants, considered her duty done, and left her to
follow her own devices with but the one condition, that she was not to be troubled with the
sight of her. Indeed, the intense bitterness of
Madame Robiera's nature was a matter of wonderment. A West-Indian by birth, and of Spanish
descent, her precocious loveliness early attracted
a visitor to the islands, a native of New York,
whose golden charms proved all-powerful with
her father, and she was wedded at an age when
she should still have been in the school-room.

Vincent Elmore was a man of irreproachable integrity and undeniable respectability, but the cold northern blood in his veins could not keep time with the fiery torrent that leaped and surged in hers, and this marriage was a most unhappy one. Tyrannized over by her husband, frowned at and tutored by his relations, her affections, turned back on herself at every point, became a lava-tide, scorching and devastating where they should have warmed into life and verdure.

Even the birth of a little son failed to afford a channel for her pent-up powers of loving. The child was taken from her and put out to nurse, and when, after a decade of stormy years, a fortunate railroad accident released her from her bondage, she could feel no emotion save rejoicing at her freedom. Now she would claim her child, and seeking once more her own dear sunny South, court the happiness of which her early youth had been so pitilessly defrauded. But no! even here the same cold, calculating policy that had marred her life still pursued her. A carefully attested will committed her child to other guardianship, making him sole heir to his father's ample wealth, in which she could claim but a life-estate. After some futile attempt to contest this, she submitted quietly to the inevitable, and meeting shortly after with Signor Robiera, a wealthy Spanish gentleman, she married him, and retired with him to his estates in Florida. Here at length happiness began to dawn upon her. Her husband was tender and devoted, and soon a lovely little girl came to add to their bliss. But the serpent that since the days of Eve has haunted every earthly paradise, lurked even amid this Eden. A malignant fever carried off the fond husband, and henceforth all the intensity of her devotion was concentrated on the child still left to her.

She grew up a marvel of beauty, and as lovely in heart and mind as in person. Suitors wealthy and noble thronged about her, but she looked upon all with indifference, until Robert Lyle, with his sunny locks and broad, fair brow, on which intellect sat enthroned, bowed before her. Then her woman-nature responded to the magic of his presence, and her whole heart went out to him. In vain her mother expostulated; in vain she reprimanded; in vain she threatened; in vain she sneered at his pale northern blood, and poured out on his devoted head the bitter hatred of years.

"Love was stronger than hate," and there came a morning when the bird was flown, the golden cage empty, and the proud woman once more desolate.

From that time she denied herself to all visitors, and closed her gates alike to friend and foe. A periodical letter from the son at the north, whom in all these years she had never seen, or a communication from her lawyer, formed her sole intercourse with the outer world. Feeding upon her own bitterness, shut out from all companionship, she seemed lost to all kindly or tender emotion. Even the sad return and early death of the daughter, once her heart's idol, apparently aroused within her no feeling save that of anger. Prematurely old and withered, she retained no vestige of her early beauty but the dark eyes, which could still flash with the brilliancy of youth. What wonder, then, with a nature thus turned to gall, she hated and shunned the child of the man who had robbed her of her last remaining treasure! And what wonder that after all these years of neglect, Marcia marvelled at a summons into the presence of her grandmother!

CHAPTER II.

"For the ocean is broad, and the wave in its track
Must follow, and follow, and never come back!"

H. T. STANTON.

MARCIA marvelled, and yet she lingered. A strange, weird feeling came over her; a vague, half-conscious presentiment that she was leaving her wild, free life behind her, and impelled her to pause and look lovingly upon the fair old garden which had so long been her retreat and her refuge. The noonday sun rested goldenly on the gay parterres, where the rarest flowers bloomed and exhaled their sweets in tropical profusion, casting its lengthening shadow on the time-worn sun-dial, and lighting up even the marble Naiads around the fountain with a semblance of life. The adjacent orange and magnolia groves freighted the air with their intoxicating perfume, and the twittering of the birds and the drowsy hum of insects made themselves heard above the hush of the noontide hour. Marcia stood awhile, silently drinking in all this beauty and sweetness, and then, with a sigh, half of enjoyment, half of regret, she turned and walked slowly towards the house. There are such moments in the lives of all of us. Moments that come to us fraught with the shadows of the untried, far-reaching future, in which our footsteps cling lingeringly to the verge of the present, reluctant to tempt the dim unknown before us.

Madame Robiera had long since exhausted her impatience at the non-appearance of her grandchild, and now sat, stern and rigid, awaiting her arrival. Even in the midst of her seclusion she never neglected the elegance of attire befitting a gentlewoman. So the dress that enveloped her wasted form was of the richest and softest satin; the ruffles that fell over her withered hands were of the costliest, daintiest lace, and the cap that surmounted her blanched but still abundant tresses was of the same rare material. The fiery lines traced by a stormy, uncontrolled temper, even more than the furrows planted by sorrow and disappointment, effectually marred the beauty of features which had once been perfect; and as she sat there, a lonely, unloved, unloving old woman, she·inspired the sentiment which most of all she would have scorned and rejected—pity. And her surroundings were like to herself: God's free air and blessed sunshine were sedulously excluded from this apartment, in the dim twilight of which could be discerned furniture of indisputable antiquity and richness, but unsuggestive of comfort, and as rigid and uncompromising in detail and arrangement as the stern old lady herself. The silence was so profound that one might well imagine herself transported to one of those enchanted palaces that play such an important part in all old-fashioned fairy tales, and indeed, except for an occasional nervous tightening of the clasped hands, no fabled princess had ever fallen under a more potent spell than that which enthralled the presiding genius of these domains.

At least some such idea came to Marcia, when, after a low, hesitating knock which elicited no response, she opened the door and crossed the threshold, over which she never remembered to have been summoned before. The gathering gloom and intense stillness formed such a marked contrast to the bright sunshine and teeming life without, that no wonder she stood for a moment awe-stricken and irresolute whether to advance or retreat.

But as she stood thus, her grandmother turned her head and said harshly, "Who is there?"

"It is I—Marcia, grandma. Aunt Phillis told me that you wished to see me."

"And a pretty time you have taken to make your appearance. However, I must acknowledge you come honestly by your wilfulness. But why do you stand there by the door? I am not an ogre, that you should be afraid of me."

"Afraid of you? Why should I be afraid? True, you have never smiled on me, never given me the right to press my childish lips to yours and say '*I love you;*' but fear is for the coward or the slave, and not for Marcia Lyle, your grandchild!"

"Indeed! So you deal in heroics?" But despite her supercilious words, a gleam of something akin to pride and even tenderness flashed across the old lady's face as she gazed on the kindling eyes and proud bearing of her grandchild.

"Perhaps I do," said Marcia simply; "for all my heroes, all the brave knights and faire ladyes I love so to read about, have always despised fear and reverenced courage; but grandma, even as I despise fear do I adore truth, and only the thoughts of my heart find utterance at my lips."

"That is all very well; but I wonder how you came by such lofty sentiments. You certainly did not imbibe them with the cold northern blood of your fair-faced, false-hearted father."

"Hold, grandma! respect the dead. I do not say that my father did not wrong you, or that you have no right to think of him with bitterness; but at least you should not speak of him thus to me—his child. That he was false-hearted, I cannot believe, else how could he have been so loved by one as pure and gentle as my mother. O grandma! perhaps you were pitiless; perhaps you frowned upon them, as you have sometimes frowned on me when I crossed your path unbidden, and thus forced them from you."

"Hush, child! Beware!" said her grandmother hoarsely, her eyes flashing and her whole form dilating with suppressed passion. "Since the day that I laid my child—your mother—in the grave, no one has dared to recall the miserable past. I warn you once more, beware! lest I curse you, even as I cursed your father."

"No, grandma, you could not curse me," said

Marcia passionately. Even if you could feel the curses in your heart, your lips, more kind, would refuse to utter them. But why will you not let me love you? I am so young and yet so lonely; I yearn so for love, and in all the wide world I have none but you. Cannot all this lapse of years blot out the wrong, and bring back the time when my mother sat perchance in this very room and looked at you from eyes like mine, rejoicing in the caresses for which I plead in vain?"

"No! a thousand times no!" said the old lady vehemently. "If you are your mother's child, I cannot forget that you are also your father's. Years cannot quench a hatred like mine. They but add fuel to the flame. I will not again nurse into life the viper that shall one day turn and sting me. Strange as it may seem, I once trusted, hoped, and yearned for love like you; and, like me, you shall live to learn that love is a dream, hope a phantom, and faith a mockery."

' No! no! no! no!'" cried Marcia, shuddering. "Refuse my love, spurn me if you will; but leave me my hope and my faith. Let me still believe in my childhood's heroes, and dream of a future all sunshine and flowers."

"Well, dream on. No doubt the awakening

will come soon enough without my assistance. But have you no curiosity to learn why you have been summoned here, or is that one of the passions too ignoble for your very exalted code of honor?"

"On the contrary, your message filled me with wonderment, and as I walked to the house, my only thought was, 'What can my grandma have to say to me?' But when I entered this room and saw you sitting alone in the gloom, I forgot it all in the longing, 'Oh, if she would only let me love her!'"

"Really, your rhetoric does you credit," said the old lady contemptuously. "I sent for a child, and I find a woman. How have you managed so to outgrow your years?"

"That is a question which I am still too much of a child to answer, unless it may be, that being constantly alone, with no one to think or act for me, I have unconsciously learned to think and act for myself. As for rhetoric, I know nothing about it; but doubtless my manner of expressing myself has been taken from the books that are my only companions."

"And you may be thankful that they are," retorted her grandmother. "But why am I prolong-

'ing an interview that has certainly afforded me no pleasure ?" And yet she paused nervously before she continued : "Have you ever heard that your mother was not my only child ?"

"Never !" exclaimed Marcia in extreme aston- ishment.

"And yet it is true—that I have been married twice, and that I have a son by my first marriage, who has always resided, and who is still resid- ing, at the North."

"But why does he never come to see you, and why have I never heard of him ?" questioned Marcia eagerly.

"Ah, there is the cold northern blood again," said the old lady bitterly. "He was taken from me when a mere infant, and brought up in such total disregard of the tie between us, that doubt- less he would long since have forgotten my very existence, had it not been convenient occasionally to remember it. But he is coming at last, and it was to tell you this that I sent for you."

"But when ?" asked Marcia, filled with bewil- derment at the suddenly discovered relationship, and yet vaguely delighted at the prospect of any break in her monotonous existence.

"He was to have left New York on the thirtieth, so he may be expected here to-morrow; and I hope he will find you looking less like a wild Indian than you do at present, And now go, child, go! I would be alone. I had thought that the past was buried and forgotten; but you have evoked phantoms from its darkest depths to mock and haunt me. Go!" and with an imperious wave of the hand she motioned Marcia from her, and sank back in her chair exhausted.

CHAPTER III.

"And the sweet song died, and a vague unrest,
And a nameless longing filled her breast—
A wish, that she hardly dared to own,
For something better than she had known."

WHITTIER.

MARCIA left her grandmother's presence in a state of the wildest excitement, and once beyond the depressing influence of the shadowy apartment, her imagination busied itself in conjuring impossible pictures of the uncle whom she had never seen, but whom, with the impulsiveness of her ardent nature, she was prepared at once to welcome to her heart of hearts. For once her beloved books failed to charm her, and she flitted restlessly about, vibrating between the spacious drawing-room and grand old dining-hall, which, under the skilful manipulations of "Sassy Chloe" and "Deaf Uncle Mose," were undergoing a thorough airing and cleaning, and the sunny

west chamber, where Aunt Phillis was presiding
over a similar renovation, till she drove those
worthies to the verge of distraction.

"Lor'! Miss Marshy, honey," said Aunt Phillis
imploringly, "can't ye manage for to sit still one
mite of a minit? Jes' look at the tracks your
bressed little feet done made on my nice floor, and
I'se been waxin' and a-rubbin' till de lookin'-glass
ain't nowhere—not dat I spec young marse been
used to much, way up dar at de Norf, but I jes
like to show him dat we darkies know what's
what, ef our skin am black and spotted like de
leopard."

"O Aunt Phillis! Aunt Phillis!" said Marcia, laughing. "I am sure that your quotations
from Holy Writ would astonish good Father Baptiste himself;—but," she added contritely, "I am
sorry that I made tracks on your floor, which does
look too bright and too pretty to be spoiled. But
what am I to do? I cannot sit still, and I don't
want to go in the garden; Chloe is keeping guard
over the drawing-room like a dragon, and when I
ventured just now to peep inside the dining-room,
Uncle Mose looked as sour as a vinegar-barrel."

"He did!" said Aunt Phillis in a rage, forgetting her own annoyance; "I'll larn him what vin-

egar-bar'ls is made for ; and as for dat Chloe, I'll
let her know dat if some people can sot up for
dragons, dar is some as is born lions, and de lions
allus 'vours de dragons, head and tail."

"Never mind, Aunt Phillis," said Marcia soothingly ; "I dare say I was in the way. It seems
to me that I was born to be in the way. I wonder," she added musingly, "if my new uncle will
think so."

"Lor' ! chile, don't be settin' too much store by
dat new uncle. I'se hearn tell o' blood as is thicker
nor water ; but it's my 'pinion dat dese Yankees'
blood is all water. Shoo !" and the old darkey
gave an indignant punch to the bed which she
was robing in its snowy covering.

"I am sure that is true of other people besides
the Yankees. My grandma could not care less for
me, if no drop of her blood coursed in my veins."

"Now, Miss Marshy, don't be a talkin' 'bout
her blood ! As if she had any. Land sakes ! it's
snow ; it's ice ; or if dar's anything colder up yon-
der, it's dat berry thing. Dem Yankees done
froze it for her long ago."

"Poor grandma !" said Marcia, half to herself,
"how I would love her if she would but let me !
My very heart ached for her to-day, when I saw

her sitting there, looking so lonely and desolate."
Then, going back to the all-absorbing topic, "I
hope that my uncle is not cold and stern like her.
No ; I will picture him to myself kind and gentle.
Perhaps he has a happy home, and a dear wife, and
merry, rosy children—it may be, daughters like
me—and for their sakes he will lay his hand softly
on my head, and speak tenderly to me who have
no father !" and she fell into a reverie, which
might have lasted *ad infinitum*, had she not been
aroused by Aunt Phillis with a—

"Come, Miss Marshy ! you must get out of this.
I'se done my do, and now I'se gwine for to shut
up. I reckon dey'se got nuffin at de Norf dat'll
take de shine off dis 'partment."

And very inviting it looked, with its cool, polished floor, its snowy muslin curtains and toilet-
cover, and its tempting bed, whose spotless linen
was redolent with a faint odor of crushed rose-
leaves. The wreath of eglantine that surmounted
the mirror, the sprays that confined the flowing
curtains, and the tastefully arranged flower-vases,
scattered here and there, were Marcia's contribu-
tion, permitted under protest by the practical and
order-loving Aunt Phillis. ·

The long day wore to an end at last, and notwithstanding many promises to herself of an early rising, the sun was high in the heavens the next morning, when Marcia was awakened by the hearty voice of Aunt Phillis exclaiming, as she opened the shutters and let in a flood of golden light, "Bress dat chile! am she gwine to sleep till doomsday?"

"No indeed!" said Marcia, springing out of bed; "I am wide awake now, and I'll be dressed before you can turn round."

"Not so fast, honey! I'se 'sponsible for your twilet dis mornin.' Ole Miss, she said to me last night, tossin dat proud old head o' hearn, which I don't b'lieve'll ever lay low, even in her coffin, 'Phillis, I wish you would try to make your Miss Marcia look like a lady!' 'Thank you, ole Miss,' says I; 'what's born in de blood is sure to come out in de bone.' 'Very true,' says she, 'but I am afraid that no one would pick your Miss Marcia out as a specimen. Tie up those Indian locks of hers, and see if you can find a whole dress for her to wear. I would not like my son to think that I keep an asylum for beggars!' P'raps you don't think I was a bilin, but I bit my tongue with my teeth, and I didn't tell her how you 'fused to let me comb your pretty har

afore you went to her room 'dat mornin, and how,
when I tole you dat you'd tore your dress on de
bushes, you said, 'Never mind, she'll never notice it!' But don't cry!" said she, in consternation
at the tears which Marcia could not restrain at
this fresh evidence of her grandmother's harshness.
"You's worf more'n de whole lot shuk up in a
bag togedder, Yankee Marse frowed in; and if
you'll jis promise to hold still I'll make you so
pooty, dat ole Miss 'll open dem eyes o' hearn
wider dan ebber!" .

And Aunt Phillis made her word good, and the
transformation was very complete from the elfish,
unkempt damsel of yesterday to the trim, daintily
dressed young maiden that a half hour later
emerged from Marcia's bed-chamber. Her luxuriant black hair, brushed smoothly back from her
temples, hung in glossy plaits below her slender
waist, and her neatly fitting dress of spotless muslin formed as simple and appropriate a costume as
Aunt Phillis could have selected, even if she had
had the shop of a Parisian modiste at her disposal.

"Dar, honey, you look sweet enuff to eat!" said
she, gazing admiringly after her nursling as she
descended the broad staircase.

Reaching the hall, Marcia stepped out on the

veranda to claim her usual floral tribute from
the rose-bush that clambered so ambitiously almost
to the very roof of the gray old mansion, indulging in numerous conjectures as to when her uncle
would probably arrive, and whether her dress
would retain its freshness till that auspicious
moment; inwardly resolving to be the first to her-
ald the expected guest. As she passed the open
dining-room, she looked in and saw Uncle Mose
putting the finishing-touches to the already carefully arranged breakfast-table, and lo! gazing out
of the bay window which looked to the sea, stood
a gentleman, at the sight of whom her heart gave
a great bound, and she paused as if transfixed to
the spot. As she had said truly to Aunt Phillis,
no masculine ever entered their gates except Father
Baptiste or Monsieur Moreau; this gentleman was
clearly neither of those, so it must be the uncle
for whom she had projected such an ardent welcome and prepared so many pretty speeches. He
must have come in the night; and she almost felt
that in coming thus, he had defrauded her of some
of her just rights; not that she had much time to
think: her uncle had evidently heard her step,
light as it was, and turned quickly around, with
an expression of surprise, indeed, but mingled

2

with a look of such kindly interest, that Marcia
decided at once that he was not in the least like
her grandma, and that she was certain to love him
very dearly. And indeed Vincent Elmore bore
but little resemblance to his stern old mother, being in form and feature almost the exact prototype
of his father. But it was in form and feature alone.
The Vincent Elmore who, years ago, had won the
proud heart of the young West-Indian, only to
crush and trample upon it, could never have looked
out from eyes so true and tender as those which his
son turned upon Marcia that summer morning, nor
could a smile so grave and sweet have been at
home on the face of one who counted his favors by
dollars and measured his friendships with gold.
Ah, no! very different was the son, who, a man
past the middle age, his hair tinged here and there
with silver, stood now, for the first time, beneath
the roof of the mother from whom he had been so
cruelly estranged in his very infancy. Perhaps,
being born to wealth, he had been spared the sor-
did influences and petty cares that in the race for
gold too often contract the soul and harden the
heart of the merchant-prince ; or it may be that the
warm, generous blood of the young mother had
mingled with and tempered the frozen current

transmitted from father to son. Be this as it may, it would have been hard to find a warmer heart or a kindlier nature than filled the . breast of the uncle,—truly the uncle of Marcia's dreams,—who, drawing the young girl towards him as he spoke, said :

"Can this be Marcia ?   I was not led to expect anything half so civilized."

"Ah ! then you have already seen my grandma ?" said Marcia naïvely.

"Yes ; last night, soon after my arrival, when these dark eyes were peering into dreamland. But how did you so quickly divine it ?"

Oh ! because—because my grandma does not like—I mean she does not care for me," said Marcia hesitatingly.   "But I wish she had been kind enough to say nothing about me. Now I know I shall never be able to make you love me," and the tears actually started to her eyes.

"Cela depend," said her uncle cheeringly, stroking the trembling little hand which he still held in his. "Suppose I prefer trusting to my own observations and forming my own conclusions ?"

"Then I am not afraid," said Marcia, brightening ; "for I really believe I am careless only because there is no one to notice me or take an interest in me. Grandma never forgave dear mamma for marrying my poor father, and she cannot endure me because I am his child. Although we live in the same house, I sometimes do not see her for weeks at a time, and she never speaks to me if it is possible to avoid it. No one ever comes here. The servants like me as well in a torn dress as a whole one, and I fear that I have learned to be careless about it too."

"Poor child! poor child! I know a brace of merry girls who are often forced to plead guilty to dishevelled locks and torn dresses, without half your excuses."

"And they must be your children and my cousins!" said Marcia, gayly clapping her hands. "I pictured you to myself before you came, kind and gentle as you are; and I thought you must have children, and when I saw you I felt sure of it. I am so glad they tear their dresses too. Do tell me what are their names; how do they look; how old are they; and do you think they would like me?"

"What an avalanche!" said her uncle, comically. "Let me see: one, two, three, four questions, all in a breath! Really I am not equal to answering them till I have fortified myself with some of this nice coffee Uncle Mose is just bringing in, the mere fragrance of which confirms the traditional excellence of southern cookery. And there comes my mother. Marcia, we should be very gentle with her, for she has had a hard life. Poor mother! I fear I will never be able to forgive the cruel policy that has kept me from her all these years;" and he hastened to meet her and offer his arm to escort her to the table.

Accepting her son's courtesy as a matter of course, and yet with all the courtly dignity of the old *régime*, Madame Robiera, for the first time in many long years, sat down to do the honors of her own table. Glancing at Marcia, she said, not altogether ungraciously, " Well, I am glad to see that Phillis has succeeded in toning you down a little. But I suppose you have not yet been presented to your uncle ?"

"Oh, Marcia and I took that ceremony in our own hands, and are already the best of friends," said the latter good-naturedly, busying himself in selecting the choicest bit of chicken for his mother, and showing her throughout the meal a delicate attention and consideration which, stern as she was, she could not wholly withstand. Nor did

he by any means ignore Marcia; addressing
pleasant little remarks to her from time to time,
that made her feel as if a new era had indeed
dawned in her life, and filling her with a fervor
of admiration that I fear was inimical to the
fealty she had always sworn to the heroes of her
childhood's romance, causing even her favorite
Black Prince to shrink for the nonce into inglori-
ous obscurity.

CHAPTER IV.

"These struggling tides of life, that seem
In wayward, aimless course to tend,
Are eddies of the mighty stream
That rolls to its appointed end."

BRYANT.

BREAKFAST over, Mr. Elmore was at once at his mother's side, ready to attend to her; but at the door of her apartment she paused, saying:

"I am well aware that the business which after the lapse of so many years has procured me the presence of my son must be of urgent importance.".

Mr. Elmore colored, and would have remonstrated; but with a wave of her hand she silenced him, and continued:

"I find myself not so young as I once was, and the unusual excitement of last night has so far overtaxed my strength, that I must beg you to defer the discussion of it for the present."

"Willingly. I am entirely at your disposal, and I trust that I shall be able to convince you that my long neglect is not quite so culpable as it appears. But," said he, gazing anxiously on her aged face, where the traces of recent agitation were too plainly visible, "if you would but allow me to minister to you, and, late in the day as it is, to do a son's part—"

"Enough!" returned she. "I need neither your ministrations nor your sympathy. I am unused to both, and expect to die, as I have lived, without them. "But," she continued, not unmindful of the duties of hospitality, "I trust that you will consider the house and the servants entirely at your disposal, and amuse yourself as well as the limited resources at your command will permit."

Mr. Elmore bowed, and, opening the door for her to pass, turned away with a deep sigh. Ah, terrible are the phantoms of duties neglected—possibilities that may never return! The golden sands run out so quickly; the flowers, that might have made our lives beautiful, are left to fade unplucked, and then,

> ". . . . . God pity us all,
> Who vainly the dreams of youth recall;

" For of all sad words of tongue or pen,
    The saddest are these,—' It might have been ! ' "

But such thoughts are not very pleasant companions, especially on a bright southern morning,
when the air is redolent with sunshine and
flowers, and voiceful with melodies but little in
accordance with sorrow and regret ; and Mr. Elmore was not sorry when a soft hand was laid in
his, and he saw Marcia at his side, holding a very
suggestive-looking key-basket.

"Come, uncle," said she, "as grandma has
deserted you, you must be content to take me for
a hostess. See, I have coaxed the keys from
Aunt Phillis, and I am going to entertain you by
showing you our old house. But perhaps you do
not know that it was built by the Spaniards, who
first settled our beautiful State, and who were
my grandfather's ancestors. I don't wonder they
scared the Indians away, for if they at all resem-
bled their portraits, they were certainly grim and
ugly enough."

"Not a very flattering criticism," said her uncle
as he rose to follow her. "I fear you have not
much pride of ancestry."

"On the contrary, I glory in having descended from a long line of grave Senors and

proud and beautiful senoras ; for I forgot to tell
you that the women are as beautiful as the men
are ugly. I love the picture-gallery better than
any spot about the place ; and whenever I can pre-
vail on Aunt Phillis to let me in, I spend hours
gazing on the portraits hanging so mutely on the
wall, till they seem to step out from their frames
and fill the silent room with the pomp and pa-
geantry of ages past."

"So you are enthusiastic ? But, my dear child,
your language and your ideas surprise me. Who
has been your teacher ?"

"As to that," said Marcia simply, "Father
Baptiste taught me to read when I was preparing
for my first communion, and grandma has a whole
library full of books. But if you were to question
me on grammar, or arithmetic, or anything that is
useful to know, I am afraid I should lose your
good opinion. Ah !" said she, unlocking a door
at the end of the long corridor that they had been
traversing, " here is the narrow passage that leads
to the old part of the house, and as it is very dark,
you must mind your steps."

Obeying orders, Mr. Elmore picked his way
carefully through the obscurity, and soon found
himself in a large hall, heavily panelled with

some dark wood, whose elaborate carvings would have formed the delight of an antiquarian. Opening out of this hall were several apartments which had evidently been used as bedrooms, as the worm-eaten furniture, rich with gilding and quaint ornamentation of a century agone, served to testify. One of these apartments presented a much more modern appearance than the rest, and had evidently been freshly swept and dusted. The bed, with its faded hangings of blue and gold damask, occupied an alcove ; gilt-framed chairs, covered with the same rare fabric, were scattered here and there ; curiously fashioned mirrors reflected from tapestried walls, and in one corner stood a stringless lute, still tied with a faded blue ribbon. Mr. Elmore uttered an exclamation of surprise.

"Ah !" said Marcia with something like a hush in her fresh, young voice, "this is the apartment of Donna Inez, the fairest and most ill-fated of my race. Tradition relates, and her portrait, which I will presently show you, certainly confirms, that she was young and wondrously beautiful. But alas ! she was pledged in marriage to Don Pedro, old and ugly, though fabulously rich, and of great renown, and he bore her from her native Spain to his Florida home, while her heart remained with a handsome young lover over the sea. Discovering her secret, he became fiercely jealous, and made of this boudoir a prison, where the poor lady pined and sang herself to death. And as all old mansions have a ghost, I must inform you that Donna Inez is our ghost. The servants have a superstition, that whenever she finds her apartments neglected she leaves them to wander through the rest of the house, so that their fears cause them to be particular, as you see. It is also said that she haunts the chapel, and that the death of a member of the family is always foretold by strange, wild notes from the old organ, said to be called forth by her ghostly fingers."

"Poor Donna Inez!" said her uncle, "what tales these walls might tell if they could speak, and what heart-broken echoes one might awaken from this slumbering lute. But I should not think the disfranchised spirit would care to revisit a spot where it had known such bitter grief."

"Nor I," said Marcia; and yet she closed the door with a subdued reverence, which was in itself an involuntary declaration of faith in the superstition her reason should have taught her to reject.

"Now for the picture-gallery!" she exclaimed, leading the way to another door; and in a moment they stood in the presence of the smiling ladies and frowning knights who, once crowned with honors and heralded by fame, now lived but in the canvas on the silent walls. Mr. Elmore passed from one to another, and did not wonder at Marcia's fascination for the spot. Each face seemed to suggest its history, and he could fancy the weird romances which her vivid imagination might have called into being. They paused before a portrait representing a young girl of exquisite loveliness. The dress of white satin and the veil of rare old point, worn in the graceful Spanish fashion, might have been her bridal robes; and even without Marcia's prompting, her uncle could have told that this was the unhappy Donna Inez.

Leaving the picture-gallery, they descended a quaintly-carved staircase, and after glancing at the ball-room and banquet-hall, passed into the gallery that led to the chapel, which, though not, as formerly, in daily use, was still kept in repair. Even in the noontide of this bright, sunshiny day, the light in this consecrated spot, coming as it did through stained and mullioned windows, was so dim, that Mr. Elmore did not at first discern the

exquisite beauty of the frescoing on the walls and
ceiling, or the floor beneath their feet, which was
laid in a mosaic of colored marbles. Once perceived, however, they so engrossed his admiration
and his scrutiny, that Marcia turned to the music-
books on the organ, which, although they could
not claim the antiquity of the other belongings of
the chapel, had always possessed a peculiar charm
for her, as exponents of an art she adored, though
utterly ignorant of it. She, however, left them
hastily, as she saw her uncle approaching the
altar, being anxious to be the first to call his attention to the Agnes Dei, which formed the frontis-
piece, and to exhibit the wonderfully carved
crucifix, the rarest of all the family heirlooms.
Then she pointed out the entrance to the vault beneath, and the marble tablets, recording the names
of those that slept therein. They then left the
chapel ; but just as she closed the door, and with
difficulty was turning the key in the ponderous
lock, a wail from the organ smote upon her astonished ear. Trembling with affright, she
clutched her uncle's arm, just as another one
echoed through the silent halls.

"Donna Inez! the omen! the omen!" she

gasped, and would have fallen if her uncle had not supported her.

"Nonsense, Marcia!" said he; "you are too sensible not to know that the spirits of the departed are not permitted to come back to earth. And besides, the high noon of a bright day is not the traditional hour for ghosts. But give me the key, and I will return and investigate the cause of these unwonted sounds."

"No! no!" said Marcia, but her uncle insisted; and taking the key from her hand, re-entered the chapel. He soon returned, saying smilingly, "I think your own carelessness has evoked the spirits this time. No doubt you did not securely replace the music-books which I saw you examining, for I found that two of them had fallen. In doing so they must have struck the key-board and produced the sounds which have so terrified you."

Marcia was silenced, but evidently not convinced.

"Let us go into the garden," said she, shuddering, and she gave a sigh of relief as they stepped out into the sunshine. Her elastic spirits soon rose, though the shadow had not quite vanished as she said, "Now I am going to show you the grotto, the fountain, the old sun-dial, and all my favorite haunts."

"That is right; I am glad to have my bright little cicerone restored to me."

"O uncle, you are so kind, so good, to have so much patience with what I know you must consider my foolish weakness. But oh! it was not, it was not!" she exclaimed, the old look of terror and distress coming back.

"There!" said Mr. Elmore, drawing her more closely to him as he spoke, "don't think about it. We will talk of something more pleasant. So this is the scene of your gypsying," he continued, glancing around. "I'll venture a wager that I can discover the very spot that you have selected for a studio;" and to Marcia's delight, he walked at once to the tree in whose leafy recesses we first made her acquaintance

"The very place!" said she, gleefully; "but how did you know?"

"Because these spreading limbs form such a convenient seat; and still more, because that could not belong to any one but you," pointing to a garden hat dangling among the branches.

"My hat! I forgot it yesterday when grandma sent for me. Was it indeed only yesterday?

it seems so long ago. Then I had never even heard of you, and now I feel as if I had known and loved you always."

"I am glad of that; for in truth, I have been busy making plans for you for the last hour."

"Making plans for me? how kind. But what are they?" questioned Marcia eagerly.

"I must plead guilty of a Yankeeism, and answer your question by asking you one. How would you like to go home with me?"

"Oh, so much! so much! But grandma! What will she say? and even if she does not love me, would it be right to leave her here all alone?"

"Of course she shall be consulted, and everything will depend on her decision. If she evinces the slightest inclination to retain you, I will not urge your departure, but consider it your highest duty to remain; but it seems to me, that if your presence in the house is as painful to her as she makes it appear, she will be relieved to have you away in good hands. The life you are leading is not a natural or a healthy one, and although, thanks to your taste for books, you have laid up a goodly store of general knowledge, your mind wants discipline and training; all of which I pro-

3

pose. that you shall receive in common with my own children."

"Ah, your children! my cousins! how could I have forgotten them all this time? But you are not too tired to tell me all about them now, dear uncle?" said Marcia beseechingly.

"On the contrary, I can imagine no more pleasant task, especially with such a listener," said Mr. Elmore, gazing kindly at her glowing face. "To begin, there's Paul, a great, tall—and by this time bearded—fellow, who is across the seas, pursuing his studies in a German university. Next comes Jennie, our bright-eyed, sparkling brunette, who, having held all our hearts in her thrall during the seventeen summers that have passed. so lightly over her, is now, like Alexander, sighing for 'other worlds to conquer' in the shape of the hapless beaux who may see fit to singe their wings in the light of her smiles, when she makes her début next winter. Then my loving, golden-haired, blue-eyed Lottie, who will be your companion, and who, I am sure, will love you dearly. And last, there are our mischievous, fun-loving Nita and Dick, aged respectively six and seven— a precious pair of spoiled darlings, but the very sunshine of the whole household."

"Nita! that is my grandma's namesake?" questioned Marcia.

"Yes, Nita is our diminutive for Anita; heigh-ho! I wish I could see the little fairy."

"And I wish I could see them all. But my aunt! tell me about her."

"Ah, words are too poor to describe her. My children are jewels, but she is beyond and above them all. With the poet:

> "'I think this wedded wife of mine
> The best of all that's not divine!'"

And he fell into a reverie, which Marcia did not disturb, as she too was dreaming, and had drifted so far away, that she started when her uncle interrupted her with: ,

"A penny for your thoughts, Marcia dear!"

"Oh!" said she, "I was wondering how many persons there may now be in the world whose lives are destined one day to mingle with and make a part of mine. Until yesterday, it seemed to me as if I might live on alone forever; or if I did sometimes picture to myself a different future, I could conjure up no personages more real than the heroes and heroines of the books from which I had learned all I knew of life. And to-day you are here, and you tell me of a blessed aunt and a whole troop of cousins, whom I am sure I shall yet know and love. And if one day can bring forth so much, it bewilders me to think what may happen in all the years of a long life."

"Child, child, you think too much! I am more than ever convinced that you ought to go home with me. But let us return to the house; perhaps by this time your grandma may be ready to receive me."

But in this he was mistaken, and it was evening before he was admitted to her presence. The solitary lamp seemed rather to heighten than dispel the obscurity of the apartment; but as Madame Robiera turned to greet her son on his entrance, its rays fell full on her face, which looked so wan and haggard that he started involuntarily, saying:

"Mother, you look ill; let us postpone this business till you are stronger."

"I am as well as usual," said she grimly. "One cannot pass through a life like mine, made up of winters, without bearing traces of its tempests and its snows. Produce your papers; delays are dangerous. The tree which the lightning has scathed may for a time bid defiance to wind and storm, but its sap is dried up, its vitality withered, and who can tell but the next fierce blast may lay it low ! "

Mr. Elmore looked sadly at her ; but without venturing further remonstrance,. laid before her certain papers which, he proceeded to explain, had reference to her life-estate in the property now his, and which required her signature. She listened indifferently to his explanations, and then, drawing the documents towards her, signed them without a word, merely saying, as she returned them to him :

" All this might have been transacted through a lawyer. I wonder that you took the trouble to come so far to attend to it."

"I am aware of that. But mother, these papers are but my excuse for troubling you with my presence. The real object of my visit is to convince you that I am not the unworthy son you have had reason to suppose me, and to endeavor, late as it is, to make amends for the past."

"That is quite unnecessary," said the old lady impatiently. "You have been no worse than your antecedents might have led me to expect."

" Yes ! " said he, without noticing the reproach, " you and I have been cruelly estranged. I can hardly find it in my heart to forgive those who, not content with tearing me from your breast when a mere infant, poisoned my tender years with stories of your desertion and neglect, and when, as I grew up, despite all this, I would have sought you out, deterred me by assurances of your implacable hatred to all that bore my father's name."

"How and when did you learn the truth?" said she calmly; but her whole frame shook with suppressed emotion.

"Only a few months ago, when I accidentally met with one who had known you well in those early days, and who told me of your trials: of your exultant joy when I was born, and your passionate grief when I was taken from you, and also of your vain attempts to regain possession of me after my father's death. After learning this, I felt as if I could not take my own little ones upon my knee and enjoy their innocent prattle and fond caresses till I had sought my long-lost mother, and obtained her blessing and her forgiveness. So here I am; and mother, you will not refuse what I have come so far to claim?"

"As to my forgiveness, I do not consider that you need it, since the blame rests not with you but with others. But," she continued, vainly struggling to retain her composure, "why do you

ask for my blessing? Of what advantage is the
blessing of one whose very blood is turned to
gall, and whose heart is dead to all tender and
kindly emotion?"

"A parent's blessing can never be valueless to
a child. O mother! give me yours before we part
to-night, if only as a pledge that my years of neglect are not remembered against me!"

"God bless you, then, my son, if you will have
it so. But now leave me. These scenes are too
much for me. I am faint; I am weary! Yesterday that child, with her wonderful eyes—her
mother's eyes—must evoke the dead past from its
deep, dark grave to haunt me, and to-night you
have brought up memories and awakened chords
of my heart that I thought were silenced forever.
Oh, the phantoms! the phantoms! how they press
on me from every side! But go," said she, in a
tone that would not be gainsaid; "I would be
alone with them."

"Then good-night, mother," said he, stooping
to kiss her. "But I do not like to leave you thus.
Let me at least send your servant to you."

"No, no! I will ring when I need her!" And
Mr. Elmore, closing the door gently, left her alone
with her thoughts.

CHAPTER V.

Oh, hearts that break and give no sign
Save whitening lip and fading tresses,
Till Death pours out his cordial wine,
Slow-dropped from Misery's crushing presses."
HOLMES.

LONG after Mr. Elmore left his mother, her solitary figure haunted him ; and at length, taking his hat, he went out in the grounds, in the hope that the quiet influence of the still moonlight would calm his perturbed spirit. Wandering aimlessly about, he found himself in the vicinity of the chapel, and paused to admire the picturesque beauty of the gray, moss-grown walls and stained windows, over which the moon was now shedding a silvery halo. As he stood thus, the memory of Marcia's fright recurred to him, and despite himself a vague feeling of apprehension stole over him, which he vainly endeavored to dispel.

"Nonsense!" said he. "There is some magic about this spot: I shall end by becoming as superstitious as the negroes themselves!" And turning, he re-entered the house. Here all was still, the whole household apparently wrapped in slumber; and as he passed his mother's apartments, the extinguished light and unbroken quiet convinced him that she too had retired to rest. Still the evil spirit would not be exorcised, and it was long before sleep visited his eyelids. Neither was Marcia's rest that night as unbroken and profound as it was wont to be. In the solitude of her apartment the mysterious sounds she had heard still rang in her ears, and she could not accept the simple and natural explanation her uncle had suggested. Her imagination persisted in conjuring the most frightful images and impossible catastrophes, and the night was far advanced when at last she sank into a fitful slumber, from which she was awakened by the unusual sound of wheels upon the gravel. Rubbing her eyes to assure herself that she was really awake, she sprang out of bed, and reached the window just in time to see, stopping in front of the house, a carriage from which alighted a gaunt little personage whom she had no difficulty in recognizing as Monsieur

3*

Guerin, the village doctor. The night had gone, for there was the broad daylight streaming through the windows, but in her bewilderment Marcia could scarcely persuade herself that she was not still dreaming. Filled with a dread of something terrible, she knew not what, she hurried on her clothes, and descended the stairs with trembling steps.

Just then the doctor came out of her grandmother's room, and with him her uncle, looking pale and agitated.

"Nothing to be done, sir! nothing to be done!" the doctor was saying in his brisk, professional tones; "the poor lady must have been dead for hours. Heart-disease, I should say. Yes, decidedly, heart-disease! If I can be of any service, command me!" and with a bow he had vanished.

Marcia stood for a moment motionless, and then, like an arrow, she flew to her grandmother's bedside. Yes, it was all true! The "silver cord was loosed," at last, "the golden bowl broken." "Beyond the sleeping and the waking," "beyond the watching and the weeping," that form, upon which earth's storms and tempests had done their worst, had passed whither none might follow. Upon the aged face rested a calm smile, strangely at variance with the troubled life, as if the welcome death had brought a benediction with it. And let us hope that it had, and that the long dark record of hate was forever folded out of sight, and the burden of sin laid down with the burden of life at the feet of the Saviour.

At least there was no room for bitterness in Marcia's heart, as she knelt by that solemn bed-side.

"O grandma, grandma!" she sobbed, "if you had but smiled on me once, only once," and seizing the withered hand, she covered it with kisses.

The servants stood by, too awe-stricken to interfere, till Mr. Elmore entered, and passing his arm tenderly around her, said:

"Come with me, my child; this is no place for you."

But she would not go, only clinging more closely to the hand that could not now refuse her caresses. However, his gentle authority prevailed at last, and he drew her out into the garden, where the calm face of Nature was all unchanged, and the birds sang as cheerily and the flowers smiled as gayly as ever.

"Oh!" said Marcia, "it seems so strange that

everything should be the same, while"—but here she broke down and her tears broke forth afresh.

Her uncle let them flow awhile unchecked, and then he said kindly :

"All this serves to show how much more wisely things are ordered for us than we could order them for ourselves. I fear that if the sun should cease to shine every time an affliction is sent to a poor mortal, we would all soon be compelled to live in the shadow."

"But all this was her own, her very own," said Marcia passionately, "and I cannot bear to see those naiads holding their marble shells to catch the falling drops, just as they have done ever since I can remember. It seems to me that even the birds should sing more softly, and the flowers hide their gay hues under their sheltering leaves, in the presence of such a sorrow."

"Such feelings are very natural. Grief falls so crushingly on the heart of youth. But, Marcia, remember that you are my little girl now, and you must learn to subdue and control this rich, wild nature of yours."

And thus he talked, gravely and kindly, till Marcia felt soothed and calm, and wondered what she would have done if this trouble had come to her when he was not there to comfort her.

Father Baptiste called in the course of the day, full of concern for his little favorite, as he had always styled Marcia, and was much relieved when Mr. Elmore told him that he intended to take charge of her future. Monsieur Moreau and the lawyer also paid their respects; and Madame Robiera had led such a secluded life, that this exhausted the list of friends, and Marcia and her uncle were left pretty much to themselves.

Marcia saw her grandmother's face once again. It was the day of the funeral, which took place in the little chapel, and it was so calm and peaceful that the sight did her good, and she was able to control herself very well during the ceremonies, till the moment arrived for depositing the coffin in the vault, when she trembled violently; and nervously clutching her uncle's arm, exclaimed in a voice of irrepressible anguish.

"Not there! O uncle, don't let them leave her there!"

This excitement was followed by days of such entire prostration, that she was incapable of anything but lying still and enjoying an unlimited amount of coddling and petting from Aunt Phillis,

and such care and attention from her uncle, that
she almost began to doubt her own identity.

In the meantime Mr. Elmore busied himself in
settling his mother's business and making arrangements for a speedy departure as soon as
Marcia should be strong enough to travel.

Madame Robiera's will was simple and concise.
With the exception of a few trifling bequests to
servants, her entire estate was left to Marcia. A special clause empowered Monsieur Moreau to select
a guardian in case he declined to act as such
himself; and as he had a decided aversion to any
kind of business or responsibility, he was very
glad to confer the trust on Mr. Elmore. It was
also provided that the servants should be retained
on the home place, which, wherever Marcia
might make her home, was always to be kept in
order and repair, and which could on no account
be either rented or sold.

And so time passed, bringing with it at last the
eve of the departure. Marcia had spent the day
in farewell visits to each familiar spot, and despite her bright anticipations her heart grew heavy
as she realized for the first time all that she was
leaving. Tears were streaming down her cheeks,
and she looked pale and worn in her black dress,

as she sat in her little bedroom watching Aunt Phillis, who was putting one of her many last touches to the trunk, the packing of which had for days been her engrossing occupation.

"Dar, Miss Marshy, honey," said she at length, shutting the lid with a snap that made Marcia start, "I reckon de white trash where you'se a gwine can't beat that."

"I am sure they cannot!" said Marcia, and her tears flowed afresh.

"Don't, honey,—don't!" said the old nurse in distress. "You'll spile dem pooty eyes of yourn, and den you can't never git to be de princess, and do dem grand things we done talked about."

"I don't care about being a princess," sobbed Marcia; "this old house and the dear old garden are more to me than all the palaces in the world!"

"Jes' wait till you see dem palaces!" said Aunt Phillis, with more philosophy than one would have given her credit for. "I'se feared dey'll be so fine, dat you'll not stop wi' forgetting dis house, but dem odder houses made without any hands, what we read about."

"Never!" said Marcia indignantly, drying her tears. "Aunt Phillis, what do you take me for?"

" Dar, honey, dat's how I like to see you, head
up, and eyes a-flashin'. Lord! dar's no countin' de
hearts you'll smash when ye gits big 'nuff; wish
I could be dar to see!"

" Then why will you not come with me?" said
Marcia reproachfully; " my uncle said I might
take you, if you were willing."

" Gospel troof, ebry word, and marse's a gen-
man ebry inch o' him. But what 'ud 'come o' de
old place widout Aunt Phillis? No! no, honey,
it a'most kills me to leff you go, but I must stay
here and keep things straight till you come back
wi' dat grand young prince what's waitin' for
you somewhar in dis land o' promise. And now,
chile, you must go to bed, whar you orter bin
an hour ago!" and unheeding Marcia's remonstrance, she undressed her as if she had been an
infant, and laid her in the bed, where, overcome
with weeping and fatigue, she was soon wrapped
in a profound slumber.

Long after her darling slept, the faithful old
nurse kept watch beside her, while the big tears,
hitherto so bravely repressed, fell thick and fast
over her sable cheeks. The bright, beautiful
morning came all to soon for her, but the sunshine charmed away half of Marcia's sorrow, and

she was able to smile through her tears, as the carriage rolled through the gates through which she was one day to return—but we will not anticipate, for in

.

"Every venture of the chances
  Of life's sad, oft desperate game,
Whatsoever be our motive,
  Whatsoever be our aim,
  It is well we cannot see
  What the end shall be."

CHAPTER VI.

"O pleasantest of mortal things!—
That angels dwell in homes on earth,
Where silently, with folded wings,
They tarry by the hearth."

IT was a cool, pleasant apartment in one of the handsome mansions that dot the banks of our beautiful Hudson, which has been most appropriately styled the "Rhine of America." The Rhine, but without its ruins, and consequently without that delightful and mysterious charm which the shadow of a dead past ever casts over the living present.

The intermingling of the "then" and "now," the shadow and the sunshine, the gray moss-grown ruin and the fresh, springing shrub or flower, serves as much to beautify and intensify the landscape, as, in life, the sorrows bring out and heighten the joys, and in the mosaic of human existence, the dark stones, even more than the fair

ones, perfect and define the design of the heavenly
Architect. But there must be something in the
very thought of Germany, suggestive of idealism
and mysticism, since we have wandered off into
those cloud-veiled regions instead of entering the
"cool, pleasant apartment" on whose threshold
we stood at the opening of this chapter. And yet
it was most inviting: the soft summer breeze
floated in through the mist-like lace curtains that
draped the long, low windows, bearing with it
the combined sweets of the myriads of gay blossoms that adorned the terraced parterres without.
Beautiful pictures hung on the frescoed walls;
groups of rare statuary looked out from sculptured
niches; while the open Steinway, bestrewn with
the contents of the half-emptied music-stand beside
it, the spacious table, plentifully laden with uncut
pamphlets, papers, and the latest contributions to
the world of literature; to say nothing of the
lounging-chairs of every conceivable pattern and
shape, and the dainty work-stand with its domes-
tically suggestive feminine appurtenances, told
that this was the family sitting-room. But not
the least attractive feature of the apartment was
the fair, gentle lady who, in her low seat beside
the work-stand aforesaid, was endeavoring

to busy herself in the fabrication of some article
of child's apparel, an occupation which was
seriously interrupted by long, frequent glances at
the clock on the mantel.

At last she said to herself, "It is almost time ;
he will soon be here now," and the smile that
illuminated her face was tender with the love-light
of many summers, ay ! and winters too ; for hers
was one of those true woman's hearts which beat
alike in the June sunshine or the December snow.

"He has been gone so long," said she, pursuing
her musings. "But I am glad he went ; so glad
that his stern old mother blessed him before she
died. And poor little Marcia ! what would she
have done without him ? So young and so
alone ! My heart yearns for the poor motherless
child. I hope the girls will be gentle and thought-
ful with her, and not forget that she is among
strangers. And Miss Herbert, I must caution
her about the lessons. She might be too exacting
just at first—But," exclaimed she, as she caught
the sound of merry little feet upon the stairway,
"there comes Nita and Dick ; so good-by to
thoughts for the present," and she turned smilingly to welcome the intruders.

Yes ! this is Aunt Lucia, the wife of whom Mr.

Elmore spoke so lovingly; though it seems superfluous to say so, as her reverie has already served to assure us of her identity, as well as to introduce us to the "precious pair of spoiled darlings," who presently came bounding in, saying breathlessly:

"O mamma! mayn't we go in the carriage to meet papa? We have been so good all day! Miss Herbert says so!"

"Who can doubt that you are paragons with such an endorsement?" said their mother, smiling. "But what was that I overheard nurse telling Betty this morning about mud-pies, and a torn frock, and a missing cap?" It seems to me, that a little boy and a little girl, not a thousand miles off, had something to do with the woful ditty."

"O yes! that was us," said Dick, hanging his head. "But we didn't go to do it—that is, the torn frock and the lost cap. And the mud-pies! they were mighty nice—and p'raps you made 'em too when you was a little girl!"

Mrs. Elmore's delicate hands certainly appeared an emphatic refutation of the slanderous accusation; but she only laughed merrily as she said:

"O, you wise little ones! how soon you learn

to teach us that the follies of childhood are not to be measured by the wisdom of age!" And then she added in a different tone: "Yes, darlings, you shall go to meet papa. But, Nita, let me straighten your sash! and Dick, you monkey, don't forget to be polite to Cousin Marcia!"

"Oh! another girl!" said Dick in a doleful tone, shrugging his precocious shoulders. "And girls ain't one bit jolly: none but Nita," and the inseparables darted out of the room to get ready for their drive.

Mrs. Elmore reseated herself—and again took up her work; but her fingers were idle, and she was as far into dreamland as ever, when, a few moments later, a pair of soft arms were twined lovingly around her neck, and a fresh, young voice exclaimed gayly:

"My dear, sweet, lovely mamma! I don't have to be a magician to guess where your thoughts are straying—for my part, I wonder that you are even making a pretence of doing anything. As for Jennie and me—we haven't had one grain of sense all day. Now, please," she continued, putting her hand playfully over her mother's mouth, as she tried to make some remark, "don't rise to explain that this is my chronic state. I don't

deny it ; but you must admit that it is most unusual with Jenny. Poor Miss Herbert arose this
morning in one of her most rigid moods, fully intent on Lindley Murray and abstruse mathematics,
both of which she was forced to relinquish early
in the day, proposing 'Gibbon's Decline and
Fall' as a compromise (her idea of light reading,
you know). By the time the bell rang for luncheon, she was glad to suggest Shakespeare. Only
think, mamma, of Miss Herbert suggesting Shakespeare in school-hours ! But one page of Julius
Cæsar, as rendered by Misses Jennie and Lottie
Elmore, so thoroughly disgusted her, that she
actually dismissed us in despair."

"Poor Miss Herbert ! I fear you madcap girls
have tormented her sadly. But where is Jennie ? "

"Putting the finishing-touches to the grand
toilet with which she proposes to delight papa
and overwhelm our new cousin."

"I would like to know of what that grand
toilet will consist," said her mother, laughing ;
"for if I am not mistaken, Miss Jennie owns
nothing more elaborate than the white muslin
in which you have so becomingly arrayed yourself."

"Thank you, mamma ! It is so comfortable to

have you praise me, especially when you are generally obliged to reprove me for my carelessness. But something must be conceded to the beauty and belle of the family. A bow here and a flower there will make all the difference in the world between Jennie and me, and the effect will fully compensate for the extra time taken to produce it. No doubt I look very passable in my white muslin, and this blue ribbon, which is vainly endeavoring to confine these troublesome curls into something like proper limits : à la Grecque, as Miss Herbert says—'My dear Miss Lottie, arrange your hair à la Grecque!' But Jennie's tout ensemble will be positively regal. Please, mamma, give me a good mark for the French phrases. But there comes the 'faire ladye.' Did I not tell you so?" and she looked admiringly at her sister, who just then entered the room.

"I know that you are a dear, good, unselfish girl," said her mother, kissing her fondly, "and I have a right to be proud of both my daughters!"

And who could gainsay it—Lottie's fair, smiling face, in which the rival roses of York and Lancaster struggled ambitiously for ascendency, framed in a nimbus of soft golden ringlets, formed

in truth a charming picture, albeit in direct contrast to her sister, on whom none could gaze with
out yielding involuntary homage to her peerless
loveliness. Tall, slender, and graceful, the effect
of her simple dress heightened and enhanced by
those indescribable touches to which Lottie had
playfully alluded, the dark hair wound in a massive coil around her classic head, she realized the
ideal of a beautiful brunette.

> "On her cheek an autumn flush
> Deeply ripened: such a bush
> In the midst of brown was born,
> Like red poppies grown with corn.

> "Round her eyes her tresses fell,—
> Which were blackest none could tell;
> But long lashes veiled a light
> That had else been all too bright."

"And I am sure you are not prouder of us
than we are of our own dear mother," said she
with a loving glance from her dark eyes, that
made Lottie exclaim :

"Those eyes! those eyes! Such glances may
be very harmless when lavished on dear mamma ;
but my soft heart is already filled with compassion for the poor victims that are destined to
come within range of your masked batteries next
winter."

4

"Then I fear you are wasting your sympathy," retorted Jennie gayly. "I anticipate no such wholesale hecatombs to my charms. I am no Julius Cæsar that I should 'veni, vidi, vici.' By the way, mamma, did Lottie tell you about our Julius Cæsar to-day?"

"Yes; and I suppose I ought to be very much displeased, if I were not too happy to be stern to-day. But come, let us go out on the piazza. Your father will certainly be here soon, for the clock has already struck six."

"And there is the carriage just turning into the avenue," said Lottie, clapping her hands with delight; "and as I live, there is that irrepressible Dick perched up beside the coachman! Rather an exalted position for a young man of his inches."

And in a few moments more, the fond greetings had been exchanged, and Lottie, as a matter of course, had taken possession of Marcia, and carried her off to the room they were henceforth to occupy together, chattering volubly all the while.

"Here, Marcia," said she, "this is my book-self, and mamma has had that one put between the windows for you, in hopes, as she says, that

you will shame me into something like order ; for
you must know I am an incorrigible sloven."

"Oh, I am so glad !" said Marcia ; this honest
confession acting like magic in dispelling the uncomfortable, strange feeling that had hitherto possessed her.

"Glad that I am a sloven !" exclaimed Lottie,
laughing. "I fear that is hardly kind."

"Oh, I do not mean that," replied Marcia,
coloring. "Only I am so full of faults myself,
that I was afraid if you were too good and too
perfect, you would not love me as my uncle said
you would."

"And as I am sure I will," said the warm-
hearted girl, impulsively throwing her arms
around Marcia. "It must be so sad to have no
sisters and brothers. I am sure I don't know
what I should do without mine."

"And Jennie is so beautiful," said Marcia.
"I fairly held my breath when I looked at her.
It is strange, but she is so like the Donna Inez
in our picture-gallery at home."

"And who is Donna Inez?" asked Lottie, her
curiosity and her interest at once aroused.

"One of my ancestors," said Marcia simply.

"I will tell you all about it some day. But the story is too long and too sad for to-day."

"Please, Lottie, may I come in?" said a small, disconsolate voice just then, and a curly head was thrust doubtfully in at the door.

"Certainly, Queenie," said Lottie, springing up; "but Nita, pet, what is the matter? Those pretty lips are sticking out ever so far, and actually I see two big tears in those bright little eyes."

"I ain't no Queenie nor pet neither, to-night," said the little one more forcibly than grammatically. "Nobody likes me, and nobody wants me. Papa and mamma are talking so hard they can't even see me; Sister Jennie is walking on the terrace with Miss Herbert, and you're worse than any of them; for you just runned away with Cousin Marcia as if she was all yours, when she's mine,—for I went in the carriage to get her."

"So you did, you little darling," said Marcia, kissing her.

"But where is Dick?" continued Lottie; "he is generally quantum sufficit."

"He has gone to the stable with Thomas," said Nita, her tears rising with her growing sense of injury. "I wanted to go too, but he said I was too fine, and told me that I'd never be a '*brick*' till I stopped wearing blue shoes and these things," pointing to the broad sash tied around her waist.

"Ah! that was 'the straw that broke the camel's back,'" said Lottie sympathizingly. "Poor little thing! your cup of grievances is indeed running over. But what would Dick say if he knew you had been crying? Tears are even worse than sashes, according to his code of morals. Let us wipe them all off and coax back the smiles, while Cousin Marcia brushes her hair for supper, which I am sure will soon be ready."

And the little fairy was again all sunshine at that happy meal, where she was petted and spoiled to her heart's content, her papa having scarcely a word for any one else. Marcia was the delighted recipient of her kind Aunt Lucia's undivided attention; but the very depth of her feelings made her unusually silent and reserved, which, combined with her thin, colorless face, and not too tastefully selected toilet, caused the fastidious Miss Jennie to wonder what her papa could have seen in that pale, silent, unformed girl, to call forth the enthusiastic praises with which his letters had been filled.

All unconscious, however, of this hasty criticism, Marcia meanwhile was positively revelling in Jennie's beauty. Indeed, her entire surroundings filled her with a delicious sense of rest and happiness; and this day, which had introduced her for the first time to the sanctities of domestic life and the family circle, was destined to be for her a gold-lined one forever, shining all the more brightly from its contrast with the dark ones through which she had just passed; and when she laid her head on her pillow that night, she could even find it in her heart to be thankful for the past shadows which so heightened and glorified the present sunshine.

CHAPTER VII.

"Multiplication is a vexation,
Division is as bad ;
The rule of three doth puzzle me,
And fractions drive me 'mad,'"

SANG Lottie gayly one bright afternoon as she entered the school-room, where Marcia was seated, her head resting on her hands, poring disconsolately over a slate filled with a most unpromising array of figures.

"O Lottie! I am so stupid. I don't believe I will ever get this sum, and yet Miss Herbert says it is so easy that even Dick could do it."

"I suspect that is simply a little figure of speech on the part of Miss Herbert, though you know that Dick is conceded to be a mathematical prodigy. But what is the difficulty?" and she drew the slate towards her as she spoke.

"O no! you must not!" exclaimed Marcia ; adding hastily, "Not that I do not think it very kind of you, but Miss Herbert told me I must do it myself, and I don't think it would be quite right to let you help me."

"As you please," said Lottie, reluctantly giving back the slate; "but, Marcia, please make haste. The afternoon is perfectly lovely, and mamma says I may take you to see that beautiful view which I have been longing to show you ever since you have been here."

"You may be sure that I will do my very best," said Marcia ruefully; " but"—with a long-drawn sigh—"I fear there will be no views for me this afternoon."

"She ' sighs like a furnace ! ' " exclaimed Jennie in a theatrical tone, entering the room just then in search of a book. "Shade of the immortal Shakespeare, tell us what weighty matter has evoked those lugubrious echoes from their vasty depths !"

"Now, Jennie, don't mount your Pegasus," said Lottie. "It is nothing but Marcia's tiresome sums." But Marcia only moved uneasily in her seat in painful consciousness of the covert satire her sensitive nature was keen to detect.

"What! does the brilliant mind refuse to grasp the idea that two and two make four, or is the number of times that ten is contained in twenty the incomprehensible problem?"

"For shame! Jennie," exclaimed Lottie angrily, and Marcia's eyes flashed, though she bit her lips to keep back a hasty retort, and her usually pale face flushed with the effort to repress her rising tears.

"And why for shame?" said Jennie provokingly. "I am sure I have not said 'the rose that all are praising is not the rose for me,' even though I may have seen fit to indulge in a little pleasantry at the expense of the rare exotic."

"Jennie!" again burst indignantly from Lottie's lips; but at this moment Miss Herbert opened the door, and glancing from one to another in surprise, said in her coldest and most governess-like tone: "Young ladies, what does this mean? I sent one of your number hither in order that the silence and recollection which we endeavor to make the rule of this apartment might facilitate the accomplishment of a certain unfinished task; but I surely did not expect to find her holding such a levée."

"Oh, it is all my fault!" exclaimed the impulsive Lottie. "I was the first intruder. I came in to tell Marcia of a treat which mamma had

4*

promised us, and to see if I could not hurry her
up a little."

"Hurry her up!" repeated Miss Herbert.
"Really, Miss Lottie, I must beg you to be more
choice in your language. But how did you propose to do this? Not, I hope, by offering assistance?" and her countenance assumed a look of
greater severity than it had yet worn.

"Who can doubt it?" said Jennie in a tone
which told that her stinging mood had not yet
passed. "These female Damon and Pythias pro-
fess to hold all things in common; then why should
they make exceptions of such trifling matters as
talents, accomplishments, or," she added point-
edly, "mathematical proficiency."

"Why, Jennie! I do not know you this afternoon!" exclaimed Lottie in mingled grief and
anger. "What have Marcia and I done to call
forth such cutting remarks? But, Miss Herbert,
it is true that I wanted to help Marcia, but she
was too honorable to accept my offer."

"That is very well," said she, unbending somewhat; "and now, young ladies, I must beg you
to leave your cousin to her task."

As the governess was supreme in the school-
room, there was no alternative but to obey, and

Jennie walked out haughtily, while Lottie reluctantly followed her, casting a wistful glance at
Marcia as she passed.

During all this trying scene Marcia had sat perfectly silent, keeping her lips firmly closed, with a
self-control remarkable in one so impulsive and so
unused to authority or restraint ; but when Miss
Herbert also withdrew, and she felt herself at last
alone, she laid her head on her desk and sobbed
as if her heart would break. Poor child ! A few
short weeks ago, when she entered her uncle's
house, she had felt that she had entered paradise.
But already had she discovered the trail of the
serpent that lingers in every earthly Eden. The
thorns had already begun to grow on the roses, the
shadows to flit across the sunlit paths, and she was
learning the lesson which since the days of Adam
has, sooner or later, been conned by all his poster-
ity. True, her uncle was as tender and thought-
ful as ever ; her Aunt Lucia was kindness itself,
and the loving, sweet-tempered Lottie had at once
taken her to her heart of hearts. So far the picture
was all golden, but the ebon lines were not wanting.. Miss Herbert, although highly accomplished,
and in general thoroughly just and impartial, was
not calculated to enter into and appreciate a nature

like Marcia's; and though Mrs. Elmore had imparted to her all the circumstances of her neglected
childhood, she could not understand how such
ignorance of the common, primary branches of ed-
ucation could be coupled with such a varied stock
of general knowledge as Marcia undoubtedly possessed. This rendered her disinclined to overlook
any failure, and so exacting was she, that few
indeed were the afternoons on which Marcia was
permitted to leave the school-room with her
cousins. Marcia, proud and sensitive, and painfully conscious of her deficiency, never complained;
but she sometimes found it difficult to restrain
Lottie's indignation at what she termed Miss Herbert's injustice. But the sharpest thorn in Marcia's
side was Jennie's treatment of her. Her speech of
to-day was but a fair specimen of similar ones
which she was constantly making. Indeed, she
scarcely ever addressed a remark to Marcia that
did not contain some lurking satire. This seemed
unaccountable, especially as the young girl had,
from the first, conceived a passionate admiration
for her beautiful cousin. But Jennie had so long
been the idol of her family, and was so accustomed
to the adulation universally paid to her rare beauty
and talents, that she could not brook even the idea

of a possible rival; and with more discernment than Miss Herbert, she foresaw that she might some day meet with such a one in Marcia. She at once recognized the brilliancy and strength of her rich, untrained intellect; the gems drawn from the stores accumulated in her extended, though desultory reading filled her with unconscious envy, and she was even compelled to acknowledge that the expressive midnight eyes were in no way inferior to her own glorious orbs, and that the thin, colorless face possessed a delicacy and refinement of outline, and an intellectuality of expression, that not only redeemed it from present ugliness, but gave promise of future beauty. This latent spark had been fanned into a flame by the music-master, who, at Marcia's first lesson, after testing her untried capabilities by the customary gamut, had delightedly exclaimed in Jennie's hearing :

"Ah, this is one grand voice ! We will make one *superbe* singer of mademoiselle."

The languages also seemed to come to Marcia by intuition ; so that in the very paths in which her supremacy had hitherto been most indisputable, Jennie already saw her young cousin pressing hard in her steps.

In the meantime, with the true humility of genius, Marcia was entirely unconscious of all this. The idea of rivalling her peerless cousin never entered her busy brain, though she often racked it to discover a cause for the coldness and indifference, which so deeply hurt her. This afternoon, however, speculation was lost in exquisite pain, and her long pent-up tears flowed on without restraint. The afternoon waned, and the evening shadows stole into the silent room, but she marked them not, till a soft hand was laid on her shoulder and a sweet voice exclaimed in surprise :

"You here! Why, my child! I thought that you and Lottie were on the very top of Hudson Heights, enjoying the pure air and the grand scenery. And crying too! What is the matter?"

And her Aunt Lucia sat down beside her, stroking her burning brow with a kind, motherly touch that soothed Marcia at once, so that she was able to answer calmly.

"I did not have my sums, and I could not go."

"That is hardly sufficient cause for all these tears," said Mrs. Elmore, pausing ; but as Marcia did not volunteer any further explanation, she continued : "Why did you not come for me to intercede for you?"

"I did not think of it ; and if I had, I should not have liked to trouble you."

"Never say that again," interrupted her aunt. "Do you not know that a mother considers nothing troublesome that she can do for her children, and it is her highest privilege to be the chosen confidante of their joys and sorrows—and my dear, you must not forget that you are now my child."

"Thank you! thank you, dear Aunt Lucia," said Marcia, seizing her hand and covering it with kisses, and at the same time inwardly resolving that although her silence might cause her to appear ungrateful and wanting in confidence, nothing should tempt her to pain that kind heart by revealing the true cause of her distress.

But whatever her aunt may have thought, she only drew the child more closely to her, saying, "But what about those unhappy sums? I fear the tears have been as fatal to their accomplishment as the excursion with Lottie would have been."

"Indeed they have," said Marcia ruefully. "I fear that Miss Herbert will think me either very stupid or very stubborn, or perhaps both," and she sighed wearily.

"I will make it all right with Miss Herbert this

time, and induce her to wipe off old scores and begin
anew.   But go now, my dear, and smoothe these
disordered tresses, and try to reduce your swollen
eyes to something more like natural dimensions,
before your uncle sees you, or he will wonder who
has been persecuting his Southern wild-flower."

Putting her slate away with alacrity, Marcia
threw her arms around her dear aunt, exclaiming,
"Blessings on you, precious, darling Aunt Lucia!
I wish I could do something to prove my love for
you.   The perils that the brave knights of old
encountered to serve their ladye loves are nothing
to what I would do for you," and her spirits re-
bounding with the elasticity of youth, she tripped
lightly out of the room.

"Poor child!" mused Aunt Lucia, as she vanished, "if she but knew how much more highly I
would prize her confidence than all the chivalry of
the middle ages, she would not withhold it.   What
can I do to win it?   I am sure those sums could not
have been the sole cause of such a burst of grief,
though I fear Miss Herbert is too harsh with her:
I am certain that she does not understand her,
nor does she understand my loving Lottie's gentle
nature.   With Jennie, her course has been admira-
ble; but different temperaments require different

management. Ah! how much easier it is to be ruled than to rule! 'Uneasy lies the head that wears a crown' is true of all in authority, be theirs a princely diadem or the more lowly insignia of the mother of a family. But the office is so sweet, I would not exchange it. Ah! there are Nita and Dick's merry voices in the hall. And this is what Lonfellow calls 'the children's hour.' I must go to them! Ah my little darlings, if I could but keep you always as you are now. A few short years, and the others will be fledged and flown, and the time will come when you too must leave the parent nest; but for the present at least I can say with the poet:

> "I have you fast in my fortress,
>   And will not let you depart,
> But put you into the dungeon
>   In the round-tower of my heart."

CHAPER VIII.

" How sweet (while warm airs lull us, blowing lowly),
With half-dropped eyelids still,
Beneath a heaven dark and holy,
To watch the long bright river drawing slowly
His waters from the purple hill—
To hear the dewy echoes calling
From cave to cave through the thick-trimmed vine,
To hear the emerald-colored water falling
Through many a woven acanthus-wreath divine !
Only to hear and see the far-off sparkling brine,
Only to hear were sweet, stretched out beneath the pine."

TENNYSON.

THUS might Marcia and Lottie have spoken, if they could have clothed their thoughts in words as they sat, a few afternoons later, beneath the tall, spreading trees, contemplating the beautiful Hudson from one of its most romantic and picturesque localities. Both young girls were endowed with a keen appreciation of nature ; but to Marcia's poetic temperament, the feeling amounted to a passion, and she gazed as if she could not drink in enough of the beauty scattered with such a lavish hand around them. She gazed and then she dreamed till her eyes grew shadowy with visions of the mysterious land, which none but disembodied spirits may enter save in fancy.

"Marcia," said Lottie at last; but eliciting no response: "Marcia," she repeated, "where is your fancy straying? your face looks so strange and weird, that involuntarily I have thought of the beautiful Lorelei, and wondered if she could have left her fair grotto in the Rhine to charm you with her fatal song."

"O Lottie! why did you speak? This river was the river of life to me; those white-sailed boats, our barks launched on its surface. I have watched them, now floating idly with the tide, and anon struggling with the rushing current. The sunshine has ever seemed to rest goldenly on yours, while mine has often sailed beneath the shadows. See! yours is already safely moored to the shore, while mine is still breasting the rising waves, hurrying onward, where yon lowering cloud, prophetic of tempests and storms, shrouds the distant horizon in gloom."

"But your bark is not destined to be wrecked," said Lottie; "it will battle nobly with the storm.

See how bravely it mounts the white-capped breakers!" Hand in hand, the two girls silently watched the receding bark, till at last Lottie exclaimed, "There, we can see it no longer. Blessings attend it!" And then springing up hastily, she added: "But, Marcia, we must be going, and that at once, for if I mistake not, these gathering clouds betoken more mischief to us than that far-off one we have been watching so intently. Let us hasten, or the rain will be upon us."

Losing no time, they immediately descended the height; but ere they reached the valley, the lightning began to flash and the thunder to roll ominously. Lottie turned pale as the echoes reverberated through the surrounding hills; but Marcia seemed imbued with the very spirit of the storm, and her face glowed with an unnatural excitement.

"Is not this grand?" said she to her shrinking companion. "Lottie, are we anywhere in the neighbourhood of 'Sleepy Hollow'? I should so like to meet the famous Heinrich Hudson and his silent band; but I am afraid that although the elements are so favorable, the hour is not propitious."

"How can you talk so, Marcia. I am actually

trembling with fright; and there comes the rain to add to our troubles," said Lottie, as the big drops began to fall around them.

" What of that ?" returned Marcia ; " we are not so delicate that a little rain can hurt us."

"But we are a good half mile from home, and mamma will be so uneasy."

"Ah, yes, dear Aunt Lucia ! I never thought. I would not like to frighten her ; but is there no place where we can find shelter ? Those gates ! I don't remember to have seen them before, but surely they must lead somewhere ?" and Marcia pointed to a pair of massive iron gates just ahead of them.

" Ah, yes ; the Murray place ; I did not think we were so near it," said Lottie, more cheerfully. " There is nobody there but the old gardener and his wife, who is the housekeeper; but they will be glad to shelter us. Kenneth Murray, who owns the place, is the last of his family, and he is papa's ward, and is away in Europe with Paul."

By this time they had reached the gates, but finding them securely locked, they were glad to effect an entrance by climbing the fence. The rain was now falling in torrents, and their light summer clothing was completely drenched ; but notwithstanding these untoward circumstances, Marcia could not help noticing the grand sweep of the broad avenue that led to the house, which was a fine old mansion built of rough gray stone, covered here and there with creeping ivy vines, and bearing a look of venerable antiquity, unusual in this young country, where, although fortunes are often made in a day, they rarely remain in a family for more than one generation.

"Thank God, we are here at last!" said Lottie, as she ascended the steps; while Marcia raised the knocker on the great doors. The echo thus awakened half startled the two girls as it sounded through the empty halls, but in a few moments steps were heard approaching, the key turned slowly in the lock, and old Jeffries the gardener appeared, amazement pictured in every lineament of his honest face.

"Lord! Miss Lottie," said he, "be that you? How ever did you git out in sich a storm. But walk in, you and t'other miss too. It's an ill wind that blows no good, and the old 'ooman'll be precious glad to see your purty faces, if you be as wet as two ducks in a duck-pond."

"Indeed we are wet enough," said Lottie, laughing, her spirits rising now that she found herself under shelter. "But, Jeffries, this is my cousin, Miss Marcia Lyle, who has come to live with us; and I know she will be as great a favorite with you as the rest of us madcaps. You will find her quite good-looking when she is dried out a little," she added mischievously.

"I am sure of that," gayly rejoined the old man. "And I am proud to make Miss Marcia's acquaintance, and I know the Missis'll be the same, and she'll have you dry as bones in a twinklin'. But here she is to speak for herself," he added, as they had now reached the end of the hall, and a trim little dame, with cap and neckerchief as immaculate as her snowy white apron, stepped out of the housekeeper's room, and advanced to meet them.

"Bless us, Miss Lottie!" exclaimed she, 'who'd 'a thought o' seein' you! And I s'pose this is the young lady as is come from furrin parts to live with you. Sakes alive! how wet you be. But never mind, wet or dry, you are 'as welcome as the flowers o' May,' so walk in and sit by the fire, while I look up suthin warm to put on your blessed backs. It is a lucky thing that I would have the fire this evening, though Jeffries often laughs at me for kindlin' it in midsummer; but as

I tell him, it looks more cheerful like, and there's no knowin' what may happen."

All this time she was bustling about, putting the tea-kettle to boil and making the young girls comfortable ; but presently she left the room, returning in a few moments with a pile of snowy linen on one arm, and on the other two dresses of rich brocaded satin, the sight of which would at once have carried us back to the days of our great grandmothers.

"O Mrs. Jeffries, those dresses!" exclaimed Lottie. "They make me think of Kenneth. You must know, Marcia, that there are trunks full of just such as these upstairs, and in the good old times when we used to come here for a day's frolic, we considered it our greatest treat to be allowed to rummage through them. Sometimes Mrs. Jeffries was so kind as to let us put them on, and I can assure you that we felt very grand, strutting about in our borrowed plumage."

"That you did, and as handsome a set of little ones you were as ever I'd wish to set my two eyes on ; my own bairn (asking your pardon) the finest and tallest of you all ;" and the old dame wiped her eyes with the corner of her snowy apron. "You see, Miss Lottie, I knowed well enough that you and t'other miss oughtn't to sit in these wet clothes, so I made bold to get some of my own linen, which, though hardly fit for such as you, is the best I have to offer; but I was puzzled what to do for dresses, till all at once I minded those old times; and here are two gowns fine enough for a queen; but, if you don't mind my saying so, you must put them on in a jiffy, before you take cold!"

"Thank you! How kind! This is delightful!" burst simultaneously from the lips of both the girls, and they were soon attiring themselves in great glee, when Marcia suddenly exclaimed:

"But, Lottie, is there no way in which we can let Aunt Lucia know that we are safe? It seems wrong to be so merry, when she may be suffering so much on our account."

"Bless your dear heart for mindin' that sweet aunt o' yourn; but old heads is more thochtfu' than young ones, and as soon as I seed you safe in my own room, I started. Jem, the blacksmith's lad, who had been helping the old man in the garden the afternoon, to tell the dear leddy that I have you, and that I mean to keep you till the storm is over, if it lasts all night. It'll not be

5

the first night Miss Lottie has passed at the
' Ivy.' "

"But the storm is raging fearfully, and it is already dark," said Lottie, as an ominous peal of
thunder resounded in the distance and the rain
beat furiously against the window-panes. "Do
you not think that Jem will be frightened and
turn back ? "

"Not he!" said the old lady. "He's a brave
lad and fleet o' foot; and he no more minds a
storm than Heinrich Hudson himself; so, my
dears, make yourselves easy and let me hear your
blithesome laugh again."

After this the dressing went gayly on, and our
two school-girls were soon transformed into elegant court ladies of a century agone. All was
complete, even to the arrangement of the hair,
which the girls had accomplished with wonderful
skill, and the effect of which was greatly heightened by two elaborate combs which the kind
housekeeper had drawn forth from her store of
antiquities, and which the delighted Marcia and
Lottie declared to be all that was wanting to the
perfection of their toilet. Just as they were finished, and were taking an enraptured view of
themselves, old Jeffries appeared at the door with

a light, and invited them to the library, which he had opened and made ready for their accommodation. Accepting his invitation with alacrity, their fresh, young voices awakened such gladsome echoes in the long-silent halls, that good old Mrs. Jeffries smiled softly to herself as she set to work to get what she called "a bite" and "a sup," and her old man exclaimed that it seemed like the good old times.

The library was a cheerful, spacious apartment, albeit of sufficient dignity of aspect to be in keeping with the general character of the mansion. The tall, well-filled bookcases were laden with a wealth of classic lore that would have given the finishing-stroke to a bibliomaniac, and the marble bust of many a departed genius kept watch over the garnered treasures of his immortal intellect. Artistic groupings in bronze adorned either end of the mantel-shelf, in the centre of which stood a clock, whose motionless hands had long pointed to the mystic hour of twelve ; while underneath it, just above the broad fireplace, was a marble shield, on which were engraved these words :.

"Principia, non homines." (Principles, not men.)

"That," said Lottie, as Marcia stooped to read

the inscription, "is the motto of the Murray family, and such a noble race have they proved,
that it is said that none have failed to come up to
the high standard."

"That is indeed high praise!" said Marcia,
"and certainly does not tend to lessen the interest surrounding the absent Kenneth, with whose
premises we are making so free. Tell me, is he
one of those heroes to whom 'distance lends enchantment to the view,' or do you think he would
stand the test of closer inspection?"

"As for that, cara mia, I hope you will soon
have an opportunity of judging for yourself; for
as papa is growing impatient at Paul's long absence, and Kenneth's recently attained majority
makes his presence here indispensable, we may
hope soon to see 'the Duncan on his native heath!'
However, when Kenneth left us, he was as handsome a lad as one might wish to see, and in character a perfect Bayard, *sans peur et sans reproche.*
But that speaking likeness opposite will satisfy
your curiosity better than any words of mine could
do; for I could almost imagine it to be Kenneth
himself thrust into a frame and suspended from
the wall."

And truly it was a handsome face that greeted

Marcia from the canvas, as she turned to look at
it. The laughing blue eyes ; the fair hair tossed
carelessly back from the smooth, broad brow ; the
firm, proud mouth, giving even to that boyish
countenance the stamp of character and determination ; the unconscious grace of attitude, all challenged the young girl's admiration, and she gazed
so long and fixedly, that Lottie exclaimed, laughing :

"Cease those longing glances, cousin mine, or I
will make them the material of an impromptu romance !"

Marcia smiled, and then said, as if thinking aloud,
"*Sans peur et sans reproche!* Such a casket might
well enshrine a spotless, fearless soul. But I wonder where the original may be wandering this
wild night, while we are so snugly ensconced amid
his Lares and Penates."

"Somewhere in the mystic Rhine-land," rejoined Lottie : "perchance whispering soft noth-
ings in the ear of some golden-haired, rosy-cheeked
fräulein, oblivious of America and America's fair
daughters. But who can that be?" she exclaimed,
as a thundering knock at that moment fell on their
startled ears ; "I cannot think that mamma would
send for us in such a storm !"

"Nor I!" said Marcia, listening intently as the tones of a clear, manly voice now rang through the hall, followed by exclamations of wonder and delight from old Jeffries and his wife.

"I verily believe it is Kenneth himself!" said Lottie at last. "Remember the old adage, 'Speak of the rays and the sun will appear!'" and she started impulsively for the door; but before she could reach it, it opened and a young man entered, but paused on the threshold with a most ludicrous expression of perplexity and surprise.

"O Kenneth! how glad I am to see you," said Lottie rushing eagerly forward to greet him.

"Why, Lottie! is that you?" returned he no less warmly. "I really did not recognize you, until you spoke. Jeffries informed me that there was a light in the library, but left me wholly unprepared for the vision of loveliness awaiting me therein. I deemed myself returning solitary to a solitary home, and you can imagine my surprise when I suddenly found myself in the presence of two fair dames, who looked as if they might have stepped out of the picture-gallery to meet me. For a moment the relics of my childish belief in ghosts overpowered me, and then I felt inclined to rub my eyes to see if I were dreaming."

"Ah! I had forgotten my magnificent attire," said Lottie, coloring, "and," she added, "I fear I have forgotten my politeness as well, for I have not yet presented you to my cousin Marcia. However, I am sure she will take the circumstances into consideration and forgive me."

"I scarcely feel that I require an introduction to Miss Lyle," said Kenneth, bowing with courtly grace; "for you honored her with such frequent mention in your letters to Paul, that her name became, I might say, a household word to us, if it be not an anomaly to suppose that two such wanderers could claim any household words."

"But where is Paul?" questioned Lottie eagerly; "you have told me nothing of him! Of course he returned with you?"

"O yes! and he has doubtless ere this astounded the family circle at 'Glen Eden' as thoroughly as I have astounded you. I left him at the gate as we passed."

"But why did you not go in with him? I wonder that he would let you go on alone in such a storm!"

"Ah! he did endeavor to detain me, but I deemed a mother's welcome too sacred a thing for stranger eyes to intrude upon, so I resisted the

temptation and trudged on to the home that would
have been desolate indeed, had not you fair ladies
brightened it with your presence!"

"Ah, Kenneth!" said Lottie gravely, "I have
half a mind to scold you. How can you call
yourself a stranger, when you know we all consider you quite one of us? Surely you have not
forgotten how often papa and mamma have reproved you for your morbid sensitiveness!"

"No! but I cannot forget, that in all this wide
world I am an alien; that my blood courses in no
living veins, and that, sacred and dear as are the
ties of friendship, ties of kindred I have none."
And the shadow on the young man's brow deep-
ened into gloom as he spoke, and the two girls were
silent, and Marcia's dark eyes grew wistful with
their yearning sympathy. Perhaps their unspo-
ken sorrow smote him with the consciousness that
he was illy playing the part of host; for in a
moment he said gayly, "But a truce to sentiment!
Here comes Jeffries,—and adding his presence to the
fact that certain savory odors have for some time
been assailing my anticipative nostrils, I arrive at
the mathematical certainty that he brings a summons to the festal board!"

And so it proved. Dame Jeffries had not forgotten her hungry Master Kenneth of old, and her
magic had conjured up an array of "good things"
that, at such short notice, was positively marvellous. Many were her apologies that she was not
able to serve them in state in the grand dining-
hall ; but youth brought to the meal the sauce of
happy hearts and a fine appetite, and we question
if, in all the days of its past grandeur, the Ivy had
ever been the scene of a merrier banquet.

By the time they had concluded, the storm had
passed, and the moon looked out from a sky as
serene and blue as if it had never known a cloud.
Before they could return to the library the carriage
from Glen Eden was announced, and Lottie, burning with impatience to welcome her long-absent
brother, hastened their departure, at the same time
urging Kenneth to accompany them. Marcia's
eyes looked the entreaties she did not feel at liberty
to utter ; but, resisting all appeals, Kenneth was
not to be moved, merely promising to see them
early in the morning. Still as he bade them good-
night, the shadow returned to his brow, nor did it
pass away as he sat brooding over the dying embers of the library fire ; but it had lifted somewhat

5*

when at last he took up his candle to retire to rest murmuring, softly to himself:

> "Eyes that displace
> The neighbor diamond, and outface
> The sunshine by their own sweet grace!"

CHAPTER IX.

"Gather ye rosebuds as ye may,
  Old Time is still a-flying;
  And this same flower that smiles to-day
  To-morrow will be dying."

ONE sunny morning, a few days after the stormy adventure of our young friends, a merry group was assembled on the lawn in front of Mr. Elmore's residence. Croquet had evidently been the order of the day; but the mallets were now carelessly cast aside, and Dick and Nita, happy in undisputed possession of the gayly colored balls, were rolling them aimlessly through the deserted wickets. Kenneth, bearing an ivy wreath, had just approached Marcia, and, bowing before her in graceful homage, was about to crown her victor, while the rest of the party, consisting of Christabelle Huntington and her saucy brother Fred, Lottie, and the newly arrived Paul, clapped their hands in rapturous applause. Jennie alone took no part in this pretty scene, though she made quite a picture herself, as she sat, a little to one side, bending her dangerous dark eyes full upon the handsome Clifford Aubrey, apparently engrossed in the poem he was reading aloud in such impassioned tones. And yet the game had been her own proposition, and she had entered into the arrangements with all ardor and enthusiasm, till, upon drawing lots for the leadership, fickle fortune had bestowed it upon Christabelle and Marcia. Then she suddenly discovered that the day was too warm; that croquet on such a morning would be insufferable; and sailed majestically off, bearing her preux chevalier with her; not, however, able entirely to suppress a rising flush, when Nita, with more shrewdness than was agreeable, exclaimed: "Now, Jennie, don't put on airs! Cousin Marcia couldn't help getting the shortest straw."

"Ces enfants terribles!" she exclaimed, shrugging her shoulders; and then with a look at her companion that would have tempted that bedazzled gentleman to the very wilds of Siberia, "Come, Mr. Aubrey, give me something from that tell-tale volume that peeps so suggestively from your treacherous pocket!"

Alas for Jennie! She would not serve where

she could not reign. "La reine le veut!" had been her motto from early childhood, and she could not bear to have her sovereignty disputed even in trifles like the present. Young as she was, not yet fairly launched upon the world's broad tide, few masculines could withstand the witchery of her wondrous beauty, and she had already learned to know her power, and to claim this homage as her right. The Kenneth of old, too boyish and rough for her precocious ladyship, she readily yielded to Lottie and her compeers; but the Kenneth of to-day was something vastly different, and she could illy brook that he should, even in jest, yield tribute at Marcia's shrine. "Que ces enfants s'amusent!" said she contemptuously, interrupting the finest stanza. "Marcia surely does not know how frightfully that green wreath contrasts with her sallow complexion!"

Her cavalier looked up with the bewildered expression of one startled out of a dream, and said musingly:

"On the contrary, I think it is vastly becoming. Your cousin is pale rather than sallow, and I must say she bears her unwonted honors most gracefully."

If there had been less of anger and more of sorrow in the look which Jennie cast on the luckless speaker, the historic "et tu Brute" of the murdered Cæsar would have sunk into insignificance before it, and there is no conjecturing what might have transpired, if Paul had not at that moment come to the rescue of the unconscious offender.

"Jennie!" called he, "if you and Mr. Aubrey have done poetizing, we would be thankful for the honor of your company. We are discussing Kenneth's fête, and as he says you are to be presiding genius of the occasion, he won't listen to any plans that have not received your sanction!"

Thus propitiated, Jennie arose, affecting not to see the arm which Mr. Aubrey duly offered for her acceptance, and bestowing her smiles so lavishly on every one but himself, that she sent that gentleman off into such a fit of abstraction, that when, in the discussion that followed, Lottie asked him if he had ever read "Robin Hood," he astonished her by repeating:

> "O woman! in our hours of ease,
> Uncertain, coy, and hard to please— "

coloring violently, when, with a mischievous twinkle in her eyes, she interrupted him with an :

"Excuse me, Mr. Aubrey, but I don't think that quotation occurs in Robin Hood."

Meanwhile the fête was talked over most animatedly and volubly; some were at first in favor of a masquerade, but these were soon overruled by the majority, with Jennie at their head, who proposed, as an amendment, an archery-meeting, with the participants in costume. Jennie was to personate Diana, with the other ladies attired as her attendants, while Kenneth and his friends appeared as Robin Hood and his merry men. No one, not even Nita and Dick, was to be slighted on this occasion: Kenneth having promised, to their infinite delight, that they should each have a bow and arrows and shoot at the target with the rest. A promise which, by the way, was very nearly productive of disastrous results, as the pair forthwith began to test their skill in the most untoward and improbable times and places. The evening was to conclude with fireworks and a grand ball, a consummation which capped the climax of Kenneth's glory.

"O Kenneth, that will be royal!" exclaimed Lottie rapturously.

"Your munificence wins all hearts!" put in Christabel, pressing her own in comic alarm.

"We will dub you King of the Genii," said Marcia, "and your mansion the Palace of Enchantment."

"Language has exhausted itself," added Jennie; "I leave you to imagine my sentiments."

"Ladies, you overwhelm me!" began Kenneth with a profound bow.

"And we may hang our diminished heads," interrupted Fred. Huntington. "Honor bright, Murray, is not all this better than the land of castles and sauer-kraut, fräuleins and lager-beer."

"Don't be too sure of that!" exclaimed Paul. "Ken was devoted to Vaterland and the fräuleins too," he added. mischievously. "I have one in my mind's eye now—the 'Maiden of Drachenfels' we styled her."

"Now, Paul, none of your traveller's wonders!" retorted Kenneth. "You know I have always been a most loyal American citizen, albeit *not* of African descent;" thus attempting by a sorry jest to hide his embarrassment and confusion, which were in no way diminished when the irrepressible Fred, slightly parodizing an old familiar ballad, burst forth with :

> "My heart's in the Rhine-land,
> My heart is not here !
> My heart's in the Rhine-land,
> A-chasing a ' *dear !* ' "

"The 'Maiden of Drachenfels!'" said Lottie.
"That sounds romantic; and by the way, Kenneth, was it not at Drachenfels that you were detained by a sprained ankle, or something of the
kind, while Paul and the rest of your party were
obliged to proceed without you?"

"The very same," said Paul provokingly.
"And I can assure you that this damsel was as
likely a heroine for a romance as you would care
to meet—

"'Blue eyes she had, soft tresses'

of spun-gold, to say nothing of a pale, interesting
father, a wood-carver by trade, but a genius, and
intelligent and refined above his station; and a vix-
enish dragon of a mother, who doubtless made
it uncomfortable enough for the household at times.
Indeed, we can never forget Drachenfels, for we
left in a perfect blaze of glory; the eve of our
departure being some great national holiday,
which the peasants signalized by a grand ball,
tableaux, charades, etc., in which we all took
part. Kenneth and our pretty maiden—"

Here the flood-tide of reminiscence was suddenly
arrested, to Kenneth's infinite relief, by Nita and
Dick, who at that moment appeared, running
eagerly towards Paul, and shouting in one breath:

"Brother Paul! Brother Paul! Somebody's come, and he says he knows you!"

"Indeed!" said Paul coolly. "Well, who is he, and what does he look like?"

"We don't know who he is," said Nita, "but he's mighty tall, and fierce, and black, and has eyes that feel as if he was looking holes right through you!"

"And such a mustache!" added Dick. "Just as if he had swallowed a pair of Carlos and left their tails hanging out. I mean to have one just like it when I am a man."

"Eugene Castlemar to a notch!" said Paul, rising at once, and off he strode, leaving Kenneth to explain that the newly arrived was their fellow-student at Heidelberg, who afterwards accompanied them on their travels, and whom he and Paul had invited to visit them. Moreover, that he was a Cuban by birth, of Franco-Spanish descent, possessed of fabulous estates on the island, and as destitute of friends as Kenneth himself. He had scarcely time, however, to give these particulars, ere Paul reappeared with the gentleman in question, and despite the rather unflattering description of the children, each one mentally voted him undeniably and unmistakably handsome. Tall and distingué in person, with an innate air of "noblesse oblige" that seemed to have been born in him, he presented indeed a fine type of Southern manhood. His hair was black as midnight, and even through the heavy mustache, which had so challenged Dick's admiration, could be discerned the scornful curve of his proud, firm lip, while Christabel, at least, endorsed Nita's opinion of his eyes, for she nearly convulsed Marcia by whispering tragically at intervals, "My poor heart!"—"I'm riddled!"—"I'm transfixed!"—"I'm done for!" etc., etc., though Marcia afterwards told her laughingly that she did not consider his orbs at all dangerous until they were fixed on Jennie, and then the flash that illuminated them might have penetrated the very depths of Hades.

As for Jennie, she was in her element, witching smiles and beaming glances; sparkling sallies and melodious ripples of laughter made her so fascinating, so charming, that even those who knew her best were astonished. True, Fred Huntington was not so overpowered, but that he could still chat gayly with Marcia and Lottie; and Paul (being a brother) was not to be lured from Christabel's amusing companionship; but Mr. Aubrey

looked on pale and moody; Kenneth hovered
around her in undisguised admiration; and as for
the poor Cuban it was easy to see that he was irre-
trievably lost; chained from that hour, a willing
victim, to her car of triumph.

But in this world all things must have an end,
and even this long bright summer day came to a
close at last, though Mrs. Elmore claimed the entire
party both for dinner and for tea; and the moon was
casting her silvery shadows where the golden sheen
had been, before they finally dispersed. Kenneth
in virtue of his superior loneliness, took possession
of the young Cuban, and bore him off to the Ivy,
while the Huntingtons, under the treble escort of
Paul, Lottie, and Marcia, took the short-cut across
the shrubbery to their domicile, followed by Jennie and Clifford Aubrey, who was again in the
seventh heaven of delight, forgetful that when the
sun is absent it is easy to say, "Vive la lune!"
But we have introduced the Huntingtons so un-
ceremoniously into our midst, that we have not
taken time to explain that they are the nearest
neighbors of the Elmores, and that the friendship between the families is of such long standing
as to be almost traditional. Deprived of their
mother when mere infants, their father has made

it the object of his life to pet and spoil both Fred
and Christabel, an undertaking in which he has
been most ably seconded by Miss Arabella Huntington, his maiden sister, to whom her brother and
his motherless children are the very centres of existence. Clifford Aubrey was the son of an old
friend, who, on dying, bequeathed him to Mr.
Huntington's care ; but he has some time since
arrived at man's estate, and for a year past has
been located in New York City, where he is already
spoken of as a young lawyer of brilliant promise.
His adoration of Jennie dated back to his very
childhood, and although no words had ever passed
on the subject, his claims as her privileged attendant had always been tacitly acknowledged, and
until this morning it had never occured to him
that they might one day be disputed. The pang
of the awakening had been so bitter, so intense,
that now that she was smiling again, he was glad
to lull it to sleep and dream once more. But when
she had gone, the pang returned, and the visions
that haunted him were not all rosy ones, as he
paced the terrace till long past midnight, smoking
his solitary cigar.

Jennie, too, was wakeful that night, and sat a
long time absorbed in thought, not of the young

Cuban with his eyes of flame, nor yet of the solitary smoker ; but, as she did not tell her thoughts
even to the silent moon, it is not for us to betray
them.   Sufficient to say that the expression of her
beautiful face, despite the softened radiance that
fell around it, was neither gentle nor loving.   And
Marcia! long after Lottie was locked in slumber,
she sat at her window and gazed at the broad
Hudson spreading out in the distance like a sheet
of molten silver, saying with a sigh, as she turned
to seek her couch at last :

"I wonder if the moon shone as brightly at
Drachenfels ! "

CHAPTER X.

"And who with clear account remarks
The ebbings of his glass,
When all its sands are diamond sparks
That draggle as they pass?"

THE day of Kenneth's fête dawned, bright and beautiful as even our young friends could desire. Kenneth had spared neither trouble nor expense, and the Ivy had donned a festive aspect in marked contrast, though not out of harmony, with its venerable antiquity. Within, flowers were massed in every conceivable manner of adornment, even festooning the walls, garlanding the pictures, and depending gracefully from the chandeliers; while without, the grounds were gay with brightly colored marquées for ices and refreshments; impromptu bowers, that seemed transported from fairyland for the occasion, and the trees were hung with Chinese lanterns which were to be illuminated at nightfall. As the ap-

pointed hour drew near, bands of musicians dis-
coursed lively strains from various quarters;
carriage-load after carriage-load of guests swept
up the broad avenue to be duly welcomed by Aunt
Lucia and Miss Arabella Huntington, who had
consented to matronize the entertainment. The tall
mirrors of the guest-chambers, polished by Mrs.
Jeffries to the last degree of brightness, once more
reflected youthful forms and smiling faces; the
halls resounded with peals of merry laughter; the
disused ball-room was thrown open to the free air
and blessed sunshine, and the deserted mansion,
awakened from its long Rip Van Winkle sleep,
teemed at once with life and animation.

Toilets retouched and curls adjusted, the archery-
meeting of course became the central point of attention, and every one made a rush for that portion of the grounds where the targets had been set
up. As the bugles gave the signal to advance, and
Jennie appeared attired as Diana with her band of
attendant vestals, a murmur of admiration passed
through the throng. Regally beautiful she looked
in her robes of green and silver, the satin vest with
its rich embroidery displaying to advantage the
superb outlines of her rounded form; while the
deepening flush that glowed upon the damask

cheek served to render becoming a color not usually favored by brunettes; and the silver quiver
filled with feathery arrows hanging at her side,
the bow with its many colored ribbons, which she
held in her hand, and the crescent which surmounted her raven tresses, all seemed the perfect
parts of a most perfect whole. Close behind her
walked Marcia. Her dress, as that of the other
attendants, corresponded exactly with Jennie's, except that a silver star twinkled where the crescent
gleamed in the bright June sunshine; but there
was an exquisite refinement in the delicately
chiselled features and the clear, pale face, to which
not even the excitement of the moment could lend
more than the faintest tinge of rose; a wondrous
light in the shadowy eyes; a witching charm in
the smile that played about the finely curved
mouth; a nobility in the fair broad brow, above
which the star shone so fittingly, that caused more
than one pair of eyes to turn from her handsome
cousin and rest admiringly on her. With her
usual forgetfulness of self, Marcia was unconscious
of this, but Jennie saw it and was vexed. She did
not begrudge the smiling tribute paid to the brown-
haired Lottie, the golden-haired Christabel, and
the others of her band who could all claim their

6

meed of loveliness ; but to Marcia she could not
spare one drop of the adulation with which her
cup was overflowing.

But although we agree that the ladies should
be first, we have not the gallantry to say with the
courteous Frenchman : " Toujours les dames ! "
and must devote a few words to the gentlemen, who,
with Kenneth at their head, certainly made a most
presentable band of outlaws. Their plumed hats
and doublets of Lincoln green, and the silver
bugles at their sides, made a most picturesque costume, contrasting charmingly with the more dazzling and ethereal attire of the ladies.

The shooting began, and at the first round Jennie's arrow was declared to be nearest the magic
centre, even excelling that of the Cuban by the
moiety of an inch.   Kenneth and Paul, fresh from
the shooting-galleries of Germany, were astonished to find themselves wide of the mark ; Fred
Huntington was no better off, though in fact the
misfortune was shared by a score of others ; and
as for Aubrey, he was too engrossed in the contem-
plation of Jennie to make any but random shots.
On the next trial, Marcia's arrow was found close
to Jennie's, a trifle nearer the inner circle ; but on
the third and decisive round, victory declared

itself in another and most unexpected quarter.
Whether the result of one of those blind chances
which fickle fortune sometimes casts in the way of
us all, or of a skill acquired at the imminent risk
of all mirrors, statuary, and other fragile commodities of Glen Eden, Dick's final arrow pierced the
very centre, proclaiming him, to the unspeaka-
ble delight of his boon companion, Nita, and his
own infinite amazement, undoubted winner of the
prize, a handsome bow and arrows, which the
umpire presented to him with due ceremonies and
congratulations.

After this dénouement, the fair archers dispersed; and as refreshments were next in order,
the inviting marquées, dotted around so temptingly, came in for their share of attention. In the
gayest of all these receptacles Jennie held her
court. Her position as young lady hostess of
course entitled her to Kenneth's especial escort;
the smitten Cuban had not taken his eyes off her
during the entire afternoon ; and Clifford Aubrey,
fully awakened to the precarious nature of his
claims, followed her about in desperation, half
expecting each moment to see her vanish from
his sight, while numerous lesser constellations
swelled her train, and vainly endeavored to shine

by her reflected light. Jennie, true to her co-quettish instincts, was fully equal to the occasion.

"Mr. Castlemar," said she, "my cavalier, in his capacity of host, is overwhelmed with responsibilities. Please consent to be my Gannymede, and bring me a glass of that delicious lemonade."

"Oh, my pretty bouquet! Save it, Mr. Aubrey!" detaching a bud as he restored it, and bestowing it upon him with a gracious smile that thrilled him with delight.

"I suppose, Mr. Leslie, this is to be cherished for the giver's sake," said she, with a light laugh, but a look that spoke volumes, as she accepted a bon-bon from another of her devotees, who, being young and rather diffident, actually colored with pleasure.

And thus, a smile for one, a look, a nod, or a word for another, she held them all spell-bound, to the wonderment of Lottie, who, innocent of such wiles, was enjoying herself hugely, near by, with a crowd of what Jennie would have contemptuously designated "*girls and boys.*"

Marcia was not quite so fortunate. Fate had destined to her a gushing young collegian, whose specialty seemed to be to string together all sorts of meaningless phrases about starry eyes, alabaster brows, and raven tresses, illustrating them with occasional quotations, brought out with such spasmodic rolling of the eyes and surprising contortions of face and limb, that Marcia at first did not know whether to be amused or alarmed. For example, having rather exhausted the eyes and the hair, and his stock of literature pertaining thereto, he said, after a pause:

"Miss Lyle, those spotless gloves look chawming on your lily hands. They do, indeed. And I'm a judge of gloves; anybody can tell you I was the best judge of gloves at college. That reminds me—aw—who is it? Shakespeare? Yes, it must be Shakespeare who says—aw—

> "' Would I were the glove upon thy hand,
> That I might touch thy cheek!'"

And here his pale blue orbs disappeared so alarmingly, that Fred Huntington, who was just then passing by with an ice, whispered mischievously:

"Miss Marcia, where's your soothing-syrup? Fitz-Noodle's cutting his eye-teeth, and he takes it hard."

Marcia turned her head away to hide her smiles, shaking her finger reprovingly at the naughty

Fred; and at the same moment, the handsome Harry Clifton came up, and protesting against monopolies, bore her off in triumph, while her companion was pondering in what direction he would take his next Parnassian flight. The rest of the evening was like a fairy-tale. Marcia had never seen a ball-room before; and the brilliant lights, the inspiring music, and the mazy dance, seemed to her a beautiful dream. Partners crowded around her, and when the knight of the gloves appeared, he found his chances already at telescopic distance. Paul laughingly declared that his were entirely out of sight; and even Kenneth's turn came late in the evening; but it came at last, and once secured, he seemed loth to relinquish it. For Marcia's dancing was, in truth, the very poetry of motion, and she entered into it with a grace and animation that fairly idealized it. But when their long waltz was finished, and Kenneth, instead of giving her a seat in the ball-room, led her out on the terrace, where the full moon was lending the brightness of noonday to the fair June night, she gave a sigh of relief. The strains of the band still came to them through the open windows; but mellowed by distance, they seemed no longer gay but exquisitely soft and sweet.

The colored lights still glimmered in the foliage, but the lawn was deserted ; and the peace and quietness of the hour brooded over the late scene of revelry and mirth.   For a time they walked up and down without speaking ; one, at least, drinking in the loveliness around her, till her whole countenance seemed transfigured ; and when at last her companion interrupted her with :

"What are you thinking about, Miss Marcia ?"

She answered him slowly, as if reluctant to come back to earth again :

"Oh, of a great many things—almost too many and too vague for speech; but at that moment this line was in my mind :

"'The moon looks on many brooks; the brook sees but one moon.'

And I was thinking what a pity it is, that anything so fair and bright should have been chosen as the emblem of inconstancy."

"Then you must rank constancy among the cardinal virtues ?"

"Certainly ; Constancy and Truth, twin blossoms of Faith, the highest and noblest of all virtues.   Indeed, I cannot well imagine any true nobility of character without them."

"And yet in the long list of heroes held up to

us for admiration, there are few who have not
been sadly lacking both in the one and the other.
In fact, the most brilliant successes have been
achieved by diplomacy and intrigue ; and in the
world's record there are few George Washing-
tons."

"That is too true ; but I still maintain that constancy and truth are not only the insignia of all
real nobility of character, but, in a certain sense,
the essential elements of success. The laurels of
victory are won only by those who, having made
for themselves some great aim, have remained
true to it in spite of dangers and difficulties, pursuing it steadfastly even to the goal."

"Well argued, my fair enthusiast ; but that is
not so broad a view of the subject as I antici-
pated. And yet what could a broader view bring
but sad thoughts. Heads that are crowned with
the silver of age and experience tell us that those
who have the most faith in the world's chivalry
suffer the greatest disappointment. In the morning of youth, we take 'Excelsior' for our motto,
and start out clad in the armor of high thoughts
and lofty aspirations, our Ithurial spears levelled
against the Protean forms of falsehood and deceit ;
but alas ! the evening finds us with our armor

riven by many a shock, our spear shivered, our banner trailing in the dust. Ah! it is well that we cannot read the future! But," he added, "how strange that, with such a sentiment upon my lips, our wanderings have led us to the very spot tradition has made sacred as the abode of the oracle!"

And in fact, absorbed in conversation, they had unconsciously left the terrace, and now stood at the entrance of what appeared to be a subterranean grotto of considerable extent. To-night, however, it was brilliantly illuminated with colored lights, and rustic seats were scattered here and there for the accommodation of those who might wish to penetrate its recesses.

"Has not Lottie initiated you into the mysteries of 'Sybil's Cave'?" asked Kenneth, observing Marcia's look of surprise. "Then let us enter and I will do so. The legend says, that some time far away in the misty long-ago, one of my ancestors, while journeying in the sunny land of the Alhambra, encountered a young gypsy maiden, who so captivated him that he married her in spite of the opposition of her tribe, and bore her off to his own home. But the chilly clime and the customs of civilization did not suit

6*

this child of the wild wood, and she pined away and died. Strange to say, on the very morning of her death a band of gypsies made their appearance in the neighborhood; and one of them, a withered old hag, by what means could never be discovered, found an entrance to the death-chamber. It was the old grand-dame of the maiden, and long and loud were her lamentations over her poor withered blossom. At length she raised her fleshless hand to curse my stricken ancestor, but she read the grief that was in his face, and forbore. He would have lavished gifts upon her, and welcomed her to his home for the sake of his lost darling; but she would accept no favor at his hands, except the privilege of encamping on his grounds, and the exclusive right to this cave, where she would mysteriously reappear at long intervals, reading the future of the credulous who offered their palms for her inspection, and if the legend may be believed, making predictions that were startlingly accurate. The precise time and place of her death are not known, and indeed there is a supposition extant, that her spirit still haunts the spot that was her refuge in life."

"What a wonderful influence the imagination has over us!" exclaimed Marcia, who had been listening intently. "A moment ago I entered this cave with but a passing thought of its beauty, and now I almost fancy I can see the form of the old grand-dame lurking in the shadows, and hear mysterious, inarticulate whispers echoing from the enchanted walls."

"Nay! to temperaments lofty and poetic like yours, transparent indeed is the veil that divides this material world from the world of spirits; and visions may be vouchsafed to you, of which our grosser natures would have no conception; and I prefer to think that those shadowy eyes have indeed penetrated the unknown land; that your pure soul has indeed caught breathings of the celestial sphere; that—"

"Beware!" at this moment uttered a voice so near them, that they both started with one common impulse, while a light, mocking laugh rang upon their ears. Before them stood, not indeed the old grand-dame, but a veritable gypsy maiden, her long, black hair flowing unconfined over her shoulders, from which hung a scarlet cloak, while her gold-laced velvet bodice, her many-colored short skirt, and her sandalled feet gave a picturesque effect to her weird beauty.

Marcia was speechless with awe and amazement, but Kenneth exclaimed :

" Who are you !' and how came you hither ? "

> " Oh, I am a merry, merry, merry Zingara,
> From a golden clime I come ! "

sang she gayly, while her feet kept time to the stirring measure.   Then with a sudden change of mood, she gravely approached Kenneth, saying :

"I came here with a portion of our tribe, who have spread their tents in your woods to-night, but who will vanish with the dews of the morning. The legend of the 'Sybil's Cave' is not lost among us, and I had a mind to visit it.   But," said she, extending her hand coaxingly towards him, "you will cross my palm with silver, and let me read what the fates have in store for you and the beautiful senora ? "

" Nay ! I have no wish to unveil the shrouded future ! " said he, springing back ; and then with a laugh at his own reluctance, he added : " but stay ! this is the 'Sybil's Cave,' and the time and place give you an ancestral right to display your powers.   Miss Marcia, what say you ? shall we entrust our destiny to this oracle ? "

Marcia assented, and extended her hand to the

gypsy maiden, who took it in her own, gazing at it long and fixedly, and at last murmuring in a low, chanting tone :

> "Maiden of the midnight eyes,
> Danger in the present lies ;
> Sunshine lingers on thy way,
> But the hidden storm-fiends play
> In each circling gleam of light,
> Heralds of a starless night ;
> Yet awhile thy bark shall glide
> Smoothly o'er the slumbering tide ;
> But the tempest shall at last
> Bend and break it 'neath the blast,
> Ere the wrathful fury o'er ;
> Frowning skies may smile once more.
> On a still and pulseless breast,
> Weary hands must folded rest ;
> Asure eyes must cease to glow ;
> Golden locks, in death lie low,
> Ere the heart thy tendrils twine,
> May responsive beat to thine."

A long, shuddering sigh burst from Marcia's lips as the incantation ceased ; and Kenneth, extending his hand, said mockingly : "Your predictions are too melancholy, my fair seeress! could you not invoke a brighter destiny for so lovely a lady?"

"I can only repeat what it is given to one to utter," said the gypsy gravely, looking earnestly at the broad palm before her ; and, im-

pressed, in spite of himself, by the solemnity of
her manner, Kenneth remained silent till she again
burst forth:

> "Scion of a knightly race,
> Tall of form and fair of face,
> Would you to that race be true,
> Do no deed that you may rue.
> Have a care!   Have a care!"

> "Azure eyes and locks of gold
> In their thrall your future hold;
> Thrall you may not, cannot break.
> For the dark-haired maiden's sake,
> Oh beware!   Oh beware!

> "Ask not smiles you may not give,
> Wake not hopes that may not live;
> Bear the grief that none may share,
> Win not hearts you may not wear.
> Have a care!   Have a care!"

As the last words died away, Kenneth looked
up; but the gypsy had already vanished, and
leaving the grotto, he and Marcia retraced their
steps to the house, with a shadow on their bright
mood, which they vainly tried to dispel.   They
found the guests already preparing to depart, and
soon the Ivy was once more left to darkness and
obscurity, and Kenneth's fête had become a memory of the past.

Jennie and Lottie were in high spirits, and

chatted gayly all the way home, so that Marcia's abstraction was not noticed till, as they entered their room to retire for the night, Lottie exclaimed: "Why, Marcia! what is the matter? you look as if you had seen a ghost!"

"And so I have! the ghost of the future!" replied the young girl; but nature and youth asserted themselves, and when she went to bed, she soon fell asleep, dreaming strangely enough that she was drowning in the torrent of Drachenfels, and that the gypsy maiden was trying to rescue her with a braid of her long black hair.

CHAPTER XI.

"Break, break, break,
  At the foot of thy crags, O Sea!
But the tender grace of a day that is dead
Will never come back to me."

                                        TENNYSON.

" What is there left for me to do,
    But fly, fly
    From the cruel sky,
    And hide in the deeps, and die ! "

T was market-day in a small town of one of the little hamlets on the Rhine, and the Herr Pastor had been literally besieged with callers. It was plain to be seen that his worthy flock, while they availed themselves of this opportunity to dispose of their various commodities, and provide themselves with whatever was useful or needful, did not neglect to apply for sympathy in their sorrows and counsel in their difficulties to the good man who had proved

himself to be so truly their friend and father. Indeed, Frau Witka, the house-keeper and maid-of-
all-work, whose face was usually as shining as the
great brass knocker she rubbed each morning with
anxious care, looked almost cross, when, just as
she had closed the door upon what she devoutly
hoped might prove the last visitor, a summons
smote upon her ear, louder and more peremptory
than any that had preceded it.

"Oh! is it you, Frau Waldemar?" said she,
as she admitted the new-comer. "The master has
had many a visitor this day, poor bodies, who
must run to him if they but lose a groschen or
scratch a little finger; not like you, who are feeling the hand of the Lord too heavy to come gab-
bling at trifles."

"You never spoke truer, Frau Witka," said
the other, glancing at her black gown as if she
felt a sort of complacency in her woe; "but after
all, the dead trouble is not so bad as the living
one, and it's about that I have come to the master."

"And you could not come to a better. If ever
there was a good man it's the master; so go in at
once, and maybe when you have talked with him,
you will feel like having a word with me in my

kitchen. There's nothing so good for a trouble as talking it over."

Frau Waldemar shook her head with an air of mournful superiority, as if to insinuate that talking could do no good in her case, and tapping on the door of the study, was admitted at once.

"How are you, my good woman?" said the pastor, rising to meet her, "and how is the Fräulein Hilda?"

"Bad enough! bad enough!" replied his visitor. "She has fretted and moped till her cheeks are as white as a wheaten-loaf, and her eyes are almost lost with weeping."

"Poor child!" said the pastor compassionately; "she had a great love for her father."

"So great that there was naught left for her mother!" said the frau sharply. "They were forever clacking with their books, and their flowers, and what not, and who was to help me with the scrubbin' and the spinnin'? But it's my mind (God forgive her!) that it's not her father (peace to his soul!) that she grieves about, so much as it is her lover!"

"Ha! are there yet no tidings? She should have heard ere this?"

"Not a word; and it's enough to put one beside one's self, to see how red her cheeks get and how bright her eyes, every evening as the boat passes the landing, only to look paler and duller than ever when it goes on without stopping!"

"Poor child! poor child!" again exclaimed the pastor. "But if that young man is false, there is no faith in the human countenance. And yet," he added hesitatingly, "his manner always seemed to me more that of a friend than of a lover!"

"Ay! ay!" retorted the frau. "So says the silly girl herself, whenever I begin to rate him. 'Mother,' says she, 'it is all my fault: he never told me that he was my lover!' As if I had not eyes and ears of my own—as if Farmer Gottlieb's son wouldn't have kissed the very dust of her feet before she turned her back on him for the young foreigner. Lover or not, she has claims on him, and we will see if he dares to deny them!"

"She has indeed; God help them both!" almost groaned the good pastor. "Poor fräulein! Poor young man!"

"Poor young man!" fairly shrieked Frau

Waldemar, forgetting her awe in her wrath. "Poor young man! Is my child's heart then worth so little, that it may be despised and cast away, and you, who have held her in your arms a little baby, have naught to say but, 'Poor young man!' I will follow him to the world's end, but what I will find him, and the curse—"

"Hold!" interrupted the pastor authoritatively. "Remember the young man is perhaps still in ignorance of the tie that binds him to your daughter. I believe them both to be victims of a cruel joke, and Hans Gottlieb will yet live to rue his sorry revenge for the slights of his lady-love. If the Divine Master did not teach us to bless rather than curse, my curses should rest on him, the author of so much misery. "But," he continued more calmly, "perhaps my letter has not been received. I will write again, this very night; and in the meantime, my good friend, be patient and keep your own counsel, and oh! be tender and gentle to my poor little Hilda!"

Frau Waldemar raised her head, as if to utter an indignant remonstrance at this parting injunction; but there was something so commanding and at the same time so sorrowful in the face of the pastor, that it checked the words on her lips and she silently left the room and wended her way homeward, without the bit of gossip with the expectant Frau Witka.

Unfortunately this softening influence had time to die away in the course of her long walk thither, and in its stead arose a feeling of resent- ment, that the Herr Pastor should have thought it necessary to bespeak consideration and kind- ness from her (model mother as she had always considered herself) in behalf of her only daugh- ter.

"No doubt," muttered she to herself, as she toiled up the hill, that led to her cottage, "her ladyship thinks it's very fine to sit with folded hands, while I am blamed for her white cheeks and tearful eyes! But I'm going to make an end of it. There's as good fish in the sea as ever were caught, and though the Lord knows the net that's caught her is tight enough, there's no telling what may happen, and I'm not going to have her fretting away the good looks that may yet get her a rich husband!"

In the meantime, where was Hilda? Alone in the silent kitchen she sat, her entire attitude indicative of utter despondency. The tall clock ticked cheerfully in the corner; the great fireplace was gay with polished tiles of varied colors; while the high dresser, groaning with rows of shining delf and ·pewter, and the floor, dazzling in its snowy whiteness, gave unmistakable evidence of Frau Waldemar's skill in housewifery, and combined to lend an air of comfort to the homely apartment. But no portion of their brightness was reflected in the face or form of the young maiden: her spinning wheel stood idle before her; her arms drooped listlessly at her sides, while with her pale face pressed against the vine-wreathed casement she gazed aimlessly and hopelessly on the distant river. The rays of the setting sun stole tenderly in, resting lovingly on her golden tresses, as it were with a touch of kindred; but she heeded them not, and the rosy clouds that tinged the horizon might have been black as midnight for all she knew or cared. Heedless of clouds, heedless of sunshine, heedless of time, heedless of life itself, she dreamed on her own sad dream, 'till the sharp voice of Frau Waldemar recalled her wandering senses, as she came in at the open door, exclaiming angrily:

"A pretty daughter you.are! Sitting there as idle as a duchess or a countess at least, and not a bite ready for me after my long tramp! The fire burnt to ashes! Not a drop of water in the bucket!" she continued, with increasing wrath, as she bustled about; "Hilda Waldemar, what do you mean?"

' I know it is too bad, mother dear!" said the girl, rising hastily and bending over the fire as if to mend it, while the ready tears dropped upon the dying embers. "But please forgive me! I forgot—"

"Ay! ay! it is easy to say you forgot. But you are always forgetting. Do you ever stop to think what would become of you, if I should take it into my head to do the same? Get up from there!" she added, taking her place among the ashes. Those everlasting tears are doing the fire more harm than your clumsy fingers can do good; and if you will condescend for once to make yourself useful, take this bucket and go to the spring for a draught of fresh water."

Hilda obeyed at once, and the energetic frau soon had their evening meal ready; but of this repast the poor girl could not do more than make a feint of partaking, a fact which did not escape her watchful mother, though she said nothing till the table was cleared away and they had seated themselves for the evening. Then, looking up with a frown, she said sternly :

"Hilda, how long is this to last?"

"A long time, I fear, if I am to judge by past progress," said Hilda, with an attempt at a joke, holding up the stocking on which she was knitting, as if she supposed it to be the subject of her mother's query.

"You know very well I am not talking about that. I mean this eternal fretting and moping. How long, I ask you again, is it going to last?"

"God knows! God only knows! Until the grass is green on my grave. For oh! he will never come back! He will never come back!" and covering her face with her hands, the young girl sobbed uncontrollably.

"And who says he will not come back?" retorted the frau fiercely. "He will never dare to stay away! You may be weak, and I may be weak; but the law is strong, and it will go hard with me if it does not find him out."

"Mother, no more of that!" exclaimed her daughter, with a stern calmness that amazed her.

"He never said he loved me, and though I have hoped against hope, I know now that he never did love me, and I will die before I will be forced upon him!"

"Don't be a fool! it is easy to talk about dying; but youth is strong, and life is sweet, and you have never counted the long years that are in store for you."

"Ay, but I have! counted them slowly and wearily, as the hermit tells his beads; for I know that I must pass them alone, alone!"

"Alone indeed! We will see about that when the lover comes, which may be sooner than you think," added the frau knowingly. "The Herr Pastor has already written once, and he promised me this very day to write again to-night, and we will see if his letters won't bring him!"

"Mother!" said Hilda, in a voice that sounded like a wail; "how could you do this? and after your promise, your solemn promise! O God! am I sunk so low? Is it not enough that he does not love me? must he also learn to despise me? But," and her cheeks flushed and her eyes glowed, "even if he comes he shall not see me! I will hide somewhere, anywhere, so that he can never find me!"

7

"Ungrateful child! and did you think I was going to let you sit here, fretting your good looks away, and fitting yourself to be a burden on me the rest of my days, without doing aught to pre-vent it, when there is Fritz Anschen, the rich brewer, that would marry me and make a lady of me to-morrow, if you were but safely out of the way with your own proper husband."

"Mother!" fairly shrieked Hilda in her an-guish, recoiling as if an adder had stung her. "Fritz Anschen! and the flowers scarce yet with-ered on my dear father's grave! Oh, this is more than I can bear! Unsay those cruel words! Tell me that you were but jesting, mother!" But the stern face turned to hers was unrelenting, and with a low moan she rushed wildly from the room, bolt-ing her chamber door as if she would shut out some horrible vision.

How long Frau Waldemar sat thus, silently thinking, she knew not; but she was still there when the door slowly opened, and Hilda, with a face pale as a corpse, and almost as rigid and cold, threw herself at her feet, and moaned rather than gasped, "Mother, tell me it is not true!"

But the stern frau merely shook her head, and would make no denial, though a feeling of awe stole over her, when her daughter, rising, said solemnly:

"Then may God judge between you and me! and whatever I may do in the future, remember you drove me to it!", and left the room as silently as she had entered it.

For a moment she felt inclined to follow her; but checking the impulse as an unworthy weakness, she proceeded to close the house and retire to rest, muttering as she did so:

"Poor, silly, stubborn child! she thinks to move me with her airs and graces. A night's rest will teach her better; and after all, such an offer as Fritz Anschen's is not to be had every day."

And she soon fell asleep; but great was her consternation in the morning when Hilda appeared not in answer to her usual summons. The little white bed was smooth and untroubled; the neat chamber was in its usual beautiful order; but it was empty. And in that moment Frau Waldemar felt that she had lost her child, and lost her forever.

CHAPTER XII.

"Alas! that woman, not content
With her peculiar element
Of gentle love, should ever try
The meteor spells of vanity!
Her world should be of love alone,
Of one fond heart, and only one."

L. E. L.

WELL, Jennie! what's on the tapis now?"
said Lottie, making an unceremonious entrée into her sister's boudoir, one bright afternoon in mid-winter. "As Marcia and I came in
from Madam —— just now, we beheld Eugene
Castlemar's fiery bays spiritedly pawing our unfortunate paving-stones, while Clifford Aubrey's
groom, page, Mercury, or whatever you choose to
call him, was cooling his heels in the vestibule.
Pardon my curiosity; but 'when Greek meets
Greek'—you know the rest of the adage."

"You absurd girl!" said Jennie, laughing;
"there is nothing the matter except that I am go-

ing to drive in the park with Mr. Castlemar, and,"
holding up a tiny rose-colored missive, "I have
just declined a like invitation from Mr. Aubrey."

"That is too bad! I wish it was vice versa;
for between you and me, Jen, I think you are
treating Clifford Aubrey shamefully. But I hope
that at least you have said something to soften the
disappointment?"

"I have simply told him that his note came too
late," said Jennie haughtily.

"Too late! Poor Clifford! It seems to me he
is never in time for anything now. His invitation
for the opera found you already engaged for half
the season; it was too late for his promised waltz
at Mrs. Ashton's; and even those exquisite camelias
that he sent last night came so late that it was impossible to comply with his request to wear them
in your hair. But as if it were not enough that
you are trifling with one true heart, and plunging
a score of other luckless wights into bliss or woe
by your alternate smiles and frowns, you have led
that jealous Cuban on till he is positively dangerous; and for my part, I would rather encounter a
cargo of nitro-glycerine or any other explosive
compound."

"Ha, ha!" laughed Jennie gayly, arranging

her hat before the glass. "Don't be so tragic. Wait till your own time comes, ma chère, and we will see if you are not as anxious for '*strings to your bow*' as the rest of us. But why do you blame me?" added she innocently. "How can I help it?"

"Ah, Jennie, Jennie! In the words of the immortal Susan Nipper, 'I may not be a peacock, but I have eyes;' and I hope you may not yet learn to your sorrow that other things besides Clifford Aubrey's civilities may come too late. Remember,

> "'While we send for the napkin, the soup gets cold;
> While the bonnet is trimming, the face grows old;
> When we've matched our buttons, the pattern is sold;
> And everything comes too late, too late!'"

"No more an' thou lovest me!" cried Jennie, clapping her hands to her ears. "I will buy you an owl, and you shall go as Minerva to our first masquerade."

"A parrot or a magpie would suit her better," said Paul, putting his head in at the door. "But Jennie, if you have no mercy on Castlemar, please have some on our sidewalk, which will certainly be demolished if those horses stand there much longer."

"If it is, charge it to Lottie," said the wilful beauty, tripping lightly down to the parlor, where her cavalier was awaiting her.

His face glowed as he heard her step on the stairs, and his dark eyes fairly burned with the passionate love that thrilled his whole being, as he unconsciously murmured to himself:

> "She is coming, my own, my sweet!
>   Were it ever so airy a tread,
> My heart would hear her and beat,
>   Were it earth in an earthy bed;
> My dust would hear her and beat,
>   Had I lain for a century dead,—
> Would start and tremble under her feet,
>   And blossom in purple and red."

"La belle des belles!" said he, rising as she entered.

"None of that, Mr. Castlemar," returned she; "remember my rules: no flattery!"

"And when was the truth called flattery?" exclaimed he passionately. "The garnered gems of all the poets would still leave us poor in words to picture you."

"That may be; pen-portraits were always my abomination. But as we do not propose to devote ourselves to the artistic or poetic on this occasion,

let us be off for our drive while we can have the
benefit of the sunshine."

"The sun can never set in your presence," said
her adorer; but Jennie interrupted him with:

" O Mr. Castlemar! I fear you are incorrigible; but you must really proclaim a truce to such
sentiments, or I will be obliged to reconsider my
acceptance, and forego the drive."

"I can safely promise to sin no more, if such be
the penalty," rejoined he; and giving the rein to
his horses, he made himself so agreeable as they
flew along, that his star rose high in the ascendency, till a bow from Clifford Aubrey and another
from Kenneth Murray as he passed with his lovely
bays and the stylish Miss Lawrence (a rival belle
and beauty) turned Jennie's thoughts in another
channel, and she came home so tired and so cold
that even Nita saw it and asked shrewdly:

" What's the matter, sister Jennie? Did you
meet anybody that was nicer and prettier than
you?"

But every trace of this had vanished later in
the evening, when she entered the drawing-room,
where the family had already assembled, looking
so lovely that there was pride as well as pleasure
in the tone in which her father exclaimed:

"At home this evening, my daughter? This is refreshing. The claims of society have interfered sadly with our claims of late."

"Very little to your loss," said Jennie lightly, seating herself on a low stool at his feet; "but in fact, though I find it all charming,—the beaux, the opera, the driving, and the dancing, and everything,—I am not sorry for a little breathing-spell."

"Yes, these little pauses in the journey of life are refreshing alike to body and soul. But, by the way, I hope that contact with the world has left your freshness and bloom of spirit as unimpaired as these glowing cheeks?"

"Don't be afraid of that, papa," said Jennie, though she colored slightly as she detected a shade of anxiety in the kind eyes bent so lovingly upon her. "When all this rush and glitter is over, I shall be glad to go back to Glen Eden, and you will find me quite the same, if not more truly your own Jennie than ever."

"You at home?" said Paul, entering at that moment. "Let me congratulate the family circle on the presence of the belle of the season, though an unfortunate engagement prevents me from sharing in the honor. But, my fair lady, I thought

7*

you were going to the opera to-night with Sid
Howard; at least, I heard you make some such
agreement, with a smile so sweet that it left me
under the impression that you were not only glad
to accept, but duly thankful for the invitation."

"Nonsense, Paul!" returned Jennie. "But if
I did, I have claimed a woman's privilege, and
changed my mind."

"Cool! I'm glad I'm only your brother. But
tell me, Jen, how is it that you manage to have so
many fellows dying for you, and to make each
one think that beyond a doubt he is the prime
favorite?"

"Manage!" said Jennie, a little indignantly.
"There is no management about it. I can't help
it if they choose to think themselves in love with
me, and I really like them all so much that the
last seems the best."

"Take care, my daughter! A woman loses the
glory of womanhood when she so far uncrowns
herself as to descend to the arts of a coquette."

Paul took up his hat to depart; and Jennie was
beginning to think that, in Dick's expressive
phraseology, she was "*in for it*," when the door
opened, and the footman announced "Mr Castlemar and Mr. Murray."

"Take this seat by me, Kenneth," said Mr. Elmore, after the greetings had been exchanged; "I would like to have a few words with you."

And the Cuban proceeded to monopolize Jennie, happily unconscious of the indignation of Lottie, who, with her mother and Marcia, was seated at a table in a distant part of the room, engaged in looking over a book of views and sketches which, in the superabundance of Paul's trophies of travel, had not been discovered until to-day. Devoted partisan of Clifford Aubrey that she was, she could endure no infringement on what she considered his rights; but on this occasion she merely gave vent to her impatience by a sly shake of the fist, unperceived by any one but Marcia, who could not restrain a smile at this characteristic ebullition on the part of her impulsive cousin. At last Mrs. Elmore said: ·

"Come, Kenneth, Mr. Elmore has engrossed you long enough. Devote yourself to us for a while, and add the charm of your reminiscences to this already attractive volume."

"May I come too?" asked Mr. Elmore; "I am still young enough to retain my taste for travellers' wonders."

"The more, the merrier," replied his wife; and

they formed quite an animated little group, till they were interrupted by fresh arrivals, in the persons of Clifford Aubrey and Mr. MacKensie, after which the conversation became general. For although Marcia and Lottie were not yet emancipated from the thraldom of the school-room, Mrs. Elmore did not favor utter seclusion, but considered it improving for them to be present and take part on such occasions.

Mr. MacKensie was a young man about thirty years of age, and not only, as his name would indicate, a native of the land of the heather, but a *bonâ fide* Scotch laird, although he had the good taste and judgment to drop the title while sojourning in a republican land. Although not regularly handsome, he had an undeniably fine face, and was possessed of a strong native intellect and a superior culture, which rendered him a most delightful companion. In fact, he and the young Cuban were the lions of the season, and many envied the Elmores the privilege of receiving on such familiar terms such distinguished guests. To the Cuban, as we have seen, Jennie proved a sufficient and all-powerful attraction; but to the Scotchman, although, like the rest of mankind, he yielded tribute at the shrine of the beauty, it was more Aunt Lucia's gentle influence, and the sweet, homelike feeling that pervaded everybody and everything that came in contact with her. Then, too, there was a higher mental and moral tone about this family circle than most of those to which he had been presented, for superior birth and fortune too often seemed to serve as incentives, or, at best, excuses for superior frivolity and extravagance.

Jennie, intent on making herself agreeable, divided her smiles quite equally among all the gentlemen, though Lottie noticed with delight that her favorite at last attained the vantage-ground, nor did he afterwards relinquish it.

"Your cousin certainly presents a rare combination of beauty and intellect," said Mr. MacKensie, addressing himself to Marcia.

"Indeed she does. The most difficult lessons were always mere pastime to her, and I have never seen any one so wondrously beautiful," said Marcia with enthusiasm, quite unconscious how charming her ingenuous admiration made her appear to her listener.

"If I needed such an assurance, your praises would convince me that she is deserving of the adulation so universally poured out before her.

But it is a fearful ordeal, and one at which any woman might well shrink and tremble."

"And yet it is so sweet to be appreciated," said Marcia with a sigh and a passing memory of her own unloved, neglected childhood.

"Very true ; but my idea of woman is so lofty, so exalted ; to me she is such a holy of holies, that I cannot bear to see her heart made a common thoroughfare. I would have it a sacred shrine, of which but one alone should possess the magic 'sesame.'"

"Or," continued Marcia, catching his spirit, "a sealed fountain, which only the prophet's rod should make to gush with living waters."

"May I ask what theme is inspiring you and Mr. MacKensie with such poetic similes ?" said Kenneth, who was sitting near them. "I have been listening most intently, at the risk of verifying a certain pithy old adage, and what I have heard has been like Tantalus' cup : only enough to make me want to hear more."

"The theme is one which perhaps you will call trite—women's hearts," replied Marcia.

"Women's hearts as they should be, or as they too frequently are?" questioned Kenneth. "If the latter, I fear your prophet would have to be a

Midas, and his divining-rod the crucible of an alchemist. Many a true lover might exclaim with the lover of Locksley Hall:

> "'What is that which I should turn to, lighting upon days like these?
> Every door is barred with gold, and opens but to golden keys.'"

"That is a more cynical sentiment than I like to hear from your lips, Kenneth," said Aunt Lucia. "But when I consider the marriages of the present day, I cannot wonder at it. Love seems to be entirely out of the question; or if not professedly ignored, the men and maidens find it wonderfully convenient to place their affections on the highest bidder."

"What a severe speech to come from my gentle mamma," exclaimed Lottie. "When my time comes I shall certainly look out for some poverty-stricken wight, that I may feel assured that I do not come under the ban of her displeasure."

"The daughter of such a mother need scarcely resort to such extreme measures," said Mr. Mac-Kensie, "though it is true that it is the tendency of the age to rob marriage of all solemnity."

"You speak feelingly on the subject," said Marcia; "but is not your native land noted for the ease and informality with which the sacred tie may

be contracted within its limits? Your Aberdeen
has an actually historic renown.''

"That is so ; but my native land does not stand·
alone in this respect. In some of your own States,
and also in some parts of Germany, all that is necessary to constitute a legal marriage, is for the
parties to declare their sentiments in the presence
of witnesses, and thus the idle sport of an hour has
sometimes become the misery of a lifetime.''

"I never could tolerate playing at marriage,''
said Aunt Lucia, "whether in tableaux, charades,
or—but Kenneth! what is the matter? you are as
pale as a ghost.''

"Nothing. It will soon pass,'' said Kenneth
confusedly. "I have been suffering with the
headache all day.''

"It must be very severe in its paroxysms," said
Lottie, "for it blanched your cheek as suddenly
as some ghostly memory. There, you look better
now,'' as the color mounted into his face at her
words, "and I am going to have some music. I
want Marcia to show Mr. MacKensie how much
pathos a heartless American girl can put into
one of his Scotch ballads.''

Marcia gave her a reproachful glance, and would
have retreated; but for once Aunt Lucia would

not excuse her, though, in consideration of her diffidence, she had not hitherto required her to sing before visitors, and she was led in triumph to the piano. At first her voice faltered ; but with the first note she gained confidence, and the rich, mellow tones gushed forth with an exquisite tenderness, that sank into the very hearts of her listeners. Every one was charmed, and Mr. Mackensie was absolutely enraptured. Ballad followed ballad, and when, elated at her success, Lottie artfully proposed "Robert," Kenneth's favorite, Marcia showed herself quite as much at home in opera, and executed that gem of Meyerbeer with a power and finish that carried her audience by storm.

"I did not know we had such a prima donna among us," said her uncle, drawing her fondly to his side, as the door at last closed on their visitors, and—

"The canny Scot has struck his colors," said Lottie, as she settled herself to sleep. "But Marcia, let me beg of you not to dream of the blue bells of Scotland. It would spoil a pet scheme of mine."

CHAPTER XIII.

"Hear the sledges with the bells,
Silver bells,
What a world of merriment their melody foretells!"

Dick!" exclaimed Nita, clapping her hands with delight, as she looked out of the library window one bright. frosty morning. "The ground is all covered with snow, and there goes such a lovely sleigh, for all the world like those dear, pretty, swans out at the park. I wonder if cousin Kenneth will remember!"

"Of course!" said Dick confidently; "or if he don't, Mr. Mackensie will. But I say, Nita, what a pity it is that you aint a boy; we could have such fine fun coasting."

"It is a pity!" said Nita, so ruefully, that Marcia, who was seated at a table near them, putting the finishing-strokes to a sketch she was preparing for her drawing-master, could not help smiling as she said :

"Don't be so doleful about it, pet ; I'm sure girls have a nice time too."

"But not like the boys," said Nita. "And then I hate girls ; they are so mean. They always want to know how many silk dresses you've got, and what kind of a house you live in, and whether your father keeps a carriage ; and with boys it don't make a bit of difference, so you don't sneak, or tell tales, or take a dare ! "

"What an array of virtues !" said Marcia, laughing. "But won't it be nice when you are grown like Jennie ? she has (as you and Dick would say) lots of fun."

"Oh yes ; but even she is always fussing about something. I'd a heap rather be cousin Kenneth."

"Or Mr. Mackensie," put in Dick.

"Pshaw, Dick ! ever since you've known Mr. Mackensie, and been reading about Bruce and Wallace, and all that, you think nobody's anything that wasn't born in Scotland. I asked mamma about it, and she says those men all died years ago, and I don't believe the Scotch nowadays are a bit better than other people. At any rate, I think there's nobody like cousin Kenneth, and I say it again. I'd rather be him than anybody else in the world. Wouldn't you, cousin Marcia?"

"That is rather a sweeping interrogation. But to tell the truth, I think I would a little rather be myself than any one else."

"That is right!" said Dick warmly. "I'm sure you couldn't be anything better. I heard Mr. Mackensie telling papa, the other day, that you were the most sensible and best *reformed* young girl of your age, he ever met."

"O Dick! Dick! don't murder the king's English," said Marcia, "and above all, don't think that the reason I would rather be myself is because I think I am better than any one else. Far from it! I only think that God has made us just what it is best and happiest for us to be, and that it seems like thinking we know more than He does, to wish we were different."

"Yes!" said Nita, "and no doubt he made me a girl, so that I can marry cousin Kenneth when I'm big enough. He said the other day he would wait for me."

"That would be jolly!" said Dick merrily; "and cousin Marcia shall marry Mr. Mackensie, and—"

"Not so fast, Dick," began Marcia; but at this moment the children were drawn to the window by the tinkling of bells, and exclaiming, "Here they are, here they are! Oh how nice!" they rushed out of the room, almost beside themselves with delight.

The secret of their rapture was this: Some weeks before, Kenneth and Mr. Mackensie had promised them a sleigh-ride, the very first snow; also inducing Aunt Lucia to join the party, with Marcia, Lottie, and Christabel Huntington, who was present on the occasion. Since that time, the weather had been the absorbing topic with the little ones, and this morning's snow-flakes had been hailed with a glee proportionate to their anticipation. And a merry party they made! Aunt Lucia with Marcia and Nita disposing themselves under Kenneth's guardianship, while Christabel, Lottie, and Dick claimed that of Mr. Mackensie. To Marcia the sleigh-ride was even more of a novelty than to the children, for in the sunny land of her birth such wintry pleasures were unknown, and she gave herself up to the exhilaration of the moment, and became so sparkling and animated, that to Kenneth, at least, she displayed an entirely new phase of character. So absorbed was he in contemplating her and listening to her lively sallies, that his little fiancée in prospective would

undoubtedly have given up to a violent attack of
the sulks, if there had not been so much in the gay
scene around them to interest and divert her.

"Look there, mamma," said she, as a huge om-
nibus on runners passed swiftly by, with its cargo
of smiling faces—and, "How funny!" as she beheld a hastily improvised jumper, of grotesque
form and dimensions, ambitiously striving to hold
its own in the general mêlée and, "O mamma!
just see that beautiful sea-shell, and that lovely
white robe!   It looks like foam!   And if there
ain't sister Jennie in it with Mr. Aubrey.   I wonder if she sees us.   Yes! she's laughing at us."
And thus the happy child prattled on, till her
mother said laughingly :

"Nita, dear! your tongue reminds me of that
one Dick tells about, which was 'hung in the
middle.' "

Nor was it for the children alone that this day
was henceforth to be marked with a white pebble.
The snow, pure and spotless, glistening in the sunshine, gave no hint of the corruption and filth which
it hid ; nor of the cold bleak attics into which it had
drifted, making them colder and bleaker still; nor
of the houseless poor, who had shivered beneath
its icy touch.   And the careless throng enjoyed it,

unquestioning, and none more thoroughly than our little party. The park was so charming in its wintry vesture, that Marcia was enchanted, and was silent all the way home, from very intensity of feeling ; but her simple

"Thank you, Mr. Murray ; I am indebted to you for the happiest morning of my life," seemed to Kenneth more eloquent than the most elaborate acknowledgment ; and fair were the visions that arose before him as he wended his way to his rooms in the hotel, which he had made his headquarters for the winter. The glowing anthracite in the grate, and the tempting sofa drawn up beside it, invited him to reverie ; and taking a cigar, he indulged in it, till the future floated before him on the clouds of smoke, in shapes as protean and as alluring as ever flowed from the pen of Ike Marvel. So absorbed did he become, that the waiter knocked twice before he received a summons to enter, and even then his usually welcome announcement, "Letters, sir !" elicited but an ungracious nod in acknowledgment, as he laid them on the table and withdrew. The cigar was reduced to ashes ; the fire burned low in the grate, and the early winter twilight began to fill the room with shadows, and still our dreamer mused on, till at

last, suddenly remembering an engagement to
dinner, he started up, exclaiming aloud :

"If even the dream is so sweet, what would
not the reality be ? Dare I dwell upon it, or can
it be, as the cynics say, that in life our dearest
plans, our fondest hopes, our brightest anticipations are doomed, like this glorious Havana, to
end in smoke. Heigho! I must get out of this
cloudland."

And as a first step in his descent to the practical, he took up a match to light the gas. As he
did so, the light fell on the letters, which were
still lying unheeded where the servant had placed
them. He picked them up carelessly, little thinking, as he did so, that he was taking up a burden
which for many and many a weary year he should
strive vainly to lay down; a stone of Sisyphus,
with which he must toil painfully up life's steep
hill, nor be released from it until he neared the
top. The first two or three letters were unimpor-
tant enough, and he glanced hastily at them ; but
the fourth, which was addressed in a stiff, foreign
hand, and literally covered with postmarks, had
evidently travelled far and wide to reach him ;
and he looked at it, as he broke the seal, with
some wonderment and curiosity. But as he per-

used its contents, his cheeks blanched to a marble pallor; a stony look of despair stole into his eyes; a cold, gray shadow settled upon his sunny face, and covering it with his hands, he groaned aloud; then starting up, he paced the floor in the extremity of his anguish.

"O my God!" he exclaimed, "can this be true? Oh no! it is too dreadful, it must be some hideous nightmare! Is there no hope—no escape —no alternative—nothing left for me but to sit down and bear it! me so young, with so many years of life before me?"

"Yes," whispered the tempter, always at hand to take advantage of an unguarded moment; "the ocean rolls between you and your troubles. In this country, even the law will be on your side. Ignore your cruel fate. Keep your own counsel, and no one need ever be the wiser."

For a time he listened, and the expression of his face softened; the temptation was great; but his better nature triumphed, and putting it resolutely from him, he said firmly, though in a voice broken with anguish:

"No, no, I cannot! I may not be legally, but at least I am honorably, bound, and I will not be the first Murray to prove false to our glorious

8

motto, 'Principia, non homines.' But O my
love! my lost love, whom I had hoped to win.
Marcia! Marcia!" and he was again overcome.

But as the night wore on, his agitation was
sufficiently calmed for him to determine on a
course of action. It was clear that he must go
to Europe, and that without delay. So finding, on
reference to the papers, a steamer for Bremen ad-
vertised for the next day, he at once made arrangements for immediate departure. So the
morning that had dawned so brightly, and worn
such roseate colors, vanished in a night of gloom
and sorrow; and the future, which fancy had pictured so fair, resolved itself into a long, weary
vista of exile and wandering.

CHAPTER XIV.

" 'Tis thus with our life while it passes along,
  Like a vessel at sea amid sunshine and song!
  Gayly we glide in the gaze of the world,
  With streamers afloat and with canvas unfurled;
  All gladness and glory to wandering eyes—
  Yet chartered by sorrow and freighted with sighs,
  ·Fading and false is the aspect it wears,
  As the smiles we put on—just to cover our tears;
  And the withering thoughts which the world cannot know,
  Like heart-broken exiles lie burning below;
  .And the vessel drives on to that desolate shore
  Where the dreams of our childhood are vanished and o'er."

HERVEY.

HAVE any of you seen Kenneth to-day?"
asked Paul, as he entered the dining-room
the next evening, where the family where
already assembled at dinner.

"No," replied Aunt Lucia; "and it is strange,
too, for he had promised to take Marcia and Lottie to the Art Gallery."

"And Tom Blanton called at the office to-day
to inquire for him, saying that he had engaged to

dine with him last night, but failed to put in an appearance ; and when he went to his rooms he found them locked. I intended going there myself this afternoon, but Judge Davis found some writing for me to do ; and as one can't be a famous lawyer without working for it, I went at it with a will, and have but just finished."

" I hope that nothing is the matter," said Aunt Lucia anxiously ; while Marcia looked up eagerly, dropping her eyes again in confusion as they met those of her cousin, who continued carelessly :

"Oh, there is no cause for uneasiness. I will unearth the fellow after dinner. But Lottie, whom do you think I met just now ? A very particular friend of yours."

" For the life of me, I cannot tell," said Lottie. " As the old woman said, ' I am not much at conundrums.' "

" Well, then, it was no other than Fred Huntington, just arrived and vastly improved by his Californian trip. He looks at least six inches taller, is as brown as a berry, and can boast as fine a crop of whiskers as Paul Elmore, Esq.," stroking his own luxuriant beard complacently.

" Oh, I am so glad—" began Lottie eagerly ;

then blushing and checking herself, she added—
"for dear Christabel."

"Don't separate your sentences by such long
pauses, sister mine," said Paul mischievously;
"they are calculated to throw a doubt on your
disinterestedness. I should certainly suppose
that your rejoicing was for yourself, and that
'dear Christabel' was an after-thought."

"Don't be provoking, Paul! I can't see what
has led you to imagine that I have any especial
claim on Mr. Huntington."

"Only some childish reminiscences, which doubtless have deceived me; the mirage of distance, I
suppose," continued Paul. "But what is it,
James?" as a servant, entering at that moment,
handed him a note.

"A note for you, sir. Mr. Murray's man
brought it, and he is waiting below."

"A note from Ken!" said he gayly, as he
opened it. "The plot thickens—this grows interesting." But his face became grave as he read,
and more than one exclamation of astonishment
and concern burst from his lips. It ran thus:

"DEAR PAUL :—When this reaches you, I shall
be already on the broad ocean; for having re-

ceived intelligence that renders it imperative for me to return at once to Europe, I have availed myself of the first steamer. I would not have gone without seeing you, but I thought it best to avoid explanations, which I am not at present prepared to make. This will be handed you by my groom, who will await your orders, as I bequeath to you, as my parting gift, the *bays*, for I know not when I will return. Please make my adieux to all the loved ones of your home-circle, and ask them to hold me sometimes in kindly remembrance ; for I can assure you that the thought of them, and the memory of your friendship; will ever be the one green spot in the life of

"KENNETH THE WANDERER."

A thunderbolt in a cloudless sky could not have been more startling than were the contents of this note to the assembled family ; and one and all hazarded the wildest conjectures as to the cause of this sudden departure. When Christabel and her brother came in, later in the evening, they shared in the general agitation ; so that Fred seemed to forgot that any especial attention was due to him as a newly returned absentee, and quite contentedly remained a secondary consideration.

Marcia alone spoke not a word ; but her color came and went with every breath, and a dense though impalpable shadow seemed slowly blotting all the brightness out of her life. Always enjoying Kenneth's society, she had never thought to analyze the feeling, but had been content in her youth and innocence to taste the sweetness of the present, without a thought beyond ; but in this bitter moment she learned how dear was the face which the merciless waves were bearing away from her sight, perhaps forever ; how precious the tones whose echo was stifled in their ceaseless roar. She had given her love ere it had been sought—at least in words. This consciousness burned in her proud heart, girl as she was, and she resolved to bury it deep, and guard the grave with such jealous care, that no eye should ever discover it. So, though Aunt Lucia did not fail to note her pale cheeks and languid step, she was far from suscepting the real cause, but attributed them to her studies—to which she now devoted herself with redoubled assiduity, and would fain have induced her to take more recreation. But in vain ; Marcia's only refuge was constant employment ; and meanwhile the winter wore away, and spring was at hand.

Jennie's star, far from waning, waxed brighter and brighter, and Mr. Elmore's house was always gay—the general rendezvous of young and old. Christabel, Mr. MacKensie, Eugene Castlemar, Clifford Aubrey, and Fred Huntington were, as the latter laughingly said, the fixtures, and as much at home in the drawing-room as the chairs and sofas; and they considered themselves privileged, when by any chance the outer world failed to intrude upon their charmed circle. Mr. MacKensie continued to take great interest in Marcia, and frequently delighted her with some rare book or new song, a drive in the park, or a visit to the Art Gallery, where his cultivated taste seldom failed to disclose to her some hidden beauty which even her artist eyes had not detected, and thus she was indebted to him for many valuable suggestions.

Attentions so delicately proffered could not but have their influence, especially on a nature so grateful as Marcia's; and she gradually learned to rely on Mr. MacKensie in every emergency, and to look up to him as an umpire in all mooted questions. Lottie, with wonderful discretion, though, like "*Pat's Owl*," she "*kept up a-thinking*," contented herself with remarking mysteriously, that although the blue-bells of Scotland were only second-best, they did well enough when first-best was not to be had. But her exuberant spirits were constantly effervescing in all manner of fun and frolic, in which Fred was always her sworn champion and ally, and Paul, who at the first of the season had affected only the *fully fledged* young ladies, suddenly awakening to the fact that Christabel was blossoming into a beautiful woman, this younger party was upon one pretext or another drawn so much into society, that Aunt Lucia shook her head and said it was well that the time was fast approaching for their return to Glen Eden, as she feared that, except for Marcia, Madame L'Etude's had already become a dead letter.

Jennie, meanwhile, had managed to keep the scales so nicely balanced between her ardent lovers, as to leave them in a fever of doubt as to which was the favored one. But her heart told her that the time for trifling was at an end, when one morning she received a note from Clifford Aubrey begging her in earnest but manly terms to grant him a private interview. "I must," he wrote, "put an end to this agonizing suspense which is paralyzing my energies, rendering life

8*

unendurable, and unfitting me for all higher duties. If you grant my request, I will fly to you at once with a heart full of hope; but if, on the contrary, you refuse it, I will endeavor to tear from my soul a dream which has indeed become a part of my very existence, but which I shall be convinced can never be realized.''

Jennie read and hesitated; not that she doubted her own heart, for she could not remember the time when Clifford's image had not reigned there; and although for a while, after Kenneth first returned, her allegiance had seemed to waver, she was forced to acknowledge to herself that it was more from pique at his manifest admiration for Marcia than from any latent preference. But she was not prepared to give up her liberty. She knew the stern nobility of soul that characterized her lover; his rigid adherence to principle; the exalted ideal he entertained of woman; and she knew, too, that, his claims once allowed, he would tolerate in the woman he loved no derogation from his high standard. Then, too, a remorseful thought of the young Cuban crossed her mind. But at length the great master-passion triumphed over all lesser considerations, and she replied thus:

"Come; I will see you as you request.

"JENNIE."

It was a blissful interview that followed. For once Jennie forgot the belle in the woman, and all that was ignoble or unworthy faded before the hallowed consciousness that she was supremely beloved by one so worthy of her heart's best affections. But when Clifford, in the exuberance of his joy, would at once have appealed to her parents for their blessing on the future to which they had pledged themselves, she shrank back, exclaiming:

"Oh no! not so soon!"

A cloud arose to her lover's brow; but it soon passed when she hastened to add:

"Do you wonder that, miser-like, I hesitate to share even with my beloved father and mother these first, sweet, sacred moments that can come to us but once in life?"

It was late when they parted. She was to attend a large party that night,—the last and most brilliant of the season,—and, as fate would have it, under the escort of Eugene Castlemar, and she sought her room at once, making her preparations an excuse for shutting out all intruders. But

left alone, she seemed in no hurry to enter upon
her toilet; but, throwing herself in an easy-chair
by the fire, indulged in a long fit of musing.
Never had she looked so transcendently lovely
as she did sitting there in the firelight, the color
coming and going in her glowing cheek with the
ebb and flow of feeling, and a mysterious beauty,
born of the moment, darkling in her starry eyes.
She was under the spell of the Great Magician.
The fair expanse of the future was absolutely
cloudless; its thorns were completely hidden by
its flowers, and everything was soft and tender;
for

" Love took up the harp of life, and smote on all the chords with
    might;
  Smote the chord of Self, that, trembling, passed in music out of
    sight."

What a pity it is that these exquisite moments
must be so brief! That in this cold, practical
life of ours there is so much to check our noble
impulses; to awaken us rudely from our dreams
of possible goodness; to stifle our yearnings to be
something purer and better than we are; in short,
to draw us down from the beautiful ideal to the
real, which always appears so bare and uninviting
by contrast!

For Jennie, the disenchanting touch was the necessity of dressing for Mrs. Lindsay's party; and with a lingering sigh she arose, half wondering at the mental revolution which caused her to undertake with such reluctance what had hitherto been a pleasure. Even the gold-colored silk, with its elegant though delicate embroidery of seed pearls and silver, and trimmings of rare old lace, no longer appeared tempting, though she had boasted that very morning that it would turn half the girls' heads with envy, and Madame Finnesse had assured her that one like it could not be procured outside of Paris, if, indeed, even that renowned emporium of frivolity and fashion could produce such another. But remembering that she had promised Clifford to dress early, in order that she might give him a few moments before it was time to start, she made an effort to overcome her listlessness; succeeding so well, that by the time she stood before the mirror in the full splendor of her matchless attire, the softer feelings had all died away, and she was once more the acknowledged belle of the season, the fascinating Miss Elmore, whose mere appearance on any stage was the signal for many a stout heart to surrender at discretion. And indeed it

was a faultless image which that mirror reflected ;
everything was complete, from the skilfully interwoven coronal of golden wheat and silver grapes
and the high comb, curiously wrought in gold
and frosted silver, that surmounted her raven
tresses, to the delicately tinted gloves, embroid-
ered like her dress in pearls and silver, and fas-
tening with gold buttons half way up the rounded
-arm.

"I hope Clifford won't be cross," said she half
aloud. "But this is my last evening of freedom,
and I intend to make it a triumph. By to-morrow
he will have told papa and mamma, and ere
another week half New York will be apprised of
our engagement. Poor Castlemar! I wonder
how he will take it? I hope he won't rave too
much, though I fear I have treated him badly.
But he might have known that Clifford and I
have been lovers from infancy. I will be very
gracious to him to-night. There can be no harm
in giving him one more pleasant evening, even if
Clifford should look black about it. But pshaw!
what am I thinking of? I am making a perfect
ogre of this lover of mine! If he does get angry,
I can find a way to soothe him. I must begin by
showing him that I am not afraid of him, or he

will become a perfect tyrant, like the rest of the men;" and with this dangerous resolve she went down to meet him.

Accustomed as they were to her beauty, a murmur of admiration ran through the little circle as she entered the drawing-room, and Clifford Aubrey gazed at her so fondly and proudly that she feared his very looks would betray their secret.

"Oh, for a shield!" exclaimed the mirthful Fred. "Miss Jennie, you dazzle me, and I shall be completely riddled if you look at me another moment. You will put the finishing-stroke to poor Castlemar to-night."

"I hope not," said Jennie, laughing; and Clifford whispered, "My promised wife knows too well what is due to herself," as he bowed to offer her an exquisite japonica, with a request that she should wear it in her bosom.

Lottie sprang forward to arrange it, remarking as she did so: "Jennie, you do look dangerous. Mr. Aubrey, I warn you to keep her from contact with the Nitro-glycerine."

"But alas! I am not to be her escort," said Clifford, smiling, but in a tone of genuine regret.

"You are not?" returned Lottie with perceptible disappointment. "Who then is to claim the honor?"

"None other than the inflammable gentleman himself; and, if I mistake not, here he is to assert his rights," he added, as the door opened and Mr. Castlemar entered in faultless evening attire, looking uncommonly well and handsome.

It was indeed a bewitching scene upon which Clifford Aubrey gazed when he presented himself at Mrs. Lindsay's an hour or two later. The beauty and fashion of the city had assembled to do honor to the occasion; but peerless above them all shone his queenly betrothed. When he entered she was waltzing with Mr. Castlemar, and he was whispering something to her with a look of eager admiration, while she was listening with a glowing face and parted lips that sent an involuntary pang to the heart of her lover. Dance succeeded dance, and still Mr. Aubrey approached Jennie only to see her borne off by some favored knight, happy to win even a passing notice from the reigning star. At length, taking advantage of a lull in the music, when Jennie was seated on a sofa, though surrounded by a throng, as usual, he bent over her and said:

"Have you then reserved no dance for me?"

"Yes—no—let me see," said she carelessly, glancing over her jeweled tablets. "Indeed, Mr. Aubrey, I fear my list is full; you came so late. But perhaps after supper I may give you one."

"After supper, then, I will claim it," said he gravely, and without another word he turned and walked away.

Jennie followed him uneasily with her eyes; but a delicious Mazurka with Castlemar soon put everything else out of her head. She was passionately fond of dancing—and like most of his compatriots, he danced remarkably well; and wafted upon the waves of sound, he had borne her into the conservatory before she was aware of it. This was far from her original intention, as she had firmly resolved at all risks to avoid a tête-à-tête with him. But the subdued light, the murmur of the tinkling fountains, the air laden with the breath of a thousand flowers were too tempting, and without reflecting that "ce n'est que le premier pas qui coute," she yielded, and allowed him to place her on a low divan, while he took the seat beside her.

"Would that I might sit thus, and gaze into your eyes forever!" said he fervidly. "Would that I might bear you to some lone isle in mid-ocean, where the world could not intrude, and there, rearing a shrine meet for my idol, worship you as one apart—a glorious being whose every pulse was mine and mine alone."

"O Mr. Castlemar! I fear your ideas are more poetical than practical," said she with a laugh, albeit somewhat nervous, for there was a look of passion in his dark eyes that made her tremble.

"Oh! why will you always meet my devotion, my idolatry with a jest?" said he bitterly. "Nay!" as she made a motion to rise, "you must hear me. I love you!—I adore you! My very soul—my existence—my heaven, both here and hereafter, depend upon your answer! Do you —can you love me in return?"

"Yes!—I don't know—you are so sudden!— give me time!" gasped Jennie, terrified at the whirlwind she had herself evoked.

"Time! Yes! I will give you months, years, a lifetime! I will serve for you as Jacob did for Rachel, if you can but bid me hope."

What evil genius prompted Jennie to say— "Hope, then; I cannot refuse you so poor a boon, —you, who have given so much and ask so little!"

Fatal words, for which she loathed herself as soon as they were uttered; and turning her head to avoid the enraptured gaze of her companion, she looked up just in time to see Clifford Aubrey pass out of the open door with a face white with anguish. He must, then, have seen and heard all. Oh! the agony of that moment was ample revenge for countless victims. But absorbed in his happiness, her companion had perceived nothing, till at last, observing her unusual pallor, he was filled with alarm, nearly distracting her with questions. She assured him that it was nothing but a passing faintness, at the same time acceding eagerly to his proposal to order the carriage.

The misery she endured through the long watches of that weary night none would ever know. At first she was convinced that all was lost—Aubrey never could forgive her. But youth is ever impatient of sorrow, and at length she persuaded herself that there was still hope. She would so far humble her pride as to write to him to come to her; and once at her side, she would pour out her penitence and her sorrow; she would even promise never to see Castlemar again, and he could not but relent. But it was a very genuine headache which caused her to keep

her bed next morning and send back her breakfast untasted, and although, in reply to her
mother's tender questioning, she only begged to be
left alone that she might sleep, solitude brought
not the coveted slumber. Her mood changed
again. What had she done more than scores of
others were doing daily ;—and what was Clifford
Aubrey, that he should sit in judgment upon her?
Let him alone and he would come to his senses.
If she should send for him he would only despise
her for lowering her pride. And thus she tossed
and turned, unable to rest ; and when, as the day
wore on, Lottie came softly to the door, she found
her still awake, and looking so worn and haggard,
that she exclaimed :

"Why, Jennie ! what a troublesome head you
must have ! The party last night must have been
overpowering indeed, to affect you so seriously.
To think of your having stood up so bravely under such an avalanche of them this winter, to be
so overcome by the last ! But I will not worry
you with my chatter. I have something in my
pocket that will do you more good than all my
nonsense—that is, if you like the writer as well as
I hope and believe you do. Clifford Aubrey's
man brought it about an hour ago ; and as it ap-

pears to be quite a missive, I have no doubt it contains something very sweet; so I will leave you to read it in peace and go to sleep afterwards;" and laying it gently on the pillow, she left the room.

With flushed cheeks and trembling hands, Jennie grasped the note, which she knew contained her fate. Would it confirm her hopes or would it, alas! put the seal to her despair? She paused, longing yet dreading to learn its contents. But at last, with a gesture of impatience at her own weakness, she opened it and read:

"God forgive you, Jennie! A few brief hours ago, I would have staked my life upon your truth; and now, I have not only lost all faith in that, but almost in the very name of woman. I was an involuntary witness of all that passed between you and Castlemar in the conservatory. Great God! that one so fair can be so false! Had any one told me what I there saw and heard, I would have branded him with his falsehood to his face. But no! my own senses were destined to bear me testimony of my own undoing. I have proved my idol, and found it of clay; and though it rend my soul to do it, I will tear your image from the heart

that has never known a throb that was not loyal
to you.   The dream was very sweet, and would
to God that I had never awakened !   But it is over
now, and I must crush out all lingering traces of
it, and light the less hallowed fires of ambition at
the ashes of a love which is already cold and dead.
Still there is enough of tenderness clinging to the
memory of the past, to enable me to hope, in all
sincerity, that your own future may never know
the shadow which you have cast over that of

"CLIFFORD AUBREY."

Who can describe Jennie's agony as she read
these fatal words !   In that hour her soul found its
Gethsemane ; but not in the spirit of the holy
Saviour did she accept the chalice presented to
her.   Her whole soul revolted against the bitter
draught ; and when at last she came out of the
terrible struggle, it was with a calmness born not
of resignation, but despair, and with a resolve
before which her guardian angel shrank back af-
frighted.

The next morning found her at the breakfast-
table as usual ; and although her unaccustomed
pallor elicited many sympathizing remarks, it was
attributed to her severe headache, and excited no

other comment. The smile never forsook her lips, nor the brightness her eyes, and her laugh rang out even more frequently than was her wont; but her mother, though unsuspicious, sometimes started when she heard it, chiding herself afterwards for the nervous fancy that it sounded forced and unnatural. She was first on every festive occasion, and plunged into all gayeties more madly than ever, as if to make up, so Lottie said, for the quiet time she expected to have at Glen Eden. But Clifford Aubrey came to the house no more, while Eugene Castlemar was her very shadow: facts which caused her watchful parents some uneasiness. But Paul told them that Clifford was in the far west, attending to some law-business, and they had become so accustomed to Castlemar's attentions that they were taken completely by surprise, when one morning, with a face radiant with delight, he solicited a private interview, and presented himself to them as Jennie's accepted lover. So persuaded were they that her heart was with the lover of her childhood, that they would fain have remonstrated; but Jennie denied the supposition so emphatically, and advocated Castlemar's cause so warmly, growing positively eloquent over his devotion, that they were obliged to yield a reluctant consent. But they consoled themselves with the thought of a long engagement, and were totally unprepared when Jennie united with Castlemar in appointing an early day for the nuptials. In vain they sighed ; in vain Lottie pouted and grew cross, and Paul said impatiently :

"Jennie must be crazy ; for though Castlemar was a good fellow, any one could see that he was jealous as Satan ! " Even Nita and Dick, who had never overcome their first impression of Eugene, had something to say ; but Jennie quietly triumphed over all obstacles, and when they all left for Glen Eden a few weeks later, the day was fixed, though Jennie checked her lover's grateful raptures, by telling him that she wished to devote the short interval left to her, entirely to her family ; forbidding him to come to her until the auspicious moment had arrived.

CHAPTER XV.

"Comfort? Comfort scorned of devils! this is truth the poet
    sings,
That a sorrow's crown of sorrow is remembering happier things.
Drug thy memories lest thou learn it, lest thy heart be put to
    proof,
In the dead, unhappy night, and when the rain is on the roof."

TENNYSON.

WHO will join me for a walk?" said Lottie,
as she arose from the breakfast-table one
bright morning, when they had been at Glen
Eden about three weeks. "Not a soul has been
off the place since here we've been, and I for one
begin to feel like a fossil remain or some other kind
of petrifaction."

"For my part," said Jennie, yawning, "the
grounds afford me ample space for all the exercise
I require, and I never could understand the charm
you seem to find in these long midsummer ram-
bles."

9

"Oh! you are excusable," returned Lottie; "young ladies in your position are not supposed to find anything charming but writing letters to their fiancé, or reading his over; or indulging in interminable fits of musing, with his picture for an inspiration."

"Nonsense!" interrupted Jennie, coloring, while she endeavored to check, with a light laugh, the lingering sigh that arose to her lips; and Lottie rattled on:

"There is Marcia, now; she is neither engaged —nor expecting to be, for all I know—and she looks as if a little fresh air might do her good. I intend to levy on her for a companion."

"And I have been wanting to offer myself as volunteer aid to your expedition ever since you first proposed it," said Marcia, "but you have not given me a chance."

"What do you say to that, chatterbox?" said Mr. Elmore, gathering up his papers to leave the room. "Our quiet lady makes a home-thrust occasionally. But off with you, and," stroking Marcia's pale cheek as he passed, "don't forget to bring back some roses."

The two girls were soon bonneted and equipped; but the sweet freshness of the balmy air, and the calm beauty of the woods and lanes, stole over them with such silent power, that for some time they walked on without speaking.

At last Marcia exclaimed, "O Lottie, how much better this is than New York! I never before realized the truth of the commonplace adage : ' God made the country, but man made the town ; ' and I pity those who are doomed to pass their whole lives, shut up amid brick and mortar, in unhappy ignorance of green fields and waving forests. True, the park is lovely ; but it is so artificial ! It seems as if even one's admiration must be regulated by rule and measure ; and although we may glory in these triumphs of man's skill and ingenuity, it is, after all, the beauty that comes fresh from the hand of God, still glowing with His primeval touch, that causes the soul to respond even as ' deep answers unto deep.' "

"You are a poet and an enthusiast, cousin mine," said Lottie ; " but prosaic as I am, I must confess that I partake of your mood on this occasion ; though I doubt if these gay New Yorkers would thank us for our commiseration. Their unmeaning round of gayeties is to them the epitome of all that is delightful in existence, and a winter of balls, parties, operas, and theatres, succeeded by a crowded season at Saratoga, the acme of human felicity."

"I must own to a liking for the balls, parties, and theatres in their season," said Marcia, "and the opera is always enchanting; but I like them with little interludes of the Art Gallery, home enjoyments, and something that appeals more directly to the intellect. And as for Saratoga! I would drop it out of my plan entirely: the mere thought of it makes me breathless."

"Drop Saratoga!" exclaimed Lottie, in mock consternation. "Oh, you dear, delightful little piece of verdancy, I fear you will never make one of the beau-monde: for them, that would indeed be 'the play of Hamlet, with Hamlet left out.'"

"I cannot help it," returned Marcia; "and indeed I don't believe I ever was intended for a fashionable lady. Imagine me, for instance, with such a train of admirers as Jennie. I am sure I should turn positively crazy."

"Yes, Jennie did indeed play havoc with the hearts—and I suppose her winter might be called a grand success: carrying off the laurels from every festive scene, and closing with éclat by capturing the lion of the season—ugh!" and Lottie shuddered, "I wish he were safe in his native wilds."

"Hush, Lottie! try to reconcile yourself to what cannot be helped. And after all, though we may think that Jennie would have been happier with Clifford Aubrey, she ought to know best, and any one can see that Mr. Castlemar worships the very ground she treads."

"Yes," said Lottie impatiently; "but his is not the generous worship which rejoices in the homage elicited by its object. He would keep her loveliness for himself, and himself alone, and he grows furiously jealous if one but casts an admiring glance upon her. He may be rich enough, for all I know, to give her a palace of gold studded with jewels; but, mark my words, however splendid it may be, she will find it a gilded cage, and it will be the old story of

"'Chains that gall, though wreathed with flowers.'"

"Oh no!" said Marcia, recoiling from this gloomy picture. "It is your fears that give to the future so sombre a coloring. I cannot think that so dark a fate is in store for one who seems born to revel in the sunshine."

"Well, I hope not," said Lottie gloomily; "but I cannot believe that Jennie's heart is in this marriage. There is some mystery about it. Do you remember the night of Mrs. Lindsay's party—the night that Jennie came into the drawing-room looking so beautiful ? There was an expression in Clifford's eyes, as they rested upon her, that seemed to tell me, as plainly as words could have done, that there was some understanding between them, and in my delight I could scarcely refrain from saying so at the time. Then followed Jennie's fearful headache. Clifford came to the house no more, and in less than a month she announced her engagement with Eugene Castlemar. It was all so sudden. I cannot make it out. I am sure there is something wrong."

"Oh well!" said Marcia soothingly, "let us try not to think about it, but to think only that there is One above, who keeps watch over us and over those we love, who knows better how to care for us than we know ourselves—remember,

'"Cast all your care on God : that anchor holds !'"

"Thank you, my dear comforter !" replied Lottie fondly. "I cannot be gloomy when I am with you. Do you know, if you were the earth, and I were your moon, your nights would never know darkness, for I could show you only my bright side. But do you know where I am taking you this morning ?"

"No! I have never thought to inquire; I thought we were only out for a walk."

"And so we are. But as it is better to give the walk an object, suppose we call on poor old Mrs. Jeffries ; she would take it as a great honor, and Jeffries 'who was here yesterday, says that she is grieving sadly because they have no news from Kenneth."

A pang shot through Marcia's heart at this suggestion. The last time she had visited the Ivy had been with an impromptu party of the young people of the neighborhood, who had assembled there for a parting frolic, just before they left for New York, and on this occasion Kenneth had singled her out as the object of special attention. She blushed to re-think how she had remembered and prized what had no doubt been to him mere idle courtesies ; for, as she always reasoned with herself, if he had ever cared for her he could not have gone off as he did, without a word. And thus the past ever possessed for her a double pang : she was wounded alike in her pride and her love. But there was no trace of these emotions in the cheerful tone with which she replied :

"Let us go, by all means ; it was like you to think of it."

The old house looked deserted and empty enough, with its closed shutters staring blankly through the green leaves ; for although everything around it was in perfect order, no care could divest it of the desolate, melancholy aspect that always clings to an uninhabited mansion.

" We will not make an entrée in state this time ; it will be so much nicer to take the dame by surprise," said Lottie, as she turned from the main avenue into a by-path leading around the side of the house, where a door opened from the housekeeper's room into the shrubbery.

This door was now open, and Mrs. Jeffries was sitting on the step, knitting so intently that she did not notice their approach, till Lottie put her hand on her shoulder, saying :

"That must be a very important stocking, since it engrosses you so that you have not a word for old friends."

"O Miss Lottie! Miss Marcia!" exclaimed the good old lady, rising in a tremor, and executing a perfect succession of curtsies in her delight. "I am that glad to see you, that I can't find tongue to tell it. But don't think as it was the stocking that took my wits just now—I could turn off a score of them and not give it a thought, old as I be. It's my bairn that sets me a-mooning ; and as you found me to-day, so you might find me most days—but," added she with a sudden gleam of hope, "mayhap you've come to bring me tidings?" and she looked wistfully into Lottie's face.

"I wish I could," said Lottie sympathizingly ; "but we have not heard a word since he left. But don't fret," she added, smiling, "it will all come right. Kenneth is surely big enough to take care of himself."

"Yes, but it beats my time, what could have taken him off to furrin parts agin so soon and so sudden—and the letter he writ me ! it was fit to break my heart. I've read it and cried over it, till it is e'ena'most worn out, but if you and t'other miss would like to see it, here it is," said she, taking it from her pocket, wrapped carefully in a clean white handkerchief.

Lottie read it, and then, with eyes filled with tears, handed it to Marcia.

"My dear good old nurse," it began. "I am going far away, and for a long while ; but although I have but little time, I cannot go without a word to you. If I do not find what I feel bound to seek, I may, perhaps—but no ! I dare not cal-

9*

culate upon anything in the future that will
enable me to hope that my dreams of a happy
life at the Ivy will ever be realized. I need not
charge you and Jeffries to take good care of the
dear old place, for you have always done so; but
I do charge you to keep my room always ready for
me, night and day; as to know that there is one
spot on earth where a welcome is awaiting me will
be some consolation to

Your boy
KENNETH."

"Poor Kenneth!" said Lottie, "I wonder what
can be the matter! even Paul can't imagine. But,"
she added cheeringly to the dame, "don't grieve;
he will be walking in on you some fine morning,
when you least expect him, and, who knows? perhaps he will bring a wife with him from across
the seas."

"As to that, I think he might find one nearer
home; but however he comes, it will do these old
eyes good to see him, and even the furrin leddy
would be welcome for his sake."

The two girls chatted a while longer with their
old friend, leaving her at last, as she said, with a
lighter heart than she had known for "mony a
day."

But if Marcia left any brightness behind her, she certainly reserved none to take away with her ; for she was so silent and preoccupied during their homeward walk, that Lottie assured her that an automaton would have been as interesting a companion; and her uncle, who was on the veranda when they arrived, told her that if she had obeyed his injunction about the roses, she had certainly gathered none but white ones, as her cheeks were even paler than usual.

In the meantime the day fixed for the wedding was fast approaching ; and despite all their efforts, a shadow brooded over the little circle as it drew near. To give up their child, under the happiest circumstances, would have been a bitter trial to Mr. and Mrs. Elmore ; but to relinquish her to one who was a comparative stranger, and whose home was so far distant ; and, too, with a more than half conviction that she loved another, was indeed hard to bear. Jennie alone kept up her cheerfulness,` but she seemed the very embodiment of restlessness.; and when, on two or three occasions, her mother would fain have discussed with her the duties and responsibilities of the solemn state she was about to enter, she would dwell only on the gayeties she anticipated, and the

splendors with which she expected to be surrounded.   It had been agreed that the bridal pair
were to leave immediately for Europe, to spend a
year, or perhaps two, in viewing the wonders of the
Old World before settling down on their magnificent estates in Cuba, where Castlemar was already
having arrangements made to build a perfect
palace for his beautiful bride. It was to be an
evening wedding on the grandest scale; and as
Jennie, with a carte-blanche from her indulgent
father, had devoted her last days in New York to
selecting and ordering her trousseau, loads of
finery began to arrive which might have bewildered and enchanted even a Parisian Modiste.
Castlemar, too, was so lavish in his offerings, that
Lottie suggested that it would save him trouble
to have the entire establishment of Ball & Black
transferred to Glen Eden at once, pretending at
the same time to a great fear that they would be
murdered in their beds for the sake of the jewels.
More than one gay belle would have been glad to
officiate as bridesmaid for their fair rival of the
preceding winter; but Jennie, as if with prophetic
consciousness of what was to be the great dearth
of her life in the future, would have none but loving hearts to attend her; so her train was to con-

sist of Lottie and Fred Huntington, Paul and Christabel, Marcia and Mr. MacKensie, and last, but certainly, in their own opinion, not least, Nita and Dick.

And time wore on apace, and at length but one day remained before the nuptials; Jennie's last quiet day with those whose darling and pride she had been from her very infancy; for the morrow would bring not only Castlemar, but Glen Eden would be filled with guests. During all these weeks she had never allowed herself to pause and think, and on this day she had busied herself with a thousand trifles, as if to banish reflection to the very last. But as the evening stole on, and she sat on the veranda in the midst of her dear ones, while the moon shed a silvery halo around each familiar face, and lent an added loveliness to the home that would soon be hers no longer, the lava-tide of recollection overpowered her; and making a hasty excuse, she left them, fearing to lose the rigid self-control she had marked out for herself.

Scarcely knowing whither her steps tended, she entered the library, and throwing herself down on a sofa with a gesture of despair, she moaned: "O my God! what am I doing—What am I

leaving—and for whom? `Clifford! Clifford! if
you had ever loved me, could you have been so
unrelenting! To think that I might have been
your bride!—but it is too late—too late—and to-
morrow I will be—" Here her voice died away in
an inarticulate whisper; and starting up, she exclaimed, "But what fiend has sent these memories
to torment me? If anything could add to the anguish of this hour, it is the thought of the past,
which my own hand has blotted out forever! I
can—I must—I will forget it!" But the storm of
grief, so long repressed, now swept over her in all
its fury; and believing herself alone, she did not
try to check it, and covering her face with her
hands, she bowed her head on the table beside
her, and her whole frame was convulsed with
tearless sobs.

But there was a witness to her anguish, although she knew it not, hidden in the embrasure
of the bay-window. Marcia was in the library
when she entered, although unaware of her presence till her broken exclamations reached her
ear, and then she hesitated whether to remain or
to retire. As she shrank from listening to revelations which, she knew, were intended for no human ear, and knowing that she could not leave

the room without being seen, she shrank equally
from wounding Jennie's pride by revealing to
her that she was cognizant of her secret; but at
the sight of such agony all other considerations
were lost in the longing to comfort the suffering
girl, and, if possible, save her from herself.

Springing forward, and laying her hand on her
shoulder, she exclaimed eagerly: "Jennie! O
dear Jennie! please hear me. Let me implore
you—pause while there is yet time! take not upon yourself vows which it will be sacrilege for
you to utter. Even at the foot of the altar it
would not be too late to retract—and oh! how can
you expect anything but misery to come of such
desecration of the dearest and holiest of human
ties!"

"Marica Lyle!" almost shrieked Jennie, recoiling from her touch, "how came you hither? I
thought myself alone, or tortures would not have
wrung from me the secret you have discovered.
Oh! could I not at least have been spared this
humiliation! Is there no drop of the bitter cup,
that I may leave untasted? But it is useless for
you to plead with me; I have pledged myself to
become Eugene Castlemar's wife, and I will re-
deem the pledge, even if an angel stand in the

way.   Never fear!   I have weighed the conse-
quences and I accept them.   You have witnessed
my last moment of weakness."

And in vain Marcia expostulated and entreated ;
Jennie was immovable.   And before they parted,
she had exacted from her cousin a solemn promise never to betray her.   At first Marcia had re-
fused ; but convinced at last, that to speak would
be productive of nothing but unhappiness, she
yielded ; though when she retired that night, it
was to a pillow as sleepless as Jennie's own.

The morning dawned as cloudless a harbinger
of a bridal as one could well desire, and with it
came Castlemar and the rest of the guests.   Throwing herself at once into the bustle and excitement
of the occasion, Jennie played her part with a
perfection that astonished Marcia, who wondered
whence she evoked her beaming smiles and sparkling sallies.   Indeed, her self-command never failed
her, and all acknowledged that they had never
seen a lovelier bride.   Her dress of rich, soft, lus-
trous satin, with flounce and veil of rare old
point, was marvellously becoming, and even the
most captious could find nothing to complain of
but her extreme pallor; but even this was conceded to be interesting in a bride, and so—the en-

vied of all the envious—and the admired of all admirers—Jennie was launched into matrimony in a
golden mist of glory, that seemed the brightest
augury of a blissful future.   True, in her own
home bitter tears were dropped over the place
which she had left vacant; but we are apt to put
faith in what we desire intensely—and after a
time, even those who were most doubtful, began
to believe in the reality of their darling's happiness ; and of the whole world, only Marcia knew
what an aching heart and shattered hopes lay
hidden beneath the fair exterior.

CHAPTER XVI.

"Man cannot make, but may ennoble, fate,
    By nobly bearing it. So let us trust
Not to ourselves, but God, and calmly wait
    Love's orient out of darkness and of dust."

OWEN MEREDITH.

AT the usual hour in the evening, the diligence rattled through the street of an obscure German town not absolutely unknown to us, but indebted for its name and its small measure of fame entirely to the neighboring torrent of Drachenfels. Mine host and his good frau stood in the door of the inn, ready to welcome any guests it might chance to bring; and although it was rather early for tourists, a look of unmistakable disappointment stole over their expectant countenances, when they perceived that it contained but one occupant. Nor was this disappointment in the slightest degree mitigated when, in reply to their offers of supper and their somewhat voluble enumeration of the attractions of their bill of fare, the young man said impatiently, "I want nothing but a room and lights"—turning, however, as he was escorted to his apartment, to order a cup of strong coffee sent up immediately.

"He looks like a herr; but he hasn't a civil tongue in his head for all that!" said the frau, resenting the slight to her wheaten loaf, her marvellous sausages, and the other dainties for which she was famous.

"And he would have been all the better for a glass of beer, not to speak of the few groschen it would have put in my pocket; for these Americans pay for what they get with a free hand, which is more than can be said of some I know!" and my host looked meaningly at a luckless individual in the band of village loungers who made his tavern their nightly resort.

"American!" exclaimed the individual singled out, nowise disconcerted so long as he could obtain credit for his zwei glasses as usual. "How could you tell that he was American, when he spoke German as well as you or I can?"

"As if I did not know an American!" answered mine host contemptuously. "I've seen too many of 'em. A German would surely have called for the beer; an Englishman always wants his tea; but an American must have his coffee, and it must be coffee as black as à priest's gown and strong as the giant in the legend of Drachenfels."

"Well, whatever he may be, if he's as sparing of his purse as he is of himself he certainly will not make your fortune," said a third party sneeringly, evidently considering himself in some way defrauded of his just rights in being deprived of a bit of gossip with a stranger fresh from the outer world.

In the meantime the traveller, unconscious of, and certainly indifferent to, these comments, had no sooner despatched the coffee (which, by the way, by no means realized mine host's description of its requirements), than, bolting his door, he threw himself wearily into what was obviously intended to do duty as an easy-chair, and was soon deep in thought. His face is thinner and more worn than we are wont to see it, and there is an anxious, haggard look about his eyes; but we have no difficulty in recognizing our friend "Kenneth;" and despite the lines of care around his mouth, there is an expression of quiet power and lofty resignation in his countenance that makes him handsomer and nobler than ever; in a word, he looks like one who has learned " to suffer and be strong." But his reflections were evidently painful; and rising at last, as if his emotions could no longer be controlled, he paced up and down the narrow apartment nervously and restlessly, exclaiming aloud : ·

"How vividly the past comes up before me on returning to this miserable town! Would to God that I had never entered it! How much misery would have been spared me and the poor unfortunate girl, of whom no one can tell whether she may be living or dead. Hilda! poor Hilda! I can see you now with your soft golden tresses and trusting blue eyes, lovely with an innocent beauty that was all your own. As a sister, as a friend, I could have loved you well; but as a *wife!*—Oh Heaven! that this should be, when there is another, whose name I must not, dare not breath, a single hair of whose head is dearer to me (God help me!) than your whole being. Oh, this love! —this deep, surging, overwhelming, passionate love! But I will try to smother it; and though it was a cruel joke that made you my wife, I will seek everywhere until I find you; and then—ah then! remembering that no less than myself you were a victim, I will so devote myself to you, that you shall never know my whole heart was given to another. The pastor, too, who wrote to me—he seems to think that you are but hiding somewhere, thinking in your innocence that thus you will leave me free ! Free !—ah I shall be free no more ! That was a manly, straightforward letter, and he evidently trusted me too, although circumstances seemed to point me out a villain. He must be a man of discrimination, and perhaps I will feel better after I have talked with him. I wonder if he would see me to-night. He surely cannot refuse me when I have come so far ; and," glancing at his watch, "it is not too late even for this primitive town. At all events I can but try ;" and waiting only to brush the dust from his coat, he took up his hat and descended to the public-room below, astonishing the host by asking him if he could direct him to the residence of the Herr Pastor.

Receiving in reply directions that certainly were not lacking in multiplicity, he passed out into the street, leaving the good frau, at least, convinced that he had some secret sin on his conscience, else, reasoned she, " Why should he refuse good, wholesome food, and, after shutting himself up and tramping the floor like an uneasy spirit, go out into the night in search of the pastor ? "

Unaware of these not very flattering imputations on his character, Kenneth walked rapidly down the street, and soon found himself at the residence of the pastor, who opened the door in response to his knock; and even before he had made himself known, cordially invited him to enter. As soon as he had recalled himself to the good man's recollection, Kenneth said :

"I have come to Europe, in answer to your summons, on a very painful errand ; and as I am at a loss where to be begin or in what manner to proceed, I hope you will permit me to apply to you for counsel and assistance."

"All the assistance that I can give is certainly at your service," said the pastor ; "but," and the courtesy of his tone was slightly tinged with severity, "pardon me if I say that you would have prevented a world of trouble by coming sooner."

"That is, alas! too true," acknowledged Kenneth, "and I do not wonder at the reproach your words imply ; but I owe it to myself to convince you that it is unmerited ; for until the receipt of your letter I was entirely unaware of the unhappy tie that binds me. When I consented to enact the

bridegroom in that fatal charade, it was in utter
ignorance of the peculiar laws of this section of the
country, and of the character of the one who per-
sonated the minister. I certainly never imagined
him to be a magistrate ; and indeed, in my bitter
hours of reflection it has seemed to me that there
must have been some malice at work in the affair ;
though I can think of no one likely to do me so
great a wrong. As you know, arrangements had
been made by myself and my companions to leave
at the close of the fête and we did so ; and so little
impression did the occurrence make upon me that it
passed entirely out of my mind, until, on one occasion, when some friends were discussing the
subject of marriage, one of them remarked that in
some parts of Germany it could be contracted
with the same facility as in Scotland, and without
the aid of a minister, adding that thus an idle
pastime had often proved a terrible reality. At
these words the thought of my part in the charade
flashed across me with a sudden sickening dread ;
but reflecting that it was unreasonable on such
slight grounds to suppose myself the victim of a
calamity of which one seldom hears outside the
pages of a romance, it vanished, and I never
thought of it again, till your letter came upon me

like a thunderbolt. I will not dwell upon the anguish it caused me. I saw that it had been long delayed : in fact, months had already elapsed since it was written. My duty was clear, and you can answer whether I hesitated, when I tell you that it reached me one night, and the next found me on the ocean, hurrying to meet a destiny which I would certainly never have marked out for myself."

"I believe you, young man," responded the pastor warmly, extending his hand to clasp that of Kenneth, as if with involuntary respect and sympathy. "The very fact of your being here to-night is sufficient evidence that you never intended to deny a claim which in your country, and at such a distance, you might have so easily repudiated, and I would be doing violence to my feelings did I not tell you that I reverence the nobility of soul which is thus ready to sacrifice all that life holds dear at the call of duty. But what do you propose to do, my friend ?"

" To seek for Hilda till I find her ; for I do not believe that she is dead," said Kenneth firmly ; adding : " but it is so long since your letter was written : perhaps you have had tidings ?"

"No, not a word ! My second letter to you—the

10

only one that you received—was written immediately after her disappearance, and since that time nothing has been heard or seen of the poor child. True, some fishermen, a week or two later, drew from the river a bonnet and shawl, which were identified as hers, and there is not a person except myself in the village who does not think that, in her misery, she drowned herself. Even her mother accepted this solution of the difficulty almost gladly, I fear; for she soon after married Fritz Anschen, the brewer, and her husband not six months in his grave," said the pastor gloomily.

" Poor Hilda ! " exclaimed Kenneth ; "but where can she have gone ?   Can you give me no clue, however slight ?   Had she no relatives ; no friends ? "

" Not a relative on her mother's side ; of this I am positively certain ; and I never heard of any on her father's, though he was not a native of this hamlet, and he did not talk much of his family affairs, even to me ; nor can I think of any friend with whom she might have taken refuge.   Poor child ! she seems as completely lost as if the earth had swallowed her."

Kenneth then confided to him a plan that he had formed of visiting all the neighboring hamlets.

But the good man dissuaded him from this, as he himself had instituted thorough inquiries in these localities, advising him to go at once to Hamburg, and there await further developments.

"For," said he, "although I cannot conceive how Hilda could have reached there, alone and unaided, there is no place like a large city for concealing one's identity; and she could obtain employment more easily than in an obscure hamlet. Besides," added he, "you could there employ detectives, who might prosecute investigations in the smaller towns if necessary, while you would be always on the spot if anything should transpire."

And before they parted it was agreed that Kenneth should set out for Hamburg at once, which he accordingly did the next morning, leaving mine host and his gossiping customers equally chagrined and perplexed at his mysterious movements, which afforded them a theme for speculation and conversation for many a day.

Arrived at his destination, he threw himself into his allotted task with an energy that should have insured success. He spared neither trouble nor expense, engaging the services of the detective corps, and himself haunted the gardens, the markets, and other public thoroughfares so persist-

ently, that his pale, quiet face would have been
missed if he had absented himself. But the days
lapsed into weeks, and the weeks into months, till
summer began to wane without result. True, in
this time his employées had come to him with
many startling discoveries, which had proved to
be nothing, and more than once the chance resemblance of a passing face had lured him into a long
and fruitless walk. But he seemed as far from his
object as ever, when one morning, as he was passing along an obscure street, whither his aimless
wanderings had led him, his attention was attracted by a piece of carving displayed with a lot
of miscellaneous articles in the window of a small
shop near by. There was nothing remarkable
about it, for the subject was too simple to admit
of much artistic skill ; but it reminded him
strangely of Drachenfels, and on reflection he remembered of having seen similar articles wrought
by Herr Waldemar, and it also occurred to him
that Hilda had been taught the use of the tools by
her father. Entering the shop and inquiring if
the object of his curiosity was for sale, he offered
a price for it that made the honest shop-woman
open her eyes, and she was more than ready to
oblige him when he asked her if she could tell

him how she came by it. It was, she said, the
work of a young girl who had come to her shop a
few weeks before with a lot of these carvings to
sell. Not being in her line, she had bought but
one of them, out of compassion for the poor thing,
who seemed in want; but if the Herr liked them,
she had taken the address, and could easily order
more. Kenneth immediately gave her a liberal
order, and promising to pay her well for them,
asked her if she would be so kind as to give him
the address. Anxious to oblige so profitable a
customer, and thinking, as she afterwards said,
that so grand a gentleman could mean no harm to
a poor maiden, she drew from a lot of well-
thumbed papers a scrap on which was written
"Frau Müller, 6 Volksgang," and handed it to
Kenneth, saying, as she did so:

"Here it is; but I am afraid you will find it a
poor place."

Kenneth thanked her and withdrew; and having by this time learned to know the city by
heart, turned his steps at once to the locality designated. It was indeed a wretched place, such a
one as only the miserably poor would think of
turning to for a shelter; even they would scarcely
call it a home. Tall, crazy tenements with long,

ruinous porches running around each story, and
serving only to add to the general dilapidation,
and shutterless windows, many of them entirely
innocent of glass, were crowded together, their
gaunt shadows entirely excluding the free air and
blessed sunshine : and as Kenneth knocked hesitatingly at the door of No. 6, he shuddered at the
thought of finding Hilda in such a squalid abode.
Receiving, in answer to his inquiries for Frau
Müller, directions to a room nearly at the top of
the house, he mounted the well-worn staircase
and presented himself at the door indicated.
" Come in," said a feeble voice in response to his
summons; and entering, Kenneth found himself
in the presence of a woman past the prime of life,
whose wasted form and sunken features told
plainly that disease as well as poverty had
claimed her for its victim. She started upon seeing him, but with a courtesy little in keeping with
her surroundings, begged him to be seated, and
Kenneth at once explained how the carving having reminded him of a dear lost friend of whom
he was in search, he had procured her address in
hopes that in discovering the name of the carver,
he might at least obtain some clue to the missing
one, whose name and the place of whose nativity

he also gave. The frau replied that as she had never been in Drachenfels, and as the carver in question was her daughter, Bertha Müller, she could of course give him no information, and she evidently considered these facts so conclusive a termination of the interview, as to leave Kenneth no alternative but so to accept them. He would fain have left a small sum of money behind him, but something in Frau Müller's manner forbade the liberty ; and indeed, as if interpreting his rapid glance around the room, she hastened to say that she hoped he did not imagine her and her daughter to be objects of charity, as, her husband having been a forest-ranger, she received a small sum from the government sufficient to keep them from want.

Kenneth gave a long sigh of relief when, leaving the Volksgang behind him, he found himself once more in the broad street, although his case had never yet appeared so hopeless. This monotonous life and constant pursuit of a phantom that seemed ever to elude his grasp were very wearing ; and as he sat over his cigar that night, he was revolving in his mind the necessity of a change, when the waiter announced a visitor, who wished to see him on important business—and the chief detective entered his room.

"At last I bring tidings," said he gravely, as soon as they were alone ; "but the Herr must summon all his fortitude to meet them ; for although I have not found the fräulein, I have found her grave."

" What ?—how ?—where ?" exclaimed Kenneth, starting up, and then sinking back in his chair, overcome with the varied tide of emotion.

"Pray control yourself!" said the detective, who seemed possessed of more sensibility than is usually accredited to his class. "I know she must have been very dear to you, or you would long ago have given up the search, and I wish we could have restored her to you. But be calm ; and when I have told you all, I think you can have no doubt that the grave which I have visited is really hers."

"The grave! Poor little Hilda!" said Kenneth ; and then composing himself with a great effort, he motioned to his companion to proceed.

"I was called last week," said the latter, "to a little village not many leagues distant from here, the nature of my business requiring an inspection of the records of the parish church. Being somewhat in advance of my appointment, I concluded to take a stroll through the graveyard while waiting

for the sexton. Wandering, I must confess, rather
carelessly among the graves, my attention was arrested by a head-stone—or rather a cross—bearing the inscription, 'Hilda Waldemar, aged eigh-
teen'—which you may imagine at once excited my
interest and curiosity ; and as soon as I had transacted my business, I sought the Herr Pastor, who,
in answer to my inquiries, exclaimed :

"'Hilda Waldemar ! Oh yes ! I remember !
That was a sad death ! A poor young girl who came
here with her aunt to try the waters of a neighboring Spa. Her aunt had a daughter about her own
age, and they nursed her with the greatest devotion,
but in vain. The physicians pronounced her disease a rapid decline ; but some say she died of a
broken heart, and I don't know but they were
right ; for it was whispered that the poor thing,
deserted by her lover, had been compelled by the
harshness of her mother to fly from her home. The
Frau Müller was so reserved, that I never questioned her about her affairs ; but she must have
been a good woman, for, as she herself told me,
the girl was not her own, but the niece of her first
husband ; and yet a mother could not have been
more devoted. This, and the fact that she was a
native of Drachenfels, comprised all the informa-
10*

tion she ever volunteered; the rest being mere
rumors, which, as she left here with her daughter
immediately after the burial, to go we knew not
where, she never had an opportunity either to
confirm or deny.'"

Kenneth sat some time in silence after the detective ceased speaking, and then he said slowly:
"You are right! This can be no other than the
Hilda we have sought so long and so fruitlessly.
I go to-morrow to visit her grave; and then, as there
is no longer anything to keep me here, I will
at once return to my native land. But in parting, let me thank you for the sympathy you
have shown me throughout this investigation;
while my banker will honor the draft I have
already given you in acknowledgment of your
services."

A sleepless night followed this exciting interview; but the first rays of morning found Kenneth
ready for his journey. He found all as had been
represented; and kneeling beside the narrow grave
where the daisies were already springing above
the golden head, he felt that this painful chapter
of his life was closed forever. A week later he
was on a vessel, homeward bound, blue waves
dancing around him and blue skies spreading

lovingly over him ; but between him and the vista of the future, like a tear mist, arose the memory of Hilda, softening and hallowing, though not veiling, its brightness.

CHAPTER XVII.

"Into the depths of thy dreamy eyes peering,
   Watching thy lips for some shadowy sign,
Trembling in doubt betwixt hoping and fearing,
   Stands my poor soul and appeals unto thine."

"All paths which the lady may travel,
   My blessings shall conquer, that so
No roughness may bruise her, no waters
   Be bitter or brackish with woe,
While the blue heavens brood softly above her,
   And the grass groweth greenly below."

ANON.

BUT, Miss Marcia, can you not learn to love me? May I not hope, that even as sparks elicit sparks, as flame engenders flame, the most entire and unselfish devotion will at last call forth in you emotions kindred to my own? You are so young—I have been premature! The voice of passion has not yet made itself heard in the pure depths of your unawakened soul, and in my eagerness I have swept its chords too rudely!"

"No! no! Mr. MacKensie!" said Marcia in a trembling voice, while her color came and went painfully. "Believe me, I am more than sensible of the honor you would do me, and it grieves me,— oh! how it grieves me, to be forced to decline it!"

"Then why decline it? Hear me, Marcia! I offer you no boyish passion, fervid and glowing it may be as the noonday sun, but as fleeting; it has come to me at an age when, having mingled with the world and learned that life is real and earnest, I am not likely to mistake an *ignis fatuus* for the beacon-light which God himself has sent to cheer our earthly pilgrimage. It has not been the growth of days or weeks, but of months, during which I have marked the budding graces of an intellect meet to cope with the proudest; the unfoldings of a soul pure and spotless as the petals of the lily; the glorious dawning of a womanhood so perfect that I have trembled lest some one should discover my hidden pearl, my secret treasure, ere I had dared to claim it. Men call me cold and proud, and perhaps I am to others, but my snows turn to fire before you; my pride is all forgotten at your feet, and you cannot know what I have suffered this winter when I have seen you, the magnet of every circle, the attraction of every feast, in the fear that perchance some smoother tongue and fairer face might woo and win you. But, Marcia, it is the rugged rock that withstands the tempest and the blast,—come to me, and let my great love be your shield from the storms of life, its dangers and its cares!"

"Oh no! no! no!" repeated Marcia, and this time her voice was almost a wail. "Would that I could, but I cannot—I may not!"

"But," said her companion gently, while a shadow stole over his honest, manly face, "why, if you would, can you not give yourself to me, Marcia?"

"Because—because—" gasped Marcia, covering her face with her hands, while the crimson tide rushed even to her very temples—"O Mr. Mac-Kensie, it is the misery of my life! "but I love another!"

"You—love—another!" exclaimed he, each word dropping slowly and painfully from his lips. "O Marcia! I did not dream of this! But why the misery? Surely you cannot have placed your affections on an unworthy object, and still less can I believe that one so favored could be insensible to the blessing!"

"And yet it is even so," said Marcia brokenly,

while her head dropped lower than ever. "How I struggled with this love, how I hate myself for it, and what it has cost me to tell you this, you cannot even imagine. But I feel that I owe it to you to explain why I am forced to renounce what might well be for any woman a crown of honor. Young as I am, I know what it is to be weary and heart-sick—and can you wonder, then, that I am tempted by the refuge you offer? But I cannot, dare not accept it—it would be false, not only to myself, but to you, who are so more than worthy of all that the noblest heart can give!".

"Marcia, you know not how this pains me, and not more for myself than you; for though I have so often pictured you the mistress of my ancestral home, glorifying and brightening it with your presence, and though your image is so interwoven with all my hopes and dreams and plans that it will be long before I can blot it from my future, still, even if you can never be mine, no less do I wish for you a life all blessings; and if word or act of mine can ever turn aside one cloud from your sky, one thorn from your path, you have but to command it. Let me be your friend, if I cannot be your lover; but oh! promise me, if the time should ever come when you can make me something nearer and dearer, you will not withhold from me the precious knowledge."

"My true friend now and forever!" said Marcia, extending her hand to him. "And let me entreat you to forget that you have ever sought to be anything more; for, believe me, there is many a maiden far more worthy to bear the honor you would have conferred on me."

"But alas!" said he, shaking his head sadly, "the waters of Lethe are a fable, and forgetfulness comes not for the asking;" and silently pressing her hand he left the room, which he had entered an hour before with a heart beating high with mingled hopes and fears.

As soon as she was alone, leaning her head on the table before her, Marcia gave way to a passionate fit of weeping. The pent-up emotions of months found vent in the vehement flood; and neither caring nor trying to repress it, she wept on till the day began to wane and the flickering light of the expiring embers cast fitful shadows through the room. As Mr. MacKensie had intimated, this, her first winter in society, had been a signal triumph. Her ready wit and sparkling repartee attracted even the most frivolous, while the more solid treasures of her richly

cultivated mind, enchanted those who were capable of appreciating them; and reminding her
of their former conversation on this subject,
Lottie had remarked that although her admirers
were almost as numerous as Jennie's, they did
not seem to embarrass her in the least, to which
Marcia replied :

"Ah! but mine are only admirers, not adorers,
and that makes all the difference!"

And this was true : utterly devoid of the spirit
of coquetry, she would not encourage feelings
which she could not reciprocate; and more than
one ardent swain, who would fain have constituted himself her victim, had been restrained
by her "Thus far shalt thou go and no farther,"
so that as yet no crushed hopes or broken
hearts reared their spectral milestones on her
way. Deep in the inmost recesses of her heart
still burned the love which had come to her
so unbidden. Vainly she tried to smother it :
Phœnix-like it would still rise from its ashes;
and often when her smiles were the brightest,
and the spirit of revelry was the wildest, her
thoughts were far away across the trackless
ocean following the lonely exile in his distant
wanderings; and with the foam still beading the

glass, the waters of her life's Marah would rise mockingly to her lips. But with a resolution uncommon in one so young she fought down all tender recollections, not allowing herself to dwell on the past or linger like the banished Peri at the jasper portals which she might not enter. Only to-day she allowed herself to drift with the tide that was surging over her, and the knowledge of Mr. MacKensie's love but added a new pang to a sorrow that was keen enough already.

"Oh!" said she, "if I could but love him as he deserves! He is so good, so noble, so generous! My childhood was so loveless, so neglected! The world holds for me so few ties of kindred! Must this fatal passion put the seal to my isolation, and condemn me to a life of cheerless loneliness? I will write to Mr. MacKensie; I will tell him I have reconsidered; and although I cannot love him with the ardor he deserves, I will, with God's help, be to him a true and faithful wife. But no! can I invoke God's help at the very moment that my lips are uttering vows which my heart repudiates?" And thus, torn by conflicting thoughts, she sat till she was aroused by a voice at her elbow exclaiming:

"Why, Miss Marcia! You here in the dark?

And the fire clean out, and the room cold as Christmas!"

And looking up, she saw James; who, entering the library to arrange it for the evening, had in his surprise thus accosted her with the privileged garrulity of an old domestic.

"I am not cold, and I like to sit in the dark sometimes," said she with forced cheerfulness, "but I did not know it was so late;" and rising, she took refuge in her own room.

"Somethin's wrong!" muttered the old servant, as he stooped to kindle the fire. "First I sees Mr. MacKensie coming out o' this very room, looking so white and cramped-like, that I a'most made free to offer him a bit of some'at I allers carries in my pocket as is powerful good for pains; and then, two mortal hours after, who does I stumble on but Miss Marcia a-freezin' by herself all in the dark in this same blessed room. 'Pears like ev'rything's topsy-turvy. There's Miss Jennie done gone married that black-lookin' furrin gentleman, when she'd a sight better taken up wi' Mister Clifford, who'd knowed her from a baby; and now here's Miss Marcia been doin' something to Mister Mac-Kensie, who's good enough for the best of

them, now Mister Kenneth's gone across the sea.
The Lord be praised! I'm glad I got my old
'ooman afore people turned so cranky, or p'raps
this ole head 'ud be grayer than it is. It don't
do for folks to be speering at Providence. But
I'd like monstrous well to know what it all
means!" and shaking his head mysteriously at
the fire, which was again blazing brightly in the
grate, James lit the gas and withdrew.

"Why, Marcia! how pale you are!" exclaimed
Lottie; as she presented herself at the supper-
table that evening.

"Is that a subject of remark?" returned Marcia;
"I thought that such was my normal condition."

"So it is; an interesting, intellectual pallor,
with a tinge of the Orient, as I heard one of your
gushing admirers remark the other day.; but
nothing so rigid and uncompromising as this."

"Really, my child, you are looking badly; I
hope you are not sick?" said her aunt anxiously.

"Oh no!" said Marcia, "I can plead guilty to
nothing worse than a severe headache, for which
a cup of your good coffee will, I am sure, prove a
panacea."

"I am afraid that you will not be equal to the
lecture to-night," said Paul; "and it would be a

pity: the papers are full of it, and everybody pre-
dicts that it will be *the* intellectual treat of the
season.''

"The coffee is my ark of refuge," said Marcia;
"but if that prove ineffectual, I must e'en try my
pillow,—and leave Aunt Lucia to make my regrets
to my cavalier.''

"And who may be the fortunate—or perhaps I
should say the unfortunate—on this occasion?"
inquired her cousin.

"Mr. Kingsley," replied Marcia. "And I imagine that a lecture with him would be a very
enjoyable affair.''

"Walter Kingsley! It would indeed! And
he is not a professed squire *des dames*, and an invitation from him is a rare compliment. Half the
girls in New York will envy you. It will be a
thousand pities if you cannot accept. But I
wonder how it is, cousin mine, that you are so
captivating, not only

> "'To the coxcombs of all ages,'
> But the poets and the sages."

"Perhaps it is because they do not know me so
well as you do, or you would not wonder at it,"
said Marcia, smiling. "But I am not so irresistible

as you would make out : Lottie has been far more successful on the '*war-path*' than I have been."

"Oh! that is because I am content with smaller game!" said Lottie. "I would never dare to .'beard the lion in his den.'"

"Nor do I lay claim to any extraordinary amount of courage ; but I hope to be sufficiently Amazonian to-night to overcome femininity in the shape of a headache."

And either the hope brought its own fruition, or the coffee proved endowed with all the magic due to its Eastern origin; for when Mr. Kingsley called, he found Marcia ready to accompany him ; and in her keen enjoyment of the famous lecturer's impassioned eloquence, she forgot for a time all her troubles.

The night was lovely : not too cold for the season, while the moon vied with the stars in lending brilliancy to the cloudless sky ; and as they left the lecture-room, Lottie and Christabel, who with Fred and Paul made up the party, proposed that they should dismiss the carriage and walk home, for the sake of variety. Marcia willingly assented ; but could she have foreseen what was to happen, she might have hesitated ; for in that homeward walk, Walter Kingsley, whose works, both in poetry and prose, had already made his name a power in the land, laid fame and fortune at her feet, and thus she was again forced to wound a noble heart, and cast from her a brilliant future.

These were no insignificant trials to a sensitive nature like Marcia's, and there were moments when she was so overpowered by conflicting emotions, that she felt as if she could embrace any destiny which might promise her a refuge from her own painful thoughts. Meanwhile, as the days wore on, Mr. MacKensie was still at her side, ready as ever with all friendly offices, yet never obtruding the great love which pervaded his whole being ; and Marcia learned to regard him with such esteem and admiration, that she began to reason with herself whether these feelings would not in time deepen into love, and whether she might not conscientiously accept the hand which even now seemed always extended to shield and protect her. And thus matters stood when she entered the drawing-room one evening, equipped for a conversazione àt Mrs. Seldon's—a highly cultivated lady, who, although in declining years, had given a series of delightful literary entertainments to the young people during the winter.

"What is the matter, Lottie ? are you not

going ?" exclaimed she in astonishment, on beholding her cousin, book in hand, comfortably ensconced in a low easy-chair, and evidently with no intention of leaving it.

"No;" said Lottie, "it occurred to me at the eleventh hour, that my cold would be the better for a little nursing, and I concluded to stay at home and attend to it. But don't look so rueful. I am only sufficiently indisposed to lay claim to the privileges without the discomforts of invalidism; and although Mrs. Seldon is always charming, I can assure you that an evening at home is not without its attractions."

"I can well believe that," answered Marcia with a sigh; "it is only I that will be disconsolate without my mate."

"No doubt! We do, in fact, generally 'hunt in couples.' But for once we will vary the programme. You must go to Mrs. Seldon's, and if you see or hear anything remarkable, *'make a note of it,'* like Captain Cuttle, for my especial benefit, while I will stay here and do likewise; for, do you know, I have a presentiment that something is going to happen to-night, but whether to you or to me, my powers of divination are not sufficiently developed to reveal."

"That is unfortunate," said Marcia, laughing. "But does the Delphic oracle foretell whether the coming event is to be of a painful or a pleasurable nature?"

"Rash girl! jeer not at fate!" rejoined Lottie with mock solemnity. "Enough for you that I know,

> "'By the pricking of my thumbs, ·
> Something evil this way comes!'"

"I hope, Miss Lottie, that you do not mean to be personal," said Mr. MacKensie, who had entered while she was speaking, and who stood waiting to escort Marcia.

"Not unless your conscience tells you to consider me so," retorted Lottie. "But it is time for you and Marcia to be off, if you do not want to take your champagne after the foam has subsided, for the wits and the sages will have exhausted their bon-mots before you arrive."

They reached Mrs. Seldon's, however, to find the evening at its height; and as Marcia was a great favorite with the venerable hostess, she at once advanced to bid her welcome, saying, with a smile:

I had almost begun to fear that you were going to fail me."

11

Then, with an expression of regret at Lottie's indisposition, she stepped aside to give place to the gentlemen, who were already pressing forward to claim Miss Lyle's attention, and Marcia was soon the centre of an admiring throng, parrying wit with some of the celebrities of the land, and advancing opinions with an intelligence, and at the same time a womanly dignity and reserve, that constituted her own peculiar charm. Mr. Mac-Kensie stood near by, his manly countenance glowing with unconscious pride and pleasure, and hope whispering in his heart ; for there had been an unwonted gentleness in Marcia's manner of late, that almost encouraged him to think she might yet learn to look favorably on his suit. But if the homely adage be true that "the darkest hour is just before dawn," it is equally true that the sun invests himself with the greatest glory at the hour of setting ; and even while Mr. MacKensie was yielding to an illusion, which cast a charm over his whole existence, an event transpired that dispelled it forever. He had withdrawn Marcia to a distant part of the room, to show her a picture which Mrs. Seldon had recently received from Europe ; and while he was enjoying her delighted comments, a murmur of voices, rising above the ordinary hum of conversation, attracted their attention.

"How came you hither? Did you drop from the skies? Where have you been this age?" were some of the expressions which greeted their ears in quick succession; and with idle wonderment as to who might be the distinguished arrival, Marcia turned round to see, and lo! standing near the doorway, shaking hands with Mrs. Seldon, was Kenneth: a trifle paler, perhaps, and more heavily bearded than when he left, but still unmistakably Kenneth himself and no other, and for an instant everything turned dark before her, and she would have fallen, but for her companion. Intuitively he divined her secret. But even in that moment of supreme agony, thinking more of her than of himself, he drew her into a neighboring music-room that chanced to be vacant, and seated her on a sofa, till she could have time to recover.

"My friend! my true friend!" gasped she, when they were alone. "I have betrayed myself to you. But you have spared me the misery of betraying myself to others. I have tried so hard— I had almost cheated myself into believing that I had forgotten. But it can never be ! it can never be !"

"At least," said he graciously, "it is something to know that your love is worthy of you—though I now feel indeed that it can never be. But I trust that God will give me strength to remain your friend, for, O my lost darling! with that passionate nature you have need of one !"

"Bless you for these words!" said Marcia; and seeing that her distress only increased that of her companion, she made a mighty effort to control it, and succeeded at last, just as she heard the voice of her hostess in search of her; and taking Mr. MacKensie's arm, she was greeting Kenneth Murray in a moment after, with as much composure as if a volcano were not raging in her breast.

"Is this the way that old friends meet nowadays?" exclaimed dear old Mrs. Seldon, not more than half satisfied at such a courteous interchange of civilities, for her warm heart was yet unchilled by the frost of many winters. "Mr. MacKensie, you must ensure me a warmer welcome, or I shall certainly never make that promised visit to your home in Scotland;" and taking his arm quite as a matter of course, she walked away with him, though he would fain have lingered to spare Marcia a tête-à-tête which he well knew could not but be a painful trial.

As soon as they moved off Kenneth said :

"Miss Marcia, I did indeed expect a more cordial reception. The steamer had scarcely landed, when, with my usual impetuosity, I betook myself to my dear guardian's residence, finding, of all our little circle, only himself and Aunt Lucia there to welcome me ; Lottie, being indisposed, had already retired ; Paul was entirely too uncertain and erratic to be safely followed up ; but upon an intimation that you were to be found here, I dared to presume on Mrs Seldon's friendship, and come here to meet you, certainly anticipating something less formal than 'Good-evening, Mr. Murray ; let me conglatulate you on your safe return.'"

"Indeed!" said Marcia. "My manner must be unfortunate ; for I am sure, of all your friends, no one is more rejoiced at your return than I am ; but I was never addicted to rhapsodies; and if I mistake not, enthusiasm is not one of the qualities supposed to increase with years."

"At least I shall not so deceive myself in the future," returned Kenneth, with a touch of her own chilling constraint; and after this, their conversation was limited to the veriest commonplaces, and it was a relief to both when some one came up to claim a word with Miss Lyle.

Lottie was still awake when Marcia came home that night, and called to her as she passed her door. The two girls did not, as formerly, occupy the same apartment, but their bedrooms adjoined, and a confidential chat, in dressing-gown and slippers, by one cosey fireside or the other, was considered by both an indispensable nightly ceremony.

"Have you seen Kenneth?" was Lottie's eager salutation on the occasion. "Didn't I tell you that something was going to happen. Nothing will ever convince me henceforth that I am not a distant relation of the '*Weird Sisters.*' But what did you think of him? Mamma says, that although thinner, he is, in her opinion, handsomer than ever."

"To me he appeared much as usual," said Marcia coolly, divesting herself of her wrappings.

"And is that all?" exclaimed Lottie, gazing at her in astonishment. "You speak as if his absence might be counted by days, instead of months. What is the matter with you?"

"There is nothing the matter, except that I am

very tired and very sleepy, and I can't see the use
of entering into details about a person whom you
will see for yourself to-morrow."

"Well," said Lottie, with a ludicrous air of
mystification, "not all my power as a seeress could
have led me to imagine this. Faithless creature,
I verily believe that you have gone over to the
'blue bells of Scotland.'"

"I am sure I could not do better," replied
Marcia; "but in point of fact, I have '*gone over*'
to nothing; though if you do not go bed, your
hoarseness will furnish Aunt Lucia with a text for
another lecture on our nightly confabs, in the
morning."

"I would be willing to risk the lecture, if you
were in a less impracticable mood," said Lottie.
"But as it is, I think I will find my dreams more
entertaining;" and exchanging the usual good-
nights, she turned to seek her pillow.

Although Kenneth had been disappointed in
Marcia's greeting, he certainly could find nothing
to complain of in Lottie's, and indeed everybody
petted, fêted, and made much of him, but the one
whose slightest smile was more to him than the
homage of the whole world. He could not guess
how wildly the proud heart beat beneath that

calm exterior; and hope began to die in his breast, while in its stead arose the conviction that Mr. MacKensie had already secured the prize which he had fondly dreamed of winning. The high esteem in which he held the young Scotchman only served to strengthen this belief; and he was sitting in his room one evening, thinking gloomily enough on the thorny paths by which fate was leading him, when some one knocked at the door, and in walked his supposed rival. To noble natures like Kenneth's such petty feelings as jealousy are an impossibility; and cordially bidding him welcome, he proceeded to enforce his words by stirring the fire into a bright blaze, and, bachelor-like, offering him a cigar.

"Not to night," said his visitor. "I came to see you on a little matter of business, and do not feel like smoking just now;" and then he went on to explain that he was about to return to Scotland; and as he had heard Kenneth admire his span of thoroughbreds, he had come to see if he would like to take them off his hands.

"About to return to Scotland?" repeated Kenneth; and then, as a sudden suspicion flashed across him: "How? When?" he added, in visible agitation.

"If I can so arrange matters, I will leave on the next trip of the 'Cambria,'" replied Mr. MacKensie, to whom this emotion was simply unaccountable.

"So soon!" exclaimed Kenneth, suddenly turning pale. "Of course you do not go alone?"

"I certainly expect to do so. But, my friend, what is the matter? Are you sick?"

"Yes!—no! When do you expect to return?" said Kenneth incoherently.

"It may be years! it may be never!" said his companion gloomily.

"Thank God!" ejaculated Kenneth. "Excuse me, Mr. MacKensie, but I have imagined that you were engaged to Marcia Lyle; and—and—I have loved her so long and devotedly, that the thought that you were about to take her from me, for the moment set me wild."

"You love her, then?" said Mr. MacKensie slowly.

"As my life!" returned Kenneth.

"Then may you succeed where I have failed!" said Mr. MacKensie solemmly; "for—for you are worthy of her."

"But have you indeed wooed, and failed to win her?" exclaimed Kenneth.

11*

· "Even so!" replied Mr. MacKensie. "But the fortune that frowned on me may smile on you —I bid you God-speed! I can say no more to-night;" and wringing his hand, he hastily left the room.

After Mr. MacKensie's departure, Kenneth's misgivings returned with redoubled force. True, his worst fear was relieved; but if Marcia was not engaged, what could be the reason of her unwonted coldness and reserve? He had not much whereon to base a hope; but after a torturing conflict with his doubts and fears, he at last concluded to put his fate to the test; and if the worst came, to try to bear it like a man.

Old James shook his head ominously as he showed him into the libary the next day, after taking up a card to Miss Marcia, on which was pencilled a request that she would grant him a private interview; but his face brightened as the hours passed and he did not come out; and when the growing darkness at last made it, as he thought, an imperative necessity to light the gas, the smiling faces and clasped hands that greeted him, as he entered the room, told him more plainly than words could have done, a tale that delighted his heart, and he confided to the old' ooman that "things wasn't so topsy-turvy as they used to was !"

"My dear, is this Valentine's Day ?" said Mr. Elmore to his wife, as Kenneth was pouring out to them the story of his happiness. "Because, if it ain't, it ought to be, as everybody is pairing off. "That scapegrace Fred has already had the impudence to ask me for Lottie ; Paul is only waiting to win his spurs, or, in other words, his diploma, to rob Mr. Huntington of Christabel, and now here comes this audacious fellow to claim our southern blossom. Never mind, Ken, my boy ; there is no one to whom I would sooner give her; but if all our fledglings are going to try their wings in this summary manner, we two old birds will soon be left alone in the parent nest.'

CHAPTER XVIII.

"This isle and house are mine, and I have vowed
  Thee to be lady of the solitude ;
  And I have fitted up some chambers there,
  Looking toward the golden eastern air,
  And level with the living winds, which flow
  Like waves above the living waves below.
  I have sent books and music there, and all
  Those instruments with which high spirits call
  The future from its cradle, and the past
  Out of its grave, and make the present last
  In thought and joys which sleep, but cannot die,
Folded within their own eternity."
                      PERCY BYSSHE SHELLEY.

THE "Cambria" sailed, and with it Mr. Mac-Kensie. And even in the midst of her great happiness, Marcia's heart was filled with regret at parting with one who had shown himself so noble and disinterested.

"God bless you !" said she, with eyes filled with tears, "and make you as happy as you deserve !"

"Thank you for those kindly words," replied he ;

"and though happiness, just now, may seem to me but a beautiful myth, do not distress yourself with the fancy that I intend to sit idly down and nurse my grief. No! every man has his appointed task; "and though love be dead, duty remains, and in fulfilling it I shall no doubt find a measure of content. Still less must you imagine that it would be better for me if we had never met. True love, even though hopeless, never yet existed without elevating the heart from which it sprang, and I shall never regret having known you. Nor shall I try to forget you; for as a lone star in a stormy sky, a springing flower in an arid desert, the thought of you shall ever be the one bright, beautiful memory of my vanished past;" and with a lingering pressure of her hand, he departed, "*homeward bound*" indeed, but leaving behind him that, without which these mystic words were but a mockery.

With the Ides of March, Paul won his long-wished-for diploma, taking his degree of LL.D. with the most distinguished honors; and soon thereafter the family began to talk of an early flitting to Glen Eden. The only dissenting voices were Paul's and Fred's; and as the embryo firm of "Elmore & Huntington" could not well exist without them, they did not like the idea of the separation. They had determined to be workers and not drones in the hive of Life, and for such young lawyers they certainly had fair prospects of success. Their industry and steady habits as students had impressed the older members of the profession in their favor; the prestige of family was not without its value; and, more than all, Clifford Aubrey had delegated to them, as far as was in his power, the not inconsiderable practice he himself had built up,—for his home was now far distant. His business having detained him in the West much longer than he had at first intended, he had become interested in this new field of labor, and had concluded to remain there. What part a shrinking from old associations had had in the formation of this resolution we cannot say; but at this time he had already been for some months established in Colorado, and was making such rapid strides in popular favor, that it required no prophet's eye to discern that the brow to which love's flowery crown had been denied, was destined to wear, at no distant day, the laurel wreath of fame.

As for his young successors, Mr. Elmore laughingly asserted that the diplomacy with which they manœuvred insurmountable obstacles, and managed to delay the breaking up of the household till the last of May, argued an intimacy with the twists and quirks and intricacies of the law that would infallibly make them a god-send to all the rogues and *double-dealers* in the country. However, they were at Glen Eden at last; and to Marcia,. at least, the days passed like a beautiful dream, from which she would never care to awake. Kenneth was all devotion, and seemed each day to find a new delight in her society. He was making extensive repairs at the Ivy, and old Jeffries and the good dame were almost beside themselves with delight.

The old place to be restored to even more than its pristine grandeur; their bairn about to take a wife, and that wife their own beautiful Miss Marcia—it seemed too much happiness to be real. Nothing was to be modernized, though everything was to be beautified and idealized; for both Kenneth and Marcia had the soul to reverence and appreciate the claims of age, and to understand that the reflection of the past may shed a glory even over the brightness of the present. Only some of the cumbrous old furniture, on which the hand of Time had been laid too rudely, was to

give place to the more graceful and elegant con-
structions of modern genius; for Kenneth did not
allow even his love for the antique to stand in the
way of comfort and convenience. Nor were the
grounds forgotten : the garden was already blossoming into more than its wonted luxuriance ; the
long-disused conservatories were gorgeous with
the floral treasures of every clime, and the spacious lawn was fast growing emerald and velvety
beneath the magic of sturdy arms and skilful labor. And as the days glided by, and the reign of
the mechanics was nearly over, the huge boxes
which had been arriving by every train began to
disgorge their contents ; rare pictures and exquisite statuary, collected by Kenneth in his travels,
emerged for the first time from their packing-cases ;
and the suite of apartments destined for Marcia's especial occupancy, was developing into a
miracle of loveliness. The gems of every collection were reserved for these hallowed precints :
nothing was forgotten, from the piano, the easel,
the miniature bookcase, with its choice collection
of her favorite authors, the graceful flower-stand,
the exquisite buhl writing-desk and work-table,
and their dainty appliances ; even to the low easy-
chair in which Kenneth loved to picture her—

himself seated in the more pretentious one beside it.

"Ay! but it's a bonnie nest that our bairn is a-fitting for his birdie," said his good nurse, gazing after Kenneth as he bounded lightly down the stairs after superintending the hanging of a lovely Fra Angelico in this sanctum sanctorum. "My old een never thocht to see the like of it."

"God send they may live long to enjoy it," said her husband; "but may he forgie' me for casting a doot on His Providence, or bringin' a darkness on the bonny sunshine He's a' sendin'. But a text o' His ain gude book hae' been a rinnin' i' my head this hour past, while I watched the young maister walkin' about so pleased like, and a' I canna pit it frae me!"

"Oot upon you, David Jeffries! The blessed Lord Himsel' kens that we hae' had enough o' darkness to take the sunshine wi'out a question; but let us hear what's a rinnin' in your puir old head."

"Little uns, keep yersel' frae idols," said the old man solemnly. "And if Maister Kenneth beant makin' a idol o' that sweet young miss, I never see one yet!"

"Who ever thocht you did! when the blessed

Lord has made seas to roll atween us an the puir souls as worships 'em!" retorted the old dame fiercely. "There's no need o' borryin' trouble,— it comes fast enough wi'out goin' for it; and don't you be-a-throwin' ony more o' your shadders i' the way o' Maister Kenneth and Miss Marcia!" But somehow when she glanced again around the room, the sun had hidden behind a cloud, and a dull gray shadow seemed to have stolen in una-wares; and though she scolded herself for an old simpleton, and slammed the shutters angrily, a feeling of foreboding settled coldly around her heart, as she locked the door and betook herself to her own apartments.

It had been arranged that the triple marriage was to take place at Glen Eden. The glorious summer days were already beginning to wane, and the appointed time was now only a few weeks distant. Recent news from Jennie gave reason to hope that she would be present on the grand oc-casion, and this was of course a subject of great rejoicing, and Nita and Dick had already begun to speculate on the wonderful things she would probably bring them. Jennie's letters during her year of absence had been long and frequent, and filled with accounts of incidents and scenes of tra-

vel, so entertaining, that in reading them one
might well fail to remark how little she said of
herself and her own personal experiences. The
last had been from Switzerland, which beautiful
country, she said, they had concluded to make
their Ararat for a time at least. She gave a most
interesting account of the peasantry, and the
beautiful and ingenious toys and kick-knacks
they manufactured, promising Nita a most complete addition to the embellishments of her doll-
house on her return. "For," wrote she, "you
must know that I have found a protégé, who has
undertaken the execution of this contract; and as
her skill is exquisite—and her taste is equal to her
skill,—we may expect wonderful results. This
genius resides in a picturesque chalet on the side
of the mountain, with the frau who furnishes milk
for our little menage; and it was in visiting this
chalet, to hear the famous Ranz des Vaches, that
I had the good fortune to encounter her. Now
don't laugh and say that Jennie has gone mad
over some rude, uncultivated peasant girl; for I
can assure you that my Bertha is no such thing.
On the contrary, she is a spirituelle, and refined
and beautiful enough for the heroine of a romance

—and what is more, I am convinced she has a history."

"I am glad to see that matrimony has not yet exhausted the poetical element in Jennie's nature," was Lottie's comment on this portion of her sister's letter. "It is encouraging for you and me, Marcia. I have been laboring under the impression, that when a woman becomes a wife the poetry is at an end, and the book must be read in prose to the close of the chapter."

"Now, Lottie!" returned her cousin, "you know that you have thought nothing of the kind! How could you, when we have dear Aunt Lucia, a living poem, always before our eyes!"

"As if mamma were amenable to the rules that govern ordinary mortals!" exclaimed Lottie, at which Aunt Lucia called them a pair of flatterers; and taking her letter, went to the library to read it over with Mr. Elmore, who had not yet seen it.

As the time drew near when Marcia was to become his wife, Kenneth more than once essayed to tell her of Hilda; but as if with unconscious prescience, each time she interposed some obstacle. At last one evening, as they sat talking over their plans for the future, which stretched so goldenly before them, he said, with a sigh:

"Marcia, you have never asked me a question about my sudden journey to Europe, and yet there are many circumstances which must appear mysterious and inexplicable. Would you not like to hear about it now?"

"Not if there is anything in the recital that will give you pain," said she, glancing at him and quickly perceiving the shadow that had overspread his face. "I can trust you; and whatever there may be that is mysterious, I am sure that my love is incapable of anything dishonorable or unworthy. No!" and she put her hand playfully on his lips as he would have spoken, "not a word! Let these days pass without a cloud, and in after years it will be so sweet to look back to a period of our lives that was all sunshine!"

"Then let it be as you will," replied he, and they alluded to the subject no more.

"A letter from Sister Jennie!" shouted Dick, bursting into the sitting-room one bright afternoon a few days afterwards, and waving the precious missive triumphantly above his head. "Perhaps this will tell a feller whether she is going to bring me that St. Bernard I wrote about—and—but wouldn't it be jolly! Perhaps it will tell for certain whether she is coming to the wedding!"

"Aint you ashamed, Dick?" said Nita; "you talk as if you cared more for a dog than for Sister Jennie, and I know I'd a heap rather have her than all the pretty things she's promised me for my doll-house."

"Pshaw!" said Dick, "what's all the doll-houses between here and the Rocky Mountains, by the side of a genuine St. Bernard? None of your shams, but a real, live, shaggy, knowing St. Bernard, that'll dig you out of an avalanche, and carry you on his back like a baby! But I don't see why I can't care a heap about a dog, and about Sister Jennie too—"

"Don't stop to talk about it, but hand me the letter," said his mother, a little impatiently. "Ah!" she added, glancing at the superscription as she was about to break the seal, "I am too fast; it is for you this time!" and she handed it to Lottie, who at once opened it, and began reading it aloud.

The first piece of intelligence was, that as she and Mr. Castlemar had finally determined to come home to the wedding, they would probably follow the letter by the next steamer, and this called forth so many exclamations of delight, that it was some time before Lottie could proceed. The next important item was that Dick's epistle had been received, and that the St. Bernard should, if possible, be procured.

"And now," she wrote, "I have something to tell you about my protégée, in whom I grow more and more interested every day, frequently taking my walks or rides in the direction of the châlet, in order that I may spend an hour or so with her. The last time that I was there she was not at home when I arrived, having gone for some wood, so the little peasant children told me, to make the pretty things for the lady ; but knowing that she would soon return, I passed into her little room and sat down to wait for her. An open portfolio was lying on the table, and I was carelessly turning over the leaves, when, finding it contained some beautiful designs for carving, I at once became interested in examining them, growing more absorbed as I discovered that they were interspersed with views of the Rhine, all well executed, and strikingly true to nature. But at length I came upon a sketch before which I sat actually transfixed with amazement, and I know you will not wonder when I tell you that from the leaves of that old portfolio, in that poor little châlet of an obscure Swiss hamlet, looked out the face of Kenneth Murray. The

brow, the eyes, the firm, proud mouth, even the
careless wave of the hair, all were his! I could not
be mistaken, and I was still gazing like one bereft
of sense and reason, when Bertha entered the room.
She advanced to meet me with her usual smile,
but as I held the sketch up before her, saying,
'Bertha, I find a picture of an old friend here;
how came you by it?' a change passed over her
face that was pitiable to behold. Her very lips
turned blue; a spasm as of mortal pain contracted
her features. 'Air!—water!—I faint!—" she
gasped, and fell senseless at my feet. Alarmed
beyond measure, I called loudly for the frau, who
came running to my assistance, exclaiming, as soon
as she saw Bertha: 'Her heart again, poor fräulein! the walk was too much for her!' and while
we were applying restoratives she explained to me
that the poor girl was subject to such attacks,
though she had never had one so violent as this.
I did not leave until she had quite revived, and
although, as soon as she was able, she reiterated
the frau's assurance that it was her walk that had
overcome her, I cannot help thinking that the picture had something to do with it, and a suspicion
has dawned on my mind that my protégée and the
"maiden of the Drachenfels," about whom Paul

used to tease Kenneth, are one and the same; and if my surmises are correct it was a far more serious matter to the poor maiden than either of them could have imagined. How she came here, so far from her home, I cannot conjecture; but my opinion remains the same; and although at present detained in the house by a rainy spell, and a slight cold, an impulse, that is not mere idle curiosity, prompts me to ascertain, if possible, whether I am correct. Ask Paul if his maiden's name was Bertha."

"Poor, poor girl!" said Marcia, who had been greatly agitated while listening to this narrative. "I wonder if it could be! I don't think the name was Bertha; but I will ask Kenneth this very night!"

"How strange!" said Lottie, "and how sad! But perhaps, after all, it was only a spasm, and we have been weaving a romance out of nothing;" and, somehow, Marcia felt unaccountably relieved at the suggestion.

But, absorbed in their comments and speculations, they did not hear the stifled groan that escaped from a pair of trembling lips, or see the ghastly look that crept into a white face that was gazing at them through the vine-wreathed

12

window; and even when attracted by the clatter of horses' hoofs, Dick, looking out, exclaimed:

"There goes Cousin Kenneth on Wildfire, riding like mad towards the Ivy. I wonder what's the matter!" His remark failed to make any impression; though when the evening passed and no Kenneth appeared, and even her uncle noticed his unusual absence, it recurred to Marcia, filling her with a vague uneasiness which she could not repress, though she mentally reproved herself for it sharply.

But her apprehensions fled with the night, and she was busying herself gayly about her room the next morning, the great happiness filling her heart, brimming over in occasional snatches of song, when, with a low knock at the door, Aunt Lucia entered. With an exclamation of pleasure, she sprang forward to meet her, but the words died on her lips; for never before had she seen on her Aunt's placid face such a painful expression of sorrow.

"Dear Aunt Lucia! something has happened: tell me what it is," said she, putting her arm gently around her aunt's waist.

"My child, my poor child!" replied Aunt Lucia, "sit down by me and I will tell you all."

"Oh! what is it? Kenneth, dear Kenneth! Is he ill? Let me go to him," gasped Marcia, trembling with alarm.

"Marcia, dear Marcia! calm yourself," said her aunt. "Summon all your faith, for God has sent you a severe trial. But if you can only trust Him, He will send the strength to bear it. Kenneth is not ill, but he has gone."

"Kenneth gone! How? Where?" asked Marcia, putting her hand to her head, with a dazed look, as if she had heard the words without comprehending their meaning.

And her aunt proceeded to tell her, as gently as possible, that when Mr. Elmore went out from breakfast that morning, he had found Jeffries waiting for him in great distress, and the old man had told him that Kenneth had come from riding the evening before dreadfully agitated, and, without speaking to any one, had locked himself in the library, remaining there for hours, and at last coming out to tell him that he had heard bad news and must leave for New York on the night-train, and at the same time giving him a note for Marcia, with instructions to deliver it in the morning. "Then," said the old man, "he turned to the dame, and said, 'Those rooms—

her rooms—lock them : let no one go in,' and he was gone before we could think.''

Marcia closed her fingers mechanically on the note which her Aunt Lucia placed in her hand, and opening it, read, her features growing more rigid with every word :

"Marcia ! *My* Marcia, that was so soon to be, how can I find words to tell you what you must know ! May it not break your heart as it has broken mine ! That letter, that fatal letter ! You did not see me ; but I heard it all, and Jennie's heroine is the Maiden of Drachenfels—and—O God ! can I write it and live ?—my wife ! Yes, my wife ! But do not think me quite a villain ; for, as Heaven is my witness, until that moment, I had believed her dead. But she is living, and I must go. Where, I know not ! Somewhere, anywhere, till I am calm enough to do my duty, and then—to her. I dare not even trust myself to say good-by ; for, if I were to look on you once more, I could never leave you. And now, my love, my darling !—for the last time I may call you so—farewell ! God help us to bear this agony, this worse than death in life.

"KENNETH.''

As Marcia finished, she gave a low moan and
sank back insensible, and for days she never
moved from the bed on which she was laid. But
youth is strong, and at length she began to
recover, evincing such growing impatience for
returning strength, that her friends were both
surprised and pleased, as they considered it a
more favorable symptom than the listless apathy
which usually follows upon great mental suffering. At last, she was able to go downstairs
and take a turn on the veranda; and the very
next day, she surprised her uncle by asking a few
moments, conversation with him.

"What is it, my dear?" said he, stroking her
thin hand, and looking tenderly in her poor, wan
face.

"Uncle," said she, bringing the words out with
a great effort, "I want to talk to you about my
future."

"Your future!" ejaculated he. "Of course
you will stay here with Aunt Lucia, and be our
comfort, as you have always been. I wonder
how we ever thought we could do without you."

"No! no!" said she, "that cannot be. It
is all so different now, so changed! I do not
want to stand in the way of Lottie's and Christa-

bel's happiness: their wedding must go on; it is my dearest wish that it should go on. But I don't think that I could bear to see it, and I must go away. Everything here reminds me so of—of—the days that are gone, that I shall go mad if I stay!"

"Poor child! Poor child!" said her uncle sympathizingly; "but where can you go?"

"To Florida, to my old home," replied Marcia. "I have duties and responsibilities there which I can find nowhere else, and perhaps in the performance of them I may find a measure of content, or at least forgetfulness!"

"But you cannot live there alone!" persisted her uncle.

"No! I have thought of that. And there is Mrs. Grey, our dear old Maitresse d'Anglais at Madame L'Etude's. Her failing eyesight has compelled her to give up her classes, and I think she will be glad to be my companion. I could not have a better or a kinder friend, and I only await your permission to write to her."

In vain her uncle expostulated, and in vain the whole family raised a storm of opposition, Lottie declaring that she would be in despair, if she left her. Marcia met all their remonstrances with such quiet determination, that they were finally forced to yield. The letter to Mrs. Grey was written, and she joyfully accepted Marcia's offer, and by the time the touch of the frost-king was tinging the woods of Glen Eden with his first autumnal glory, they were already far on their journey to Florida.

CHAPTER XIX.

"O sad ' *no more!* ' O sweet ' *no more!* '
  O strange ' *no more!* '
By a mossed brook-bank on a stone
I smelt a wild-weed flower alone ;
There was a ringing in my ears,
And both my eyes gushed out with tears.
Surely all pleasant things had gone before,
Low buried fathom deep with thee, ' *no more!* '"

"Half-light, half-shadow, let my spirit sleep :
  They never learn to love who never knew to weep."

TENNYSON.

"OU George Washington ! Stop dat grinnin',
and git Thomas Jefferson to help wid dis
yere pianny !" said Aunt Phillis, who was
bustling about, superintending the unpacking of
a piano, which Mr. Elmore had thoughtfully ordered from St. Augustine for Marcia. Her young
mistress was expected that very evening, and the
old woman was in a perfect fever of delight,
which was expending itself in all manner of energetic preparations and admonitions to her fellow-

servants, over whom she was "*lording it*" in the most approved style.

"Sakes alive!" continued she, "what's de matter wid you niggas? 'Pears like yer done lost eben de sense ye war born wid. Dar's no tellin' what ud come o' ye, widout dis chile to keep yer straight, and hold up de honors ub dis family."

"He! he! he! de Lor' knows she am big *enuff* to hold all dem and a heap more," said "that sassy Chloe," in an' aside to her admiring attendant, Gustavus Adolphus, otherwise "Gus," who tittered in chorus, as in duty bound, till Aunt Phillis, turning wrathfully around upon them, exclaimed:

"Hold yer mouf, yer brack varmints. I'se a thankin' my Maker, dis bressed minit, dat I ain't no bean-pole, and I 'clare to goodness, I'd be 'shamed to look at corn-bread and bacon ef I didn't make no better show for my keepin' den some folks!" And having thus effectually quenched her antagonists, she again applied herself to the matter in hand.

"Dar! dat looks somethin' like!" exclaimed she, wiping the big drops of perspiration from her dusky brow when the piano was at last

12*

safely deposited in what was to be Marcia's sitting-room. "And maybe ole Aunt Phillis won't be proud when she hears de little white hands a-runnin' ober dem dar keys. 'Spec my young miss knows 'most as much as Father Baptiste by dis time, and he's done forgot more'n all de res' ub de folks 'round here ebber larned. She was allers peert from a baby, a-lookin' aroun' wid dem big brack eyes, as ef she wanted to git at de bottom ub eb'ryting. Bress her little life!"

And there is no telling where Aunt Phillis' tide of reminiscence would have stopped, if Gus had not interrupted her at this juncture by respectfully intimating that he would feel " *obligated* " if she would be so kind as to get out the silver.

"Dat's what I call talkin'!" said she, with a gratified sniff. "And dis yere table looks like white folk;" as she eyed with complacency the snowy cloth, the spotless china, and polished glass. "Dar's no 'nyin', Gustavus, dat you'se a berry good nigga, 'cept when dat no-account Chloe's around, and she's 'nuff to c'rupt de Lord Gabriel heself! What yer come for, Coriolanus?" as a little woolly head poked itself in at the door.

"Please, Aunt Phillis, mammy's a-waitin' for dem eggs!"

"I'm a-comin'," replied Aunt Phillis. "And mind you, Coriolanus, git Columbus and pack yerself to de big gate dis minit, and hold it wide open fur yer young miss to ride froo; and de fust one dat goes to noddin'll git his head cracked!"

Unawed by this dreadful threat, the two urchins were soon rolling and tumbling like a pair of young acrobats down the broad avenue in the direction of the gate; and they had scarcely time to take their appointed stations before a rumbling of wheels was heard, and the carriage rolled through, and in a few moments Marcia was folded in the arms of her faithful old nurse, who was sobbing and crying with emotion as genuine as if her skin had been white as snow, under the influence of that mysterious "touch of nature" that "makes the whole world kin."

Disengaging herself at last for a "How d'ye?" and a shake of the hand with the rest of her sable friends, who crowded around her, Marcia suddenly remembered Mrs. Grey, who was standing, all this time, an unnoticed but not uninterested spectator of the little scene.

"Forgive me, my friend, if for a moment I for-

got you. This is my good old nurse; Aunt
Phillis, this is my friend, Mrs. Grey."

"You'se mighty welcome, missus, and so's all
Miss Marshy's friends. But Lor'! honey, how
you've growed! Purty as a pink, too!" ejaculated Aunt Phillis, having as yet neither eyes nor
thoughts for anything but her nursling. "But,
Miss Marshy, whar's the prince? I thought for
sure you'd bring him along wid you."

" Oh no! Aunt Phillis," said Marcia, coloring
painfully, "there is no prince, and I have not
come back a princess, but just your child—your
own Miss Marshy!"

"Dat's all right, honey; but I 'spect de prince'll
be a-coming too, afore we're much older. But
whar am my sense?" added she, suddenly recollect-
ing herself. "A-keeping you and missis a sottin'
wid your bonnets and dusty close, and Aunt
Dinah in de kitchen cross as two sticks, case her
supper's a-dryin' up!" and she bustled upstairs
with Mrs. Grey and Marcia, while Chloe and Letty
(a smart young negress, formerly Marcia's playfel-
low, but now aspiring to be her maid) followed
with their travelling-bags, shawls, etc.

"How pleasant!" exclaimed Mrs. Grey, looking admiringly at her spacious chamber, with its

polished floor, snowy bed, spotless toilet, and the full muslin curtains draping the windows, two of which commanded a view of the ocean, and, charmed with her unfeigned admiration, Aunt Phillis set her down as a "real, sure 'nuff lady," from that moment.

A flood of mingled emotions rushed over Marcia, as she entered once more her old familiar room, and thought how she had last crossed the threshold, a careless child, full of bright anticipations of the future, to return to it, still indeed scarcely more than a child, as the world counts years, but a woman in experience and suffering, with nothing left to her but the ashes of the hopes and dreams that had made life beautiful.

But this was no time for thought; and casting it from her with the self-control that was fast becoming habitual, she was soon ready to accompany Mrs. Grey to the dining-room.

"O Aunt Phillis, you are the very queen of caterers!" exclaimed she as she sat down to the table; "but I fear that Mrs. Grey and I would have need of two stomachs, like the pelican, to do even half-way justice to all the good things you and Aunt Dinah have provided for us."

And indeed the chickens, broiled and fried as

only a darkey, native and to the manner born, can broil and fry them; the rolls, white and flaky as new-fallen snow; the waffles, done to a turn, and not, as is too often the case, *turned over and done again* ; the delicious golden-brown corn-bread; the butter, fresh as a daisy ; fragrant Mocha, rich yellow cream, and delicate side-dishes of tongue and ham, cut into almost transparent shavings ; to say nothing of the luscious ice-cream, amber jellies, and mountains of tempting cake, peeping out like an after-thought from the recesses of the side-board —were enough to justify such an exclamation. But although not able to appreciate the feast, in a material point of view, as heartily as her old nurse could have desired, Marcia certainly did not un- dervalue the affection of which it was an evi- dence; and when she laid her head on her pillow that night, she could not but acknowledge to her- self that although God had seen fit to deny her life's crowning blessing, He had certainly left her much to be thankful for.

The first proceeding after breakfast, the next morning, was the distribution of the presents which, even in the midst of her grief, she had not neglected to provide for the servants, and all of which gave intense satisfaction.   Aunt Phillis being longest and loudest in her delight over a gayly-hued silk dress, a marvellous turban, and ponderous ear-rings. For Mrs. Grey this spectacle possessed all the charm of novelty; but when it was over, she retired to her own room to attend to her un-packing, while Marcia betook herself to the gar-den. How unchanged it was! It seemed as if Time, so busy elsewhere, had forgotten this quiet spot, and left it untouched, while all besides bore traces of his way-marks. The parterres were gay with the same flowers that blossomed there of yore; the birds sang the same songs; the orange and magnolia groves breathed the same sweet per-fume; the marble naiads still smilingly guarded the sparkling fountain; the moss-grown sun-dial marked the silent shadows as it had done a cen-tury ago, and there stood the tree from whose friendly branches Aunt Phillis had summoned her on that never-to-be-forgotten morning, and as she gazed it almost seemed to Marcia that all these years had been a dream, from which she would awaken to find herself the elfish, neglected child, with her stern grandmother awaiting her in the gray old mansion. And even this lonely child-hood seemed so inviting, compared with the mis-ery of the present, that for a moment Marcia almost

wished that it could be so But then, "Oh no!"
she cried. "Kenneth! my lost love! it is agony
to give you up, but I cannot bring myself to wish
that I had never known you!"

And thus she sat, while the day wore on apace,
so deep in thought that she marked not the flight
of time, till she heard a familiar voice saying:

"Ef dat ain't Miss Marshy all ober! a-settin'
and a-thinkin', and a-thinkin', as ef dar weren't
no sich thing as dinner. Many's de time she'd a
gone hungry ef it hadn't been for me!" and looking up, she saw Aunt Phillis, come in search of her.

"I believe you're right, Aunt Phillis," said she.
"I'm afraid that I cost you many a tramp when I
was a child. And by the way, everything here
seems so natural, that I have almost fancied myself
one again."

"Well," said Aunt Phillis, a little scornfully,
"dem days weren't such gay ones for you, dat you
should keer to have 'em come back. I thought
you'd be a-thinkin' 'bout de prince."

"O Aunt Phillis!" said Marcia, changing
color in spite of herself; "don't talk any more
about princes; I've done with all that childish
nonsense, and never mean to have any prince but
those I used to read about. I will just live here

quietly with Mrs. Grey, and we will do all the good we can, and you must help us to hunt up the poor people."

"Lord, Miss Marshy! how you talk! You'd better b'lieve it beats my time, to think ub a young miss like you, pretty as a pictur', a-makin' a nunnery ub herself, and a-paddlin' roun' arter poor white trash, when she might be a-havin' balls and parties till she couldn't res', an' more beaux dan she could shake a stick at."

"Dreadful!" exclaimed Marcia, laughing; "I am thankful to be spared such an ordeal. But, Aunt Phillls, it is you that are forgetting dinner this time, and Mrs. Grey will be wondering what has become of me."

And, true to her word, Marcia entered at once on the quiet, earnest life she had marked out for herself. The visits of her neighbors were cordially received and scrupulously returned, but she neither gave nor accepted invitations to those grand entertainments of which it had been Aunt Phillis' delight to imagine her the queen, though her name soon became a household word in the homes of the poverty-stricken and the afflicted; and Father Baptiste had never found such a powerful auxiliary: for he had but to mention a

charity, and she devoted, not only her ample
means, but her personal energies to its accomplishment. In the meantime, frequent letters came to
her; first from Glen Eden, bringing news of the
marriage and of Jennie's return, looking paler and
thinner than her friends could wish, but withal in
spirits, so Lottie wrote, almost too wild to be natural. Then from New York, where Christabel and
Lottie were established for the winter, Jennie having departed for her far-off home, while Mr.
Elmore was contemplating a voyage to Europe
with his wife and the little ones. Aunt Lucia
being rather delicate, the physician had prescribed
a sea-voyage, and they were anxious to place Dick
in a university at Edinburgh recommended by Mr.
MacKensie. Thus there was a word from all but
the one that was dearest, from whom she might
not hope to hear, and whose name she never
breathed save in the silent watches of the night,
when the moon and the stars were her only listeners. And the winter wore on, and day by day,
although her gentle smile was never wanting,
Marcia's cheek grew paler and thinner, till Aunt
Phillis began to wonder sadly what they had done
to her darling up dar at de Norf, and to be filled
with a nameless dread, which she would not ac-

knowledge even to herself. Mrs. Grey, too, looked wistfully at her favorite, and her lips often framed questions, which, however, were never uttered, as there was an atmosphere of reticence about the young girl that even she dared not penetrate.

One bright afternoon, when they had, as usual, betaken themselves to the sitting-room after their early dinner, she was about making up her mind for the hundredth time to speak, when Marcia exclaimed from her seat near the window:

"There are some visitors! Now if Letty were but here, she could at once tell from a glance at the carriage the names of its occupants, and would moreover give us their entire pedigree, to say nothing of their family history, past, present, and, I was going to say, future, before they could have time to introduce themselves. But, unfortunately, she is not on hand, and we must await a more formal mode of procedure."

At this moment Gustavus entered with the cards.

"Mrs. Clayton, Miss Clayton, Mr. Louis Clayton," read Marcia. "I thought they were still abroad. They must have returned very recently. Mrs. Grey, Mrs. Clayton, though considerably older, was my own dear mamma's best friend, and the only one, so Father Baptiste tells me, who'saw her in her last illness."

But by this time the party had followed their cards, and the meeting between Marcia and her guests was all that might have been expected from these tender reminiscences. Mrs. Clayton at once felt her motherly heart warm to the lonely young girl; Blanche, with more sincerity than usually accompanies such protestations, said, with a loving pressure'of the hand, that she hoped they would be friends as well as neighbors; while as for Louis, the handsome son and heir, it was easy to see that he was charmed to discover so rare an exotic in his native wilds. The visit passed most agreeably; and when they arose to take leave, Marcia was surprised to find how much she had enjoyed it. The conversation had been so general that it was not until this moment that Louis found an opportunity to say to her:

"By the way, Miss Lyle, I travelled some distance with a friend of yours, just before leaving Europe—a Mr. Murray.

"Indeed!" said Marcia, and a quick throb of the heart, unnoticed by her companion, was the only token that betrayed that this name possessed for her any unusual interest.

"A very particular friend," continued Mr. Clayton, "if I may judge from the manner in which he spoke of you. I chanced to mention that I was from this portion of Florida, and was expecting soon to return hither, and he immediately inquired if I knew you. I told him no; though I hoped soon to do so, as our plantations not only adjoined, but our families were connected by ancient ties of friendship. 'You know not what is in store for you,' replied he. Indeed I found him most agreeable, though almost too grave and abstracted for one so young, seeming like a man under the pressure of some great trouble; and the message he gave me for you in parting was, to say the least, a little singular. 'Tell Miss Lyle for me,' said he, 'that I have found nothing, and that I am still a wanderer.' But," added the young man hurriedly alarmed at the pallor that overspread Marcia's face at these words, "you are ill, Miss Lyle; shall I call mamma?" For they were standing somewhat apart from the ladies, who were conversing with Mrs. Grey.

"No," said Marcia, mastering her emotion with a great effort. "It is nothing. See, it has already passed. I have not been strong lately." And a few moments afterwards she was standing on the veranda, watching her departing guests with a demeanor as placid as if nothing had occurred to disturb her.

"Isn't she lovely?" exclaimed the impulsive Blanche, as the carriage rolled away. "I could not have imagined so much gentleness and sweetness combined with such grace and dignity."

"She is indeed singularly attractive," returned Mrs. Clayton; "possessed of charms even greater than those that made her poor mother's name almost legendary in this part of the country. But what did you think of her, my son?"

"Now don't ask Louis, mamma; don't you see that he is mooning already? But I warn you not to fall in love, brother mine, for it is said that this dear, delightful Miss Lyle (I am going to call her Marcia) looks but coldly on your sex, and some go so far as to assert that she has vowed herself to a life of good works and single blessedness."

"I shall take care of my heart," rejoined her brother; and mentally he was connecting Marcia's indisposition with his mention of Murray's name, and wondering what mysterious fate might come between them; finally ending by acknowledging that but for this very timely warning, that very valuable little organ aforesaid might have been in danger.

CHAPTER XX.

Oh is it weed, or fish, or floating hair,
A tress o' golden hair,
O' drowned maiden's hair,
Above the nets at sea?
Was never salmon yet that shone so fair
Among the stakes on Dee.

KINSLEY.

IT was a wild night on the Florida coast, and the voice of the gale, howling through the magnolia trees in the avenue, and shrieking around the gables till it died away in a hoarse moan, at last penetrated even the cosey sitting-room where Marcia and Mrs. Grey sat with their books and work; and underneath, yet pervading all like a sullen monotone, came the roar of the angry waves, lashed into fury by the blast, and beating against the rocky coast as if clamorous for victims.

"What a fearful storm!" exclaimed Marcia, shuddering; and laying down her work she went

to one of the windows that looked oceanward, and
peered anxiously into the inky blackness without.

"God grant there may be no vessel in the
neighborhood of the reefs to-night, for surely
nothing could live in such a tempest! As I gaze,
I can see nothing but an ominous line of white in
the distance, as if the billows were rising in
mighty protest against man's impotence. Listen!" she exclaimed, her face glowing with excitement, as a lurid flash lit up the sky, followed by
a peal of thunder that seemed to reverberate in
endless echoes. "I almost fancy that I can hear
the wail of the Banshee in the rising blast. How
grand, how sublime, is this war of the elements!
Man seems so little, and God so vast. As far as it
is given to finite minds to do, we seem to comprehend His infinitude, His immensity. The Omnip-
otent, who holds the ocean in the hollow of His
hand, and yet, O incomprehensible love! has num-
bered each hair of our unworthy heads, and suffers
not even a sparrow to fall to the ground unnoticed.
But Mrs. Grey, you are so pale; you are frightened! I was thoughtless; we will shut out the
storm, and try to forget it; and we will talk, or,
if you like, I will read while you sit still and listen."

And Marcia drew the curtains. But just as she had taken a book and prepared to seat herself, there came another crash, louder and more startling than before, and Mrs. Grey, laying her hand tremblingly upon her arm, exclaimed:

"Not now, my child! I am not so courageous as you, and I don't think I can compose myself to listen just now."

And at this moment the door opened, and Aunt Phillis appeared closely followed by Chloe and Letty, their eyes staring wildly, and their shiny, ebon faces ashy with fright.

"O Miss Marshy, honey!" exclaimed her old nurse, "git down on you' knees, an' ax the dear Jesus an' His bressed Mother an' all the saints to 'tect us; for the Lord Gabriel's a-waitin' for us, an' we'se all a-gwine to kingdom come afore de broke ub de mornin'."

"Come, Aunt Phillis!" said Marcia firmly but gently, compassionating the poor old creature's evident terror, but scarcely able to forbear a smile at the ridiculous manner in which it manifested itself, "calm yourself, and tell me what is the matter; what has occurred to alarm you so? Chloe, Letty, come in and shut the door!"

"What has 'larmed me!" ejaculated Aunt

13

Phillis. "O Miss Marshy! is yer done struck deaf, dat yer habn't heerd the Almighty a-rollin' His drefful cannon-balls, and a 'mandin' ub de debbil ter rake up de fires what's a-waitin' fur de poor sinners? Dey'se done bin a-makin' de skies as light as day and as red as blood, an' de ocean's a-rarin' and a-pitchin' like mad, and de waves is a-risin' an' a-frothin' worse'n Aunt Dinah's yeast, an' it's done riz clean out o' de biggest crock!"

"It is certainly a dreadful storm," said Marcia, "but this old house has stood through many a one before; and, Aunt Phillis, don't you know and believe that our dear Lord can take care of you and keep you just as safe in the midst of the tempest as in the brightest calm?"

"Yes, Miss Marshy!" said the old woman, more subdued. "But please don't stop talkin'. I'se heerd tell o' ile on de troublesome waters, and de words as come so purty from yer sweet tongue am dat berry thing. But oh! I ain't telled yer half!"

"Why, what more can there be to tell? Surely there is nothing abroad to-night worse than the thunder and the lightning? and we know that even these are sent from the hand of the same kind Father who gave 'His only Son to die that we might live.''

"De ghostesses, honey ! de ghostesses !'' said the old woman, lowering her voice to a mysterious whisper, while Chloe and Letty drew nearer in mute terror. " Leastways dat wandersome Missy Inez be a-roamin' 'roun' like wild dis stormy night. I tell ye, honey, I'se borned an' raised on dis yere place, an' all my faders afore me ; but I never heern tell ob anything so skeery as dese two eyes done seed dis berry night. De winners ub dat poor Missy Inez am all one blaze ub light, an' de ole organ, what habn't gib a soun' since ole miss died, be a-moanin' and a-groanin' as no human han's hab power to make it !''

"'Deed, miss, dat's gospel troof!'' said Chloe and Letty as Marcia looked at them inquiringly and yet incredulously, for confirmation of this wonderful recital. "An' ef yer will step to de glass-door ub de back piazza, ye can see for yerself.''

"I will go at once," said Marcia rising ; and followed by the little throng, Mrs. Grey included, she repaired to the spot designated, which commanded a full view of the uninhabited part of the mansion. It was indeed an extraordinary sight

that met her eyes, and she stood as if transfixed.
The electric fluid was glowing and writhing along
the iron framework of the Donna Inez windows
like so many fiery serpents, investing them with
a lurid glare that contrasted strangely with the
pitchy darkness of the night, and imparted to
them a weird aspect, that, apart from all ghostly
associations, rendered the terror of the darkies
less unreasonable than it had at first appeared.
Another flash lit them up yet more vividly. But
Marcia's heart stood still, when, above the roar of
the thunder that followed, arose a peal from the
disused organ, solemn and sad, like the despairing
wail of a departing spirit. She was well enough
versed in science to know that both these phe-
nomena might be accounted for by the laws of
electricity; but for the time her childish awe
came back in full force: and remembering the superstition that from days immemorial had made
this sound a warning and an omen, the thought
involuntarily occurred to her—"A death in this
house! Whose may it be?"

Often and often, in the depth of her misery, she
had persuaded herself that she longed for the
coming of the dread Azrael; that she would welcome the touch of his icy spear. But now, standing,

as it were, face to face with the supernatural, she
shrank from the vague unknown, and shuddered
as she thought that perchance the summons, the
warning might be for her. But this was no time
for vain forebodings, and turning silently away,
she said calmly to the terrified throng about
her :

"It is only the lightning; there is no cause for
fear."

And they were retracing their steps, when suddenly there smote upon their ears a sound, more
terrible than the din of the tempest, more ominous than the wail of the organ, driving the blood
from their cheeks, to send it curdling about their
hearts. It was the gun of a ship in distress!
"Boom! Boom!" it came solemnly and with
startling distinctness. "Boom!" again; but as
yet Marcia's parted lips could utter no sound.
But at last breaking by a desperate effort the
spell that froze the speech within her, she cried :

"Quick! Letty! Chloe! light the lamp in the
watch-tower! Aunt Phillis, have hot water;
fires; blankets; beds! There's a ship on the
reefs—and—O God! it may be human souls per-
ishing within sight and sound of us! And—stay!
Ring the great bell and call the men from the

quarter, and tell them I will give a hundred dollars to the man that saves one human life!"

And thus, giving her orders with calmness and decision in the midst of her excitement, the frail young girl rose to the moral grandeur of a heroine in that trying hour. Having done all that they could below, she and Mrs. Grey ascended the watch-tower, and vainly endeavored to catch a glimpse of the ship's lights through the thick darkness. "Boom! Boom!" still came the solemn sound of the guns over the hungry waves. Now nearer and nearer, but at longer intervals, till at last there was an ominous silence; and with a long shuddering sigh Marcia buried her face in her hands; then, as if in answer to Mrs. Grey's questioning look, she said:

"Yes! we can do no more good here! We will descend!"

She insisted that Mrs. Grey, who was indeed quite overcome with agitation and excitement, should at once retire; but she herself still kept her weary vigil; though the storm, having done its worst, had quite subsided, and the dawn of a beautiful morning was already flushing the eastern sky ere the tramp of many feet in the broad avenue told her that the men had at last returned.

On they came : not noisily, but slowly and stead-
ily ; and as they drew nearer, Marcia could see
that they bore between them a burden. What
was it ? Doubtless some weather-beaten seaman,
whose superior strength and powers of endurance
had enabled him to combat successfully with the
waves that had engulfed his hapless companions ;
and Marcia at once ordered her attendants to be at
hand with the restoratives which she had had in
readiness throughout the long night.

"Here! bring the poor fellow in here!" said
she, leading the way to the sitting-room, as the
men at last passed through the great doors.
"But is this all ? Were there no more saved ?"

"Yes, missus! Dar's a sailor down at ole Cot-
ter's de fisherman's, an' he says dat de ship was
de Lone Star from New York to Havana, an' she
was chock full o' people ; but as fur as we kin
heer tell, dey'se all done drowned 'cept him an'
dis yere poor lady!"

"Lady! O God!" exclaimed Marcia in intense
excitement. "Softly, my men, softly!" as the
rough hands, with a gentleness born of kindly
hearts, were depositing their burden on the bed
which she had caused to be made up in the sitting-
room; and kneeling reverently, she folded back a

corner of the blanket. It was a lovely face that met her gaze, although it was wan and colorless, and the features seemed already stiffening in the rigidity of death. The long, wet hair clung in dishevelled masses to the neck and shoulders; and struck dumb for the moment, Marcia was mechanically passing a glittering tress between her trembling fingers, when, observing the motion, one of the men exclaimed :

" Eh, Missus, ef she be saved, it's dat dar har what's done it. Jeff he seed it a-floatin' on de water, a-shinin' like gold in de dark, and he reached clean out ub de boat fur't, and dat's how we drawed her in."

This speech recalled Marcia to herself; and putting her hand in the region of the heart, she cried joyfully :

" There is yet life ! We must save her ! Call Mrs. Grey ; and you, Jefferson, bring a doctor at once ! Go to the quarter, my men ! I have not forgotten my promise ! Aunt Phillis, Chloe, Letty, here ! we must lose no time ! "

And gently disrobing the helpless form, they chafed the rigid limbs, soon aided by the doctor, who promptly arrived, till at last they were rewarded by a faint fluttering of the pulse, then :

gasping sigh, and their patient opened her eyes
with a vacant stare. Still they did not intermit
their labors, and by noon the rescued maiden had
so far revived as to be able to take several spoon-
fuls of brandy, and was sleeping calmly, her
breathing becoming each moment more natural
and regular. Who was she, and whence did she
come? Marcia did not know; but as she watched
beside the fragile form of the sleeper, and thought
of the loved ones who, perchance, had gone down
with the wreck, whence she had been so miracu-
lously rescued, her heart went out in sympathy
for the anguish that would probably accompany
the awakening. But the day was far spent, and
she herself was taking the rest she so much
needed, when at last her patient aroused, and
looking wonderingly around her, muttered a few
unintelligible words to Aunt Phillis, who was sitting beside her. The old woman at once summoned Mrs. Grey, of whom the poor girl asked
faintly, and in French: "Where am I?"

"Safe and among friends!" replied Mrs. Grey
soothingly; and too weak to comprehend her situ-
ation, she soon closed her eyes and slept again.
For a time, quietly; but as the night wore on,
she grew restless, moving her arms uneasily
13*

about, muttering brokenly to herself, and moaning as if in pain.   Much alarmed, Marcia, as soon as it was light, sent for the doctor, who, putting his fingers on the throbbing pulse and pointing to the two red spots that glowed like coals of fire on the cheeks but now so ghastly, said : "Brain-fever of the gravest type!   I feared as much."

Then followed days of anxious nursing ; the patient sometimes raving wildly for hours together, and then sinking back exhausted in a state of stupor.   Strange indeed were the revelations that came from these incoherent wanderings. The name that was always on the lips of the poor stranger was the same that was so graven in Marcia's heart, that neither time nor absence had power to efface it ; and as she listened, while the fevered dreamings of the stricken girl before her bore her back over the weary past, she could not doubt that she was Kenneth's "maiden of Drach-enfels"—the wife whose existence had cast such a desolating blight over the future that had seemed opening so brightly for her.   What strange fate had brought her hither, Marcia could not imagine ; nor as yet had there been a lucid interval in which she could ask the question. Scene after scene, fancy after fancy, crowded upon the disordered brain with ever-changing rapidity. The fatal marriage; the father's death; the long waiting for the lover who never came; the mother's cruel words; the flight; all were enacted so vividly, as to leave nothing to conjecture. And then came wanderings, as in the busy streets of a crowded city, strangely intermingled with green hills and rushing torrents; the ship; the storm. And worn out, the poor sufferer would sink into a fitful slumber.

But one morning, when Marcia was as usual seated by the bedside, the blue eyes turned to her with a glimmer of returning consciousness; the parched lips moved; and bending over, she distinguished the almost inarticulate words:

"Who are you? How came I here?"

"I am your friend; your sister. But you have been very ill, and must ask no more now," said Marcia gently; for her heart was too noble to feel anything but the tenderest love and sympathy for the young girl, who had evidently known such deep sorrow.

"Ah! I remember now!" and a wild gleam again shot through the wandering eyes. "The storm! the wreck! Oh, the cruel waves! why did they spare me?"

"Hush!" said Marcia solemnly. "It was the dear, good Lord that saved you. Do not question His mercy and love; but compose yourself, and you will soon be strong and well."

The poor girl slowly shook her head, but remained so quiet, that when the doctor came he was astonished at her improvement; though he told Marcia not to hope too much from it, as in brain-diseases, an interval of consciousness was often but the prelude of dissolution. The favorable change, however, continued throughout the day;. but the next morning her pulse began to fail so rapidly, that, drawing Marcia aside, the doctor told her to prepare for the worst. As soon as he had gone, Hilda (for so we may now call her) called Marcia to her, and said calmly:

"My friend, I know all. I am dying! Is it not so?"

A burst of tears was her only answer, and she continued:

"Do not cry! I am content. It is better so: I will be at rest, and he will be free!" And a sweet smile stole over her face.

After this a silence followed, broken only by the sobs that Marcia could not repress. But at length Hilda spoke again.

"My friend," said she, taking her hand, "I have a request to make of you. There is one in the world who ought to know my fate. Promise me, that when I am gone, you will try to discover him, and let him know what I am about to tell you.'

With a heart too full for words, Marcia could only press the cold, damp hand she held, and listen with an emotion that cannot be described, while Hilda, in broken sentences, told her what we have already heard;—of Kenneth; the marriage and her flight; adding, that when she left her home, she made her way to the only relative she possessed, an aunt by marriage. Her first husband had been the brother of Hilda's father, and she received her kindly; and indig-nant at the Frau Waldmar's unfeeling conduct, and not putting much faith in the marriage, she willingly agreed to conceal her both from her mother and her lover. Her aunt had a daughter, bearing the same name and of about the same age as Hilda, who was in failing health; on account of which, it was resolved to visit the little village before described, in the hope that she might be benefited by the waters of the neighboring Spa. Hilda, who for greater security had taken her aunt's name, being known only as Bertha Müller, the villagers naturally mistook her for the daughter, and the daughter for the niece; a mistake which Frau Müller never thought it worth while to correct. And when at last her poor cousin died, they went at once to the city, where, as we have seen, Kenneth at one time very nearly discovered her. Uneasy and alarmed at his visit, and feeling her tenure of life very precarious, Frau Müller determined to go into Switzerland, where she had relatives whom she had hoped might befriend Hilda in case of her death. Unhappily she died on the way; and the good priest who was with her in her last moments found Hilda a home with the kind frau in the châlet, where Jennie first discovered her; and here she lived peacefully enough, until chance revealed to her that the beautiful American lady (as she called Jennie) knew Kenneth. Then the poor, hunted creature felt compelled to fly again; ever true to the impulse to hide herself, that she might not be a stumbling-block in the path of the one she loved so entirely and so unselfishly. It happened that just at this time there was a lady at the inn who was anxious to secure some one to take charge of her children. She had been abroad for several years, and was about returning to her home in Jamaica ; and as Hilda readily agreed to accompany her, they departed at once ; so that when Jennie returned to the châlet, she found her protégée gone, without leaving a trace behind her. At New York they took passage on the vessel whose sad fate we have already witnessed ; and now, after years of wandering, whose epitome of sorrow might have made the dark woof of a long life, Kenneth Murray's poor young wife lay dying in the house—nay, in the arms of the woman he loved.

When she finished this recital, she was greatly exhausted ; and Marcia could only repeat her assurance ·that Kenneth should hear all; sending hastily for Father Baptiste, who came without delay and administered the last rites of the church, which Hilda received with touching humility and devotion. Then turning to Marcia with a bright smile, she said :

"Tell Kenneth that my last thought was of him, and that I was so glad to die and leave him free to marry some grand lady, more worthy of him than poor little Hilda."

And she fell asleep, and awoke no more till the

shadows of life had merged into the glorious sunshine of eternity.

Marcia mourned tenderly the pure young life
cast up to her, as it were, a waif from the mighty
ocean, and dwelt reverently on the memory of a
love so free from earthly taint, so devoted, and
so entirely forgetful of self. She rejoiced that she
had been permitted to soothe the last moments of a
life which, though so brief, had known so much
of suffering, and felt that, in receiving Hilda, she
had indeed entertained an angel unwares. She
would not consign her to the gloomy vault where
mouldered the remains of her own stern ancestors,
but made her a grave in the sunniest nook of the
little churchyard, and there the weary wanderer
took her dreamless rest, where the grass grew
ever green, and the flowers ever bloomed, and the
birds ever sang their sweetest songs above her.

CHAPTER XXI.

"..... 'O maiden mine!'
He said, 'I pluck for thee a bud so fair,
That had it grown in any Eastern clime,
Where love is writ in flowers instead of rhyme,
And were it folded, thus, within thy hand,
Mayhap a woman's wit would understand
That her returning lover hies to bring
At last, though parted long, her wedding-ring!"

THE weeks that had elapsed since Hilda's death were fast merging into months, and the noon of a tropical summer was crowning with glory and filling with perfume the beautiful land of flowers; perfect days were succeeded by perfect nights, in which the noon's silvery radiance outrivalled even the sun's golden splendors, and the tuneful mocking-bird made hill and vale vocal with his delicious melodies.

Undeterred by false scruples, and trusting implicitly to a love that had been so sorely tried, Marcia had written at once to Kenneth, as Hilda had requested; enclosing the letter to Paul, and asking him to ascertain, if possible, Kenneth's address, and post it to him. In reply to this, Paul had stated that it would be almost impossible to discover Kenneth's whereabouts, as he was a complete bird of passage, never locating himself for more than a day or two in one spot; but that he had forwarded the letter to the banker to whom he was obliged to apply, from time to time, for funds; and he closed by urging Marcia to return to them without delay. The same mail brought one of Lottie's closely written epistles, earnestly making the same request, and adding that her father and mother were expected home early in September, and that it would be such a pleasure for them to find an unbroken household waiting to welcome them.

"If," she continued, "we could induce Jennie to come too, our happiness would be complete. But poor Jennie! O Marcia! I would not like to give expression to all my fears and dreads for her. When she was first married, her letters were bright and gay enough—the ever-shifting scenes of travel furnishing material for any number of amusing, entertaining pages. But now since she has ex-

hausted the description of her home and its surroundings (which, by the way, must be a perfect
fairyland), and has been forced to fall back on her
own personal experiences, we seldom get more
than a very few lines from her, and even these are
forced and unnatural, as if she were afraid to give
her thoughts and feelings vent. She never speaks
of having seen any one, or of giving or attending any of those entertainments of which she so
often talked, and I am convinced that Castlemar's
jealousy has cropped out, as I always predicted it
would; that her fairy palace is no better than a
gloomy prison; and if her ogre of a husband does
not actually keep her under lock and key, he at
least totally secludes her from the society she is so
fitted to enjoy and.adorn."

"Poor Jennie!" sighed Marcia. "And yet, for-
tunately, Lottie does not know what great reason
there is to tremble for her happiness;" and her
thoughts reverted to that memorable evening in
the library at Glen Eden.

Then she resumed her letter, never pausing till
she had devoured every word, even to the following characteristic postscript inserted by Fred:

"DEAR MARCIA,—Please return at once, if you

do not wish to witness the utter ruin of my domestic bliss. Lottie is so disconsolate over your prolonged absence, that she has actually become poetical, calling herself a wingless bird, a stringless harp, and I know not what other specimen of dilapidation ; and as I cannot follow her in these Parnassian flights, I rely upon your coming, to bring her down to terra firma and to me."

Marcia laughed merrily as she concluded, and then her face assumed a softer expression. It was so sweet to be thus fondly loved and faithfully remembered ! In the absence of nearer ties, Lottie was as dear to her as an only cherished sister ; while Aunt Lucia was enshrined in her heart of hearts, as the loveliest and best of mothers. She was sincerely attached to her beautiful Florida home, and here she had learned, for the first time, what happiness, even under the most painful circumstances, can spring from the performance of duty. But she yearned for these loved ones, and she was so intently revolving in her mind the practicability of a visit to them, that she did not hear the clatter of hoofs, and Louis Clayton and his sister were already at the very door, when she was aroused by Blanche's merry voice saying :

"Good-morning, Fairy Queen! You look so bewitchiug in your floral bower, that it really seems a pity to disturb you ; but we have come expressly to take you off for a ride with us."

Marcia was seated on the veranda, completely surrounded by clustering vines ; and Blanche's salutation did not seem inappropriate, and certainly Louis Clayton thought that no fairy queen could be more charming, as, taking off his hat, he said eagerly :

"I hope that your Majesty will be propitious ; for I fear that we could not bear a refusal very graciously."

"Indeed you need not apprehend one," rejoined Marcia. "But as a queen is always supposed to be at liberty to make conditions, I will go, provided you return and spend the rest of the day with me."

"Nay!" said Blanche. "Not this time. Mamma said, only yesterday, that she was going to protest against this monopoly of visits, for Louis and I either dine, sup, or lunch with you five days out of the seven, and it is a rare favor to secure you for a meal at the ' Dell.' So she gave us positive instructions to bring you home with us, and I have likewise a message for Mrs. Grey, who has for some

time been promising to come over and assist
mamma in arranging her herbarium, and mamma
will be delighted if she can make it convenient to
come to-day. Papa, too, returned from San Augustine, last night, and you know he considers you a
paragon ! "

"Thank him ! " said Marcia, "for I suppose he
means to be complimentary; but my idea of a paragon is a prim old maid, with a mouth of the
prunes, plums, prisms order. However, as it is
said that an appeal to a woman's vanity is irresistible, and I do not pretend to be an exception to
my sex, you may consider that the assurance of
your father's good opinion has carried the day.
But you must dismount, while I order my horse,
and change this airy muslin for a more appropriate riding-costume; I will likewise deliver your
message to Mrs. Grey, and I think you may be
sure of her acceptance."

Marcia descended in a very short time, fully
equipped, and they were soon cantering briskly
down the avenue, as merry a party as one might
wish to meet. A crowd of sable retainers had assembled around the corner of the house, to see
them off: a proceeding which they seemed to consider an essential part of the programme, as, al-

though the rides were of daily occurrence, they
never, by any possibility, omitted it.

"Ain't dey a sight fur sore eyes?" said Aunt
Phillis exultantly. "Dar's Marse Louis. He's
as handsome as de nex' one; gemman, ebry inch
of him, born an' bred. I know dem Claytons root
an' branch. An' Miss Blanche: she's purty 'nuff
fur any kind.o' use, though ub course, she can't
be 'spected to hole a can'le to my young miss,
bress her heart! Dar she goes, wid her long fedder a-flyin', a-settin' as straight as a born princess,
and a-lookin' as proud as ole miss he'self, an' as
soft an' as sweet as her own poor blessed mud-
der."

"Hope Miss Marshy'll gib me dat fedder when
she's done got tired ub warin' it," said Letty;
"wouldn't I take de shine out o' dem Clayton
niggers one time."

"Lor', chile! ain't yer 'shamed yerself?" ejaculated Chloe. "It beats my time how covertous
some pussons is. Now I nebber 'spires to Miss
Marshy's fedders; all I'se done sot my eyes on, am
dat striped silk o' hern,—an' Lor'! how 'jiced I
was, when Marse Louis sot his foot on de flounce
dat time. Ses I, 'Chloe, chile, yer day's mos'
cum.'"

"Shut yer moufs!" interrupted Aunt Phillis indignantly, "if ye can't make no better use o' dem. 'Pears to me, dat you and Letty am like de pot an' de kettle, and you is bof as brack as you can well be. I'd thank my Maker ef I was as sartain sure ub gwine to glory, as I be dat Miss Marshy'll gib ye triflin' niggas all yer worf, an' a heap more too. Precious little you'd git ef she didn't."

"Dat's de troof," said Jefferson, taking this opportunity to chime in; "missy's han' am allers in her pocket. 'Pears like she can't say no when a pusson axes her. Wonder what she'll say to Marse Louis?" added he parenthetically, with a doubtful glance at Aunt Phillis.

"Thomas Jefferson!" retorted that individual, with dignity; "jes' min' yer own business, an' you'll have 'nuff to do. It's 'sponsibility 'nuff fur a nigga like you, to drive missy's carriage an' take keer o' her hosses; an' I 'spec her an Marse Louis'll 'scuse you from 'tendin' to dar private an' puss'nal 'fairs. Dar's nuffin' strange ef all de young gemmen fall in love wid missy; but dat don't 'bleege her to take up along o' ebry one as runs arter her." And the old woman waddled off with all the importance consistent with her somewhat elephantine proportions.

Still the idea of a marriage between her two fa-
vorites was not displeasing to her, nor was she the
only one to whom this seemed a consummation
devoutly to be wished. Nothing would have
given Mr. and Mrs. Clayton greater delight; to
have Marcia for a sister was Blanche's dearest
wish; and as for Louis, his sentiments were patent .
to all. Marcia, alone, had never thought of anything of the kind, and did not dream that Louis entertained for her more than a friendly regard. So
she rode along by his side, chatting freely, and enjoying the delicious morning without restraint; and
never had she been more lovely, nor her companionship more dangerous. The exhilarating exercise not only imparted a tinge of color to her
cheeks, but inspired her with a most unusual
gayety. During the entire day at the "Dell," her
unwonted spirits did not forsake her, and she entered into everything with a zest even more surprising to her herself than to her friends. She
joked with Mr. Clayton, sang for Louis, and chatted with Mrs. Clayton and Blanche, till she seemed
like a different being; and it was not until after
dinner, when she was seated on the veranda with
her two young friends, watching the cool evening
shadows, as they crept refreshingly over the land-

14

scape, that she thought of reverting to her letters,
and the half-formed determination they had induced. They had been sitting for some minutes,
silently enjoying the tranquil beauty of the scene,
when she exclaimed :

"Florida is indeed a lovely country, and well deserves its name. I shall regret to leave it."

"Leave Florida!" exclaimed Louis, and his
instant pallor and agitated manner filled Marcia
with a sudden and unwelcome suspicion, which
she strove at once to banish, as she continued :

"Yes, such was the engrossing subject of my
meditations when you came upon me this morning. I had just received letters from my cousins,
pleading so urgently for my return, that I don't
think I can resist them. However, my plans are
yet vague and indefinite ; for I have not even
spoken to Mrs. Grey on the matter."

"But you will come back?" asked Louis
eagerly.

"I certainly hope to do so," said Marcia. "My
home here is too lovely, and I am too sincerely attached to it, to be willing to expatriate myself entirely."

"Do you know, Marcia," said Blanche, speaking for the first time, "that I am positively jealous

of these Northern friends of yours. I wish you had never left here ; for then we would have had the first claim to you, and no one could have disputed it. But what are we going to do without you ? Louis looks disconsolate already ; I am afraid to picture my desolation ; and, of course, papa and mamma will be miserable, when they see us so."

"Indeed," said Marcia, and there was a tremor in her voice, as she spoke, "I am more touched than you can imagine at this evidence of your affection. But I tremble to think what I might have become, if my dear, kind uncle had not found me out, and taken charge of me. I am afraid that even you would not have found my companionship desirable."

And they talked on, till the moon had fairly arisen, and Mrs. Grey announced that it was time to return home, when Louis accompanied them, remaining silent and abstracted ; for Marcia's determination, so carelessly announced, had checked his rising hopes, and he told himself that if she were indeed beginning to love him, as encouraged by her kindly manner and her returning cheerfulness he had dared to dream, she could not have spoken so composedly of a separation, the thought of which fell so crushingly on him.

Marcia, too, was sorely troubled. The bare suspicion that Louis entertained such feelings towards her distressed her greatly, for in these months of free, unrestrained intercourse she had learned to look upon him almost as a brother; and before she retired that night, she resolved that she would consult Mrs. Grey at once, and that she would make her arrangements to go north without delay. That dear, good old lady was always willing to accede to anything that Marcia desired; but it happened that on this occasion nothing could be more in accordance with her own wishes. She had an only sister living in the far west, whom she had not seen for many years, and who for some time had been writing urgently to beg a visit from her, and she had hesitated only because she did not like to leave Marcia alone. So the matter was soon settled, and they had just agreed finally to start in two weeks, when in came Blanche, making an unceremonious entrée as usual.

"Marcia!" exclaimed she impulsively, plunging at once *in media res*, "I have come to make you retract what you said last night about leaving

us. How can you look at me and have the heart to
do it? I am sure I am haggard, and worn, or, if I
am not, I ought to be ; for not more than seven
hours out of the eight that I tossed upon my restless couch, did I close my eyes in sleep. Papa and
mamma likewise are grum as bears this morning,
and as for Louis—it is positively frightful ! There
is nothing on the earth or in the waters under the
earth, to which I can liken him."

"O Blanche ! you are too ridiculous !" said
Marcia, laughing. " Your picture is truly melancholy. But in fact, Mrs. Grey and I were just
deciding to go when you came in."

"Then !" said Blanche tragically, "I may as
well order my tombstone ; for hope is already
dead within me, and I shall soon fret away what
little life is left in this mortal frame when you are
gone. But cruel, inexorable girl ! will nothing
move you? I see that you have no compassion on
our misery. But what is to become of your beloved poor ?"

"I will leave them to you and Father Baptiste,"
said Marcia ; and assuming her friend's consent
quite as a matter of course, they were soon so interested in discussing these poor dependants, and
forming plans for their benefit, that time passed

by unheeded, and the luncheon hour had arrived before they were aware of it.

Blanche left soon afterwards, protesting that, as she was at last convinced of Marcia's obstinacy, it was useless for her to remain; but adding, rather inconsistently, that she would return on the morrow, as she intended to avenge herself for the short time left to her by inflicting as much of her society on her friend as possible.

After she had gone, Marcia betook herself to the garden. It had always been her refuge in all her childish troubles, and there was no spot on the place, not even the terrace that overlooked the sea, that was half so dear to her. Taking her favorite seat in full view of the sun-dial and the fountain, she said aloud:

"Dear old garden, how I will miss you!"

And indeed it was looking particularly lovely on this especial evening, presenting, as it did, a perfect wilderness of flowers, and an atmosphere so sweet, that it stole upon the senses with almost intoxicating power, while over all hung that subtile, mysterious charm arising from the unconscious linking of the present with the past, that to natures like Marcia's is so eminently attractive.

"Sunshine, fragrance, and flowers!" said she

softly to herself. "How well I remember when I used to sit here, a poor, neglected child, and dream that of these would be made up my future. Though alone, I was never lonely, for my own glowing thoughts and fancies were companions of which I never tired, and of all the wild old romances that I so eagerly devoured there were none too brilliant or impossible to take a part in the destiny that I pictured for myself. I read of princes and princesses, and imagined myself one of them. In my heroine for the time I merged my individuality wholly and entirely—and never will I forget the delight I experienced in fancying myself Rowena, and in following my Ivanhoe through his wanderings, his reverses, and his triumphs. After a lapse of years I came again to my favorite haunt, to find it indeed unchanged but myself disenchanted, and no longer a child. True, I had known the sunshine, the flowers, and the fragrance; but ah! the sunshine had its clouds, the flowers their thorns, and the fragrance, alas! had vanished with the withered hopes that lay scattered along my path. I had met my prince, nobler, truer, purer, better, far, than the most exalted creation of my childhood; but I had met him only to lose him! The smiling spring succeeds the wintry snows;

the glorious dawn, the darksome shades of night. And will not then my life too have its Orient, or must I wait for the light of eternity to dispel the gloom that has so long enshrouded me ? No! oh no! I shall see him again. It is long—so long,— but he will come at last! My life! my love!"

And even as she spoke, a shadow fell across her path, a firm, broad hand clasped her own, and a deep, fond voice murmured in her ear.

"Marcia, my own! my wife! I am here!"

And looking up, she exclaimed :

"My Kenneth! my Prince! I knew you would come!" and in another moment she was sobbing out her happiness on his bosom.

Then followed some of those exquisite moments, having in them more of heaven than of earth ; gems from God's own diadem, vouchsafed to mortals but once or twice in a lifetime. At first it was a bliss too deep for words ; and then speech came, and there was so much to tell : Kenneth of his fruitless wanderings, and how he had flown to Marcia as soon as her letter reached him. And then Marcia told of Hilda, and Kenneth listened, and the memory of the gentle girl seemed to hallow and sanctify the reunion of the long-parted lovers. At last Marcia said :

"But how did you chance to seek me here!"

"Mrs. Grey directed me hither," replied Kennenth.

"Oh!" exclaimed Marcia, "I am so glad that my destiny came to me in the garden—the dear old garden!"

"And it seemed fitting that I should find you thus, embowered in loveliness and surrounded by flowers," said Kenneth. "If there were need to tell you of my love, I would trust their eloquence rather than my own, and plucking the fairest I would place them in your hand, and bid them speak for me."

And thus they talked on, and the daylight had quite faded, when at last Marcia proposed a return to the house, much to the delight of Aunt Phillis, who with Aunt Dinah was groaning over a ruined supper.

"It's my 'pinion," said the old nurse confidentially to the latter worthy, "dat Miss Marshy's prince done come at las', an' Marse Louis mout as well hang on de willer. Whenebber you sees de white folks a-forgittin' de warfles an' de batter-cakes, an' not keering ef de rolls an' de chickens burn up, you kin lay yer life dar's love aroun' somewhar!" And the old lady waddled off to

14*

administer a gentle admonition to Gustavus in the dining-room.

The next morning, Marcia called her, and formally presented Kenneth to her.

"Aunt Phillis," said she, "here is my prince!"

The old woman made him a curtsey, and then drawing back, much to his amazement, deliberately surveyed him from head to foot; saying at last :

"Well, massa, ef ye're as good as ye're good-lookin', I 'spec' you'll do. But de misfortin' is dat eb'rything ain't as purty as it looks. We'se all heerd tell o' dem apples full o'. ashes and dem whitewashed tombstones. Not that as I'se gwine to say you is like dem. I hopes not. But, massa, I done nussed and 'tended Miss Marshy sin' she was a little baby, an' I'se seed her growed up so gran' an' beautiful, dat I'd hardly think one ub de Lord's own angels was good 'nuff fur her, an' I must 'fess dat I fears and trembles when a stranger what I don't know 'nuffin 'bout comes an' axes fur her; an' one, too, as wants to take her 'way off, whar Aunt Phillis can't never take keer o' her nor 'tend her no more!" and the tears that she could not restrain flowed down her ebon cheeks.

"Aunt Phillis!" said Kenneth solemnly, "may God deal with me as I deal with your Miss Marcia. Her happiness will always be my first care, and she shall never know a trouble that I have power to spare her. And I do not wish to take her from you. You must come with us, and every winter we will bring you back, for a few months in your Florida home, and I hope in time to convince you that I am neither a Sodom's apple nor a whited sepulchre!"

Aunt Phillis was much pleased with this little speech, and manifested her approbation by declaring that whatever else he might be, she was "'vinced dat Marse Kenneth was a rale, sure 'nuff gen'man!" But she would not commit herself on the subject of accompanying Marcia, believing firmly that everything would go to destruction without her. But when, yielding to Kenneth's solicitations, Marcia appointed an early day for her marriage, and she found that the separation was a rapidly approaching reality, love for her nursling overcame every other consideration, and she determined to go with her, keeping all the servants in a constant state of fermentation from that time, and overwhelming them with such a multiplicity of directions, that in her bewilderment Chloe protested, with a slight variation of the original text, that she did not know her head from her heels.

In accordance with Marcia's wishes, the bridal was to be a very quiet one. It was to take place in the chapel, Father Baptiste officiating, as he had done at her baptism, and Blanche and Louis, who, convinced of the hopelessness of his love, had struggled manfully to overcome it, acting as attendants; while no one was to be present but Mrs. Grey and Mr. and Mrs. Clayton, except, of course, the servants. And now the days passed rapidly away, bringing with them the last eventful one; and never had a lovelier wedding-morn dawned on a bride than that which greeted Marcia. As if conscious that it was a festal occasion, the birds poured out their very throats in a flood of melody; the grass looked its greenest; the flowers their fairest; and over all the sunshine rested goldenly like a benediction.

Marcia stood at her window and gazed at all this beauty with a heart overflowing with thankfulness. She knew that this was the great crisis of her life; but she felt no emotion but happiness, so calm and deep, that it sent not a ripple to disturb her tranquillity. Full of confidence, not

only in the earthly love that was henceforth to be
her shield and her support, but in that other and
greater Love, which had led her so tenderly out
of darkness into light, she was ready to enter,
with unfaltering step and smiling lip, upon her
life-pilgrimage. Blanche was far more agitated;
and when she had arranged the flowing veil and
spotless wreath, and bent over to kiss her friend,
she was so impressed by the radiant peace and
beautiful serenity that beamed from her countenance, that she exclaimed involuntarily:

"O Marcia! I hope that when my day comes,
I may be as sure of my future as you are!"

"I hope so, indeed, my dear friend!" replied
Marcia; "but," she added dreamily, "I fear the
world contains but one Kenneth!"

The chapel was beautifully decorated with flowers, which relieved the sombre aspect usual to it.
Wreaths of pure white roses festooned the walls
and garlanded the windows; the altar was a mass
of lights and flowers, and extending from it almost to the ceiling was a cross of lilies interspersed with lights; while directly over the spot
where the young couple were to stand, brooded a
snowy dove, exquisitely fashioned of spotless
rose-buds. The poor school-children, who had

been Marcia's especial care, met the bridal party at the door, preceding them up the aisle, and strewing their path with flowers, while their fresh young voices rang out sweet and clear in a joyful hymn.

But at length it was all over—the wedding, the feasting, and the parting; and Marcia rolled through the great gates once more; not as formerly, a trembling child living in the future, and half welcoming yet half dreading the world before her, but a loving, trusting bride with her world beside her, and encircled by a present so bright, that its glorious halo absorbed not only the future, but the past.

CHAPTER XXII.

. . . . "Until the hour of death,
Whatever road man chooses, Fate
Still holds him subject to her breath.
Spun of all silks, our days and nights
Have sorrows woven with delights;
And of this intermingled shade
Our various destiny appears,
Even as one sees the course of years
Of summers and of winters made."

AFTER a lapse of ten busy, changeful years, we must ask our readers to go with us once more to the Ivy. It is Kenneth's birthday, and he is celebrating it; not with a brilliant fête as he did on a former occasion, which we all remember, but, as he says, with a gathering of the clan; and we must take a look at our old friends and see how time has dealt with them. In that gentleman whose hair is scarcely silvered, though we can discern here and there an incipient trace of Time's frostwork, we recognize Mr. Elmore;

and by his side is Aunt Lucia, gentle and loving as ever, and looking almost as young as when we first made her acquaintance. They have evidently been made the umpires of a foot-race that is in progress between two fine, sturdy-looking boys, aged respectively nine and ten, and are watching it with great interest. The foremost of these contestants, with fair locks flowing on the wind, is Kenneth, junior; and as he reaches the goal, and looks around flushed and triumphant, he turns to us his father's handsome face, though the dark eyes are his mother's own. His companion is Lottie's only son and her father's namesake, and with his short, thick brown curls and roguish face, he looks one to be proud of. He bears his defeat good-naturedly, and only laughs merrily when his mother, still a girlish matron, though a trifle stouter than when we saw her last, tells him he must get a pair of the famous seven-league boots before he ventures to run with Kenneth again.

But who are these fairy-like little creatures with long, golden curls, eyes like twin violets, and cheeks and brows that outshine the lily and the rose? Even their dresses are alike, and their ribbons and tiny blue shoes; and indeed it would

require a mother's eye to distinguish between
them. But they look so dainty, we must ask a
formal introduction. Ah! they are Misses Lucia
and Christabel Elmore, Paul's twin daughters,
and they tell us that they were six years old yesterday. Bending over them with the incipient
gallantry inherent in his race, his brunette
complexion, jetty locks, and large black eyes,
in striking contrast to themselves, is little Eugene
Castlemar, Jennie's son, and his grandma's especial darling. Near by is Jennie herself, watching the trio with an expression of loving tenderness that so hallows and softens her face, that,
although thinner and paler than we have ever
known her, she appears even more beautiful than
ever. Years ago she came back to the old home,
a widow, bringing with her her child, then a
mere infant, now a boy of eight. She had evidently suffered, and deeply. But her sorrows
and trials remained a sealed book even to those
nearest to her. Her husband was dead, and she
would not recall the past, or cast a shadow on his
memory. Now she is once more herself, and has
regained all her cheerfulness, though not, perhaps,
her old flow of spirits; and though she still wears
her mourning dress, she is to cast it aside in a few

months, to become at last the wife of Clifford
Aubrey, who has just been returned as Senator
from his adopted State. Standing beside her is
Christabel, her face aglow with maternal pride and
tenderness as deep as Jennie's own ; and from the
lively sallies that she makes from time to time,
we can see that she is as light-hearted and fun-
loving as ever.

But where are the *pater familias* all this time?
And Marcia, our own Marcia? Ah! here they
are! we have found them at last. And you must
bear in mind that Fred is a judge; Paul, a chan-
cellor; and Kenneth!—Ah! Kenneth is Marcia's
Husband! And rumor says he might, if he chose,
give a name to a certain unknown author, whose
works are creating a profound sensation on both
sides of the Atlantic. Well! we have surprised
all these honorables in the childish sport of playing tea-party, and Marcia is looking on well
pleased. There is the miniature table, with its
snowy cloth and tiny dishes, to say nothing of the
stores of "*good things*" so temptingly displayed.
But we are most interested in the presiding genii
of the little feast. That pretty, well-behaved
young miss is Lottie, junior. Fred would have it
so, though Lottie protests that she is entirely too

proper to be named for her. And then there are a pair of Marcias. The one, a roguish elf, the counterpart of her mischievous mamma, we easily recognize as Lottie's second daughter; and need we ask who is the lovely little creature presiding over the teapot and sugar-bowl with so much childish dignity? Kenneth's eyes, sparkling with pride and misty with tenderness, would tell us, even if we did not recognize the pure, fair face with its dreamy eyes, classic features, and raven tresses.

"You shall '*pour out*' some time," said she to her little companions. "But mamma said I might to-day, because it was mine and dear papa's birthday;" and then mamma and papa and Uncle Paul and Uncle Fred were served with an easy grace, that rendered her resemblance to her mamma still more striking.

But what has become of Dick and Nita, our little irrepressibles? Do you see that tall, bearded young man, who has just dismounted from his horse, to be besieged by the two racers with,

"Uncle Dick, please let us ride Black Bess around the circle, just once?"

Watch him as he lifts them, one after another, carefully into the saddle, and calling to old James and Jeffries, who, proud of the commission, gladly obey his summons, bids them have an eye on their young masters, and wonder if this can be the harum-scarum rogue we used to know. Yes, it is the very same, though it is difficult to recognize in this distinguished graduate of the time-honored University of Edinburgh, this devotee of the ladies, so fastidious in dress as almost to be liable to the imputation of dandyism, the Dick of old, who sneered at girls, and luxuriated in nothing so much as a well-worn suit and a dilapidated hat. But with all his elegance, he seems destined to play the part of postman in these pages, as, approaching his mother with the salutation: "What will you give me for a treat?" he lays a letter in her lap that makes her eyes glisten and her cheeks glow with pleasure. It is a letter from Nita! But why is she not here to-day? Because she is now Mrs. Louis Clayton, and with her newly-made husband is at present in Scotland, visiting his sister Blanche, who has been for two or three years the happy wife of our old friend, Mr. MacKensie. In this letter Nita describes their charming home and domestic bliss in the most glowing terms, and concludes by saying:

"But all these attractions sink into insignificance before their lovely little year-old Marcia, whom her father seems absolutely to worship. I tell Blanche I would protest against this, and I have even ventured to hint that there may be some mysterious attraction about the name. But Blanche won't be made jealous, and I verily believe she loves our Marcia quite as well as her husband does."

And there is yet another group of entirely too much consequence to be slighted! Gorgeous in a turban made up of a most impossible combination of colors, and a dress whose pattern would delight the eye of a Chinese, Aunt Phillis is strutting up and down the lawn, bearing in her arms Marcia's youngest, her little Elmore, a beautiful babe of four months and the old nurse's especial admiration, as, in truth, both the others have been in their turn. But this young gentleman, having made his appearance after an interval of six years, is considered entitled to an unusual amount of homage, and Aunt Phillis never wearies of expatiating on his perfections; though it must be confessed she has at present a very appreciative audience in the person of old dame Jeffries, who, with cap and

handkerchief as immaculate as of yore, is likewise
keeping guard upon the precious treasure.

"Dis yere young Marse am none o' yer common babies," Aunt Phillis is saying. "He'll
twis' and turn wid de colic, till he can stan' it no
longer, widout sheddin' a tear; but, Lor'! when
he does 'gin for to cry! Sich lungs! Yer never
heerd de like! But he's 'havin' heself like a
man dis eb'ning. He knows its papa's birf-day!
He does, de bressed darlin'!"

"God love him!" said the old dame. "But
he's a bonny babe. Een as blue as the skies
in June, and as like my own bairn's as two peas.
That I should have lived to nurse my boy Kenneth's bairns upon my old knees! I could die
happy now!"

"Lor' ha' massy! Ef yere so happy, what
makes you talk 'bout dyin'. I never 'tend to
'sart my Miss Marshy, an' I'se gwine to live long
as dar's any one in sight. Leastways till de
Lord Gabriel blows his horn!" said Aunt Phillis, bending over the "young Marse," who began
to show symptoms of that unbearable stage of
colic before alluded to.

But the daylight fades, and one by one the
merry groups seek their happy homes; and when

at last the rising moon sends down her silvery glory on the scene, Kenneth and Marcia are alone. Side by side, and hand in hand, they sit, with hearts too full for words, thinking of the many blessings scattered in their path; and thinking thus, they see how life's *Ebon* brings out its *Gold*, and thank God for the past trials which have enabled them so fully to appreciate their present happiness. Marcia's face, half turned towards her husband and half looking up to the starry skies that spread out so cloud-lessly above them, is as fair and lovely as ever, and the radiant peace that dawned upon it on her wedding-morn has never left it. Kenneth's glance is bent wholly on his precious wife, and there is a pure, devoted love, a hallowed tenderness in its depths, that show, that for them indeed the years of this decade have been as jewels set in a framework of gold, which, like the beads of a rosary, have passed away one by one, sparkling with good deeds and holy thoughts and lofty aspirations, to be gathered again into a resplendent diadem, which shall crown them for all Eternity!

THE END.

www.ingramcontent.com/pod-product-compliance
Lightning Source LLC
Chambersburg PA
CBHW031339070726
47496CB00017B/1299